Start
Us Up

Also From Lexi Blake

ROMANTIC SUSPENSE

Masters and Mercenaries
The Dom Who Loved Me
The Men With The Golden Cuffs
A Dom is Forever
On Her Master's Secret Service
Sanctum: A Masters and Mercenaries Novella
Love and Let Die
Unconditional: A Masters and Mercenaries Novella
Dungeon Royale
Dungeon Games: A Masters and Mercenaries Novella
A View to a Thrill
Cherished: A Masters and Mercenaries Novella
You Only Love Twice
Luscious: Masters and Mercenaries~Topped
Adored: A Masters and Mercenaries Novella
Master No
Just One Taste: Masters and Mercenaries~Topped 2
From Sanctum with Love
Devoted: A Masters and Mercenaries Novella
Dominance Never Dies
Submission is Not Enough
Master Bits and Mercenary Bites~The Secret Recipes of Topped
Perfectly Paired: Masters and Mercenaries~Topped 3
For His Eyes Only
Arranged: A Masters and Mercenaries Novella
Love Another Day
At Your Service: Masters and Mercenaries~Topped 4
Master Bits and Mercenary Bites~Girls Night
Nobody Does It Better
Close Cover
Protected: A Masters and Mercenaries Novella
Enchanted: A Masters and Mercenaries Novella
Charmed: A Masters and Mercenaries Novella
Treasured: A Masters and Mercenaries Novella

Delighted: A Masters and Mercenaries Novella
Tempted: A Masters and Mercenaries Novella

Masters and Mercenaries: The Forgotten
Lost Hearts (Memento Mori)
Lost and Found
Lost in You
Long Lost
No Love Lost

Masters and Mercenaries: Reloaded
Submission Impossible
The Dom Identity
The Man from Sanctum
No Time to Lie
The Dom Who Came in from the Cold

Masters and Mercenaries: New Recruits
Love the Way You Spy, Coming September 19, 2023

Park Avenue Promise
Start Us Up
My Royal Showmance, Coming June 4. 2024

Butterfly Bayou
Butterfly Bayou
Bayou Baby
Bayou Dreaming
Bayou Beauty
Bayou Sweetheart
Bayou Beloved

Lawless
Ruthless
Satisfaction
Revenge

Courting Justice
Order of Protection
Evidence of Desire

Start Us Up

LEXI BLAKE

Start Us Up
A Park Avenue Promise Novel
By Lexi Blake

Copyright 2023 Lexi Blake
ISBN: 978-1-957568-66-9

Published by Blue Box Press, an imprint of Evil Eye Concepts, Incorporated

Author's Acknowledgements

Thanks to the amazing staff at Blue Box Press for being willing to take this brand-new journey with me. Thanks to Liz Berry, Jillian Stein, and MJ Rose—who went so far as to find the brownstone my heroines are obsessed with. Thanks to Stacey Tardif and Tanaka Kangara. Thanks so much to the entire team at Valentine PR, especially the amazing Nina Grinstead and Kim Cermak. Thanks to my personal team—Kim Guidroz, Maria Monroy, Margarita Coale, Stormy Pate, and Riane Holt.

Special thanks to Ethan Johnson for being incredibly patient with all my technical questions. If I got anything right with this book, it is because of him. If I got it wrong, I blame it all on Kim Crawford.

Dedication

At the heart of *Start Us Up* is the deep relationship we have with the women in our lives. So much of Ivy's life is defined by the strong women she is surrounded by—for good or bad. Like so very many of my books I don't know that I understood what I was processing until I read it all again. This is about how women can shape each other, building up or tearing down, and how when we choose to do the former, we can change the world for the better. In my life I have been blessed to be surrounded by magnificent, supportive women. I was graced with older women who showed me the way, and younger ones who are blazing new trails. There are too many women to name here, so I'm picking two who've recently shown me a new way to work, who led me back to joyous writing again. This book would be very different without them.

To Mari Carr and Lila DuBois for being the best coworkers/sisters a writer could ever have. And look, Lila, no dogs on the cover.

Prologue

Manhattan
13 years ago

"I'm pretty sure we're not supposed to be here."

"Well, I'm not going back out there. Britney is awful. If I have to hear her talk about my shoes one more time I'm going to punch her in the face, and then where will we be?"

Ivy Jensen looked up at Anika Fox and Harper Ross as she closed the door behind her, ignoring the sign on the outside that stated this room was off limits to the public.

They'd managed to ditch their group. It wasn't what she'd been planning when she'd signed up for the field trip to Banover Place. She wasn't particularly interested in a Golden Age mansion. Or was it Gilded? She wasn't sure. Old houses weren't her thing. She would bet this place got crappy Internet.

The room was smaller than the ones they'd been touring and seemed to be used as some sort of storage space. There was only one half circle of a window that showed the gray skies over the Upper East Side. The teacher had tried to set the scene earlier, had talked about how the city had looked in the eighteen hundreds, but all Ivy had been able to see was rain clouds that would likely open up and leave her cold and wet because she didn't have an umbrella.

Then the class mean girls would make fun of her, too.

"There's nothing wrong with your shoes." Anika moved further into the room.

"They're ugly but they're comfortable." Harper seemed to be studying the brick walls. She was wearing her familiar uniform of jeans and a sweater. Despite the fact that it was early May, there was still a chill in the air. On most days she wore sneakers, but today she'd shown up in the boots she normally wore when she worked at her father's construction site. Which she likely had earlier today and forgotten about them. "I'm just tired of the rich kids screwing with us. Ivy, build us a robot we can set on Britney."

Now there was something else Ivy could get into. Robots. Why couldn't they go on a field trip to a robotics lab or something cool like that? "I'll get right to work."

She glanced around the space. They were on one of the upper floors. There were furnishings stacked up against one of the walls and some big boxes marked *gift shop stock*.

"What I really hate is that I was looking forward so much to today and now I feel like crap," Harper said. "I've wanted to tour this place for a long time."

"You can't let them get to you." Ivy understood how she felt. Not about old buildings. That was Harper's thing, but she understood what it meant to be obsessed with a thing. She was the class nerd, the girl who spent all her time with the robotics team and in the computer lab. She'd discovered coding a few years back and it had been her obsession ever since. "What do you think this place was used for?"

They'd toured the ballroom and the magnificent study. The large suite that served as the owner's bedroom could hold the entirety of Ivy's apartment and have room to spare.

"Servants' quarters," Harper replied. "Didn't you read the lesson?"

"She was busy working." Anika sat down on the lone chair in the dusty room.

Ivy had a part-time job that sometimes felt full-time. She'd had to work from the moment she could if she wanted to buy the things she needed. Her mom had told her food and college were more important than computer equipment. She hadn't listened when Ivy had tried to explain that college wasn't happening without a damn laptop.

Her mom didn't listen much these days, didn't talk much. Just worked and came home and stared at the TV. When Ivy had told her she was on track to graduate with honors she'd merely nodded and said that was what she'd expected.

She had no idea how to get her mom to *see* her.

"The servants would be housed in rooms close to the roof because at the time that was where all the smoke and cold would cling," Harper explained. "That's why the stairs up here are different from the main house. None of the family would use this floor and they wouldn't do any entertaining here, therefore the stairs are strictly utilitarian. I still can't believe my dad knocked down one of these a couple of months ago to make room for a high-rise."

"If he hadn't, someone else would have," Anika pointed out. "And then he wouldn't have had a job."

"Yeah." A sad expression crossed Harper's face. "He needs that job. All I know is one day I want to take a place like this and polish it up. Most of the work is in new construction, but it would be so cool to reno an old-school brownstone and live in it. We could all live here and then the Britney's of the world couldn't look down on us."

"I just want to get my mom out of the crappy building we're in," Anika said. "The landlord is creepy, and I've started naming the rats. Ivy, do you want half my sandwich?"

Ivy felt a flush go through her system. There hadn't been anything for her to pack for lunch this morning, and her mom had forgotten to leave her cash. Her mom probably thought she had some since she was working part time now. But Ivy had spent every dime she'd made on a new SIM card. She'd hoped no one would notice when she skipped lunch. "I'm fine."

She sometimes wondered how different her life would be if her father hadn't died. She wondered if her mother would smile more if he was around, if she would be one of those moms who was always up in her kid's business. If she would still be making her lunches and checking her homework.

Not that she needed that or anything.

Anika's brows rose. "I can hear your stomach rumbling. Did you eat breakfast?"

Harper pulled out her lunch box. "Sit with us. I've got plenty. I figure we have at least half an hour before Mrs. Charles realizes we're gone. She's been flirting with the docent."

It was how they'd managed to slip away. The teacher in charge of their group was fairly young and hadn't developed the Spidey-like senses of the more experienced ones.

It didn't make any sense to pass out from hunger, so she settled in and accepted half of Anika's PB&J and some of Harper's chips.

"So I would live in this room if I was back in those times." Ivy leaned against the brick wall, sliding down until she was sitting.

Anika shrugged. "We would all be right here."

But that wasn't the world Ivy wanted. She didn't want to constantly fight for every dime, worry about every meal. "I'm going to write that Cecilia person and get her to mentor me."

"The tech lady?" Harper asked.

Ivy nodded. A few weeks back a woman named Cecilia Foust had come through to give a talk about women in STEM. That had been a lecture Ivy had paid attention to. "Yeah. She's mostly on the investment end, but she could teach me a lot. She could tell me what to do so I don't end up in the servants' quarters."

It was where she lived now, and it was hard. This life had dragged her mother down. It made her hard and untouchable.

Ivy didn't want to be untouchable.

"I think that's a good step," Harper said. "Maybe I should take one of my own. Dad is only willing to teach me what he knows. He thinks renovation is useless. I'm thinking about taking some classes this summer when I'm not working."

Anika grinned. "And I have an internship this summer at Rockefeller Center. I got the news yesterday. My mom is angry because it doesn't pay, but I want to get into entertainment. I have to pay my dues and make connections."

They all had found a potential path out of the lives they seemed stuck in. This summer would be about putting those plans in motion, and sometime in the future all their hard work would pay off. That was the lesson she'd gotten from the STEM lady's talk. "One day we're going to buy this place and we're going to live on Park Avenue and we'll show them all."

"Uh, this place is a historical landmark," Harper explained. "I don't think we can buy it."

She wasn't thinking positively. "Bet if we had enough money we could, and then you could make all the rooms beautiful again, not just the ones they show the public."

"That would be so cool." Anika took a swig from her water bottle. "The city is so different here. It's only a few blocks, but it's a totally different world."

A world Ivy wanted to be a part of. "We're going to make it."

Just not without her friends. It wouldn't mean anything if she didn't have Harper and Anika. They'd become her family.

Harper started talking about architecture, and Ivy let the conversation flow around her.

All she needed was a shot. She could show everyone what a poor kid could do.

The day suddenly didn't seem so dreary.

Chapter One

"I think you need to start dating again."

The words hit me like I suspect a baseball bat to the head would. They make me a bit nauseous, and when I really think about the implications of following through with that particular suggestion, the world threatens to go fuzzy.

It's like my body's instinct is to shut down to protect itself.

"Ivy, are you okay?"

I look over the brunch table at my two best friends in the world and roll my eyes. Anika asked the question, but I turn Harper's way since I'm sure she's the one who made the suggestion that threatened to send me into a spiral. "Seriously? Do you remember what happened the last time I gave dating a shot? Should I call up any of the numerous articles detailing my downfall, or would you like an oral report on the current condition of my life and career?"

I don't have much of either one, and a big part of that had been my choice in romantic partners.

Anika leans forward, avoiding her half-empty mimosa glass to put a hand on my arm. "We know what happened."

That's the trouble. She knows. Harper knows. The server probably knows. Everyone knows. My story is out there all over every tech journal and permeating the Internet like viral video gone wrong. My life dissected and turned into a cautionary tale.

Tech Goddess Brought Down by Dumbass Man Who Can't Do Math

They'll put it on my tombstone someday. Except I won't have one.

I'm totally choosing the cremation route, and hopefully someone throws a handful of me in Nick Stafford's face and he chokes on me.

After all, I damn straight choked on the ashes of the company he single-handedly burned to the ground.

"That's exactly why I think you need to try again." Nothing deflects Harper when she gets an idea in her head. That stubborn will serves her well as a woman in the male-dominated industry of construction. "It's been six months and you're back home. You've done everything you need to concerning the sale of the company, and it's time to move on with your life."

She's right about one thing. "I agree with you. Not about dating, but about moving forward when it comes to work. I'm going to Cecelia Foust's cocktail party tonight."

More words that threaten to shake my carefully constructed calm, but this is something I'm going to do.

Anika's brows rise, and I can see she's barely managing to avoid rolling those blue eyes of hers. "Cecelia? Really?"

I'd gotten a last-minute invite to the party that would be filled with some of the world's wealthiest investors. Walking into that party is going to be rough, and it will take a whole lot of bravado I'm not sure I have anymore. After all, I'm the fallen freaking angel of the tech world, but I keep telling myself if Jobs could get fired from Apple and turn around and build Pixar and then march back in and take over Apple again, then I can figure out how to climb the mountain after a fall.

Besides, I owe CeCe. I'm calling her Cecelia like she hasn't been important to me since I was a teenage girl. The truth is I'm as freaked about seeing CeCe as I am about facing a bunch of investors who know I got my ass handed to me. I've been avoiding CeCe, and when I got that invite, I realized she was done with letting me hide away.

"You know why Ivy's doing it," Harper says. "The more important thing is she accepted the invite."

Anika's eyes widen. "Wow. Are you sure you're ready for this? Do you have an idea to pitch?"

My two best friends in the world might not understand everything about Tech World, but they know about pitching to investors. There's not much I haven't talked over with these two. Even when I lived in San Francisco and they were here in New York, we talked almost every day.

Now that I'm home again, they both offered me a place to stay.

There are days I wish my pride allowed me to take them up on that. Mostly the ones that end in "y."

"I always have an idea," I return.

That is not a lie. The problem is I don't have a big idea. I have a hundred little ones. Tinkering ideas, as I like to call them. Sometimes I look at other people's code and figure out how to streamline it, to make it work more seamlessly or to simply connect faster. When I started in the business, I was known as a fixer. I was the person who fixed other people's ideas. Then I had a brilliant idea to build a company that did exactly that. I sold that one to chase after my next big dream—the one that came crashing down.

I couldn't fix our cash flow problems because I hadn't known they existed. Not that anyone in the industry believes me. After all, I presented myself as the smartest chick in tech.

Turns out I was a dumb girl who thought her boyfriend wouldn't screw her over. A lot like the rest of the woman-identifying world.

"Are you sure you're ready for something like this?" Harper puts down the perfectly made croissant she's been enjoying. Her dark hair is up in a high ponytail, accentuating the delicate beauty of her face. No guy who meets her thinks she runs a construction company.

She likely could have been a cheerleader or prom queen if she'd fallen in with the right crowd. Unfortunately for her, she'd found us. Anika and I were the nerds of our school. I was big into robotics and coding at the time, and Anika was a card-carrying member of the AV club. She was now working her way up the ladder at a major network.

Harper hadn't had time to be popular, though. After school ended, she worked with her dad. Every day. Weekends as needed. Summers had not been about vacations for Harper. They'd been about learning how to pour a foundation and install plumbing. Her father had built a business he could share with his sons, and when they hadn't shown up and all he'd been left with was a daughter, he'd handed her a hard hat and put her to work.

The woman knows a thing or two about potential burnout, so I don't ask her to stop mothering me. "I'm almost through all my savings. If I don't find a new gig soon, I'm going to be fixing iPads at the mall or walking the aisles of Target asking how I can help."

"I don't think you would be good at that," Anika says, her head shaking as though the vision is too much to take.

It would likely end up with me being fired or in jail. I'm not necessarily a people person. I accept this about myself. I'm better in virtual worlds.

Harper nods and seems to steel herself. "All right. Let's hear it."

I need more mimosa. I think seriously about asking the waiter to bring me one but without the orange juice, and to substitute whiskey for champagne. This is something I learned at CeCe's always designer-clad feet. Alcohol helps. "It's not one thing. When I get there, I'll have a better sense of what they're looking for and I'll be able to put together a package for start-up funds."

This, as they say in some circles, is not my first rodeo. I built my first business straight out of college. It was gaming. I developed the prototypes for several games that are still popular today. Not that I make that money anymore. I only developed the prototypes and wrote the base code and then sold those suckers for the seed money to start my second company. We went into school systems and government offices and streamlined the way they did paperwork. Fill out once and not again. That was when I took it to the big time. Jensen Medical Solutions. No one does forms like the healthcare industry.

CeCe Foust had been my first investor. She'd also been the one to tell me she thought my valuation wasn't right and that I was too leveraged to survive. I hadn't believed her because surely Nick had known what he was doing, and he was my boyfriend.

She'd been right.

And yet I'm going to walk into her Upper East Side brownstone this evening and boldly ask her for more.

Okay, maybe boldly isn't the right word. But I am going to shove my stupid pride down and ask. Once I know what she's looking for.

"Have you thought about going back to gaming?" Anika asks.

"I'm not some shut-in who has nothing better to do with her time than write pay to play apps," I insist, although some can make a solid argument I'm all that and more. I'm a twenty-nine-year-old woman living in her mom's rent-controlled apartment in the bedroom I'd grown up in. The one I vowed to never come back to. Even when I visited my mom, I stayed at a hotel. I told her it was because I usually brought someone home with me, but I think she knew the truth.

Maybe that's why she seems equal parts bitter and strangely satisfied with the way everything's gone down.

I believe her when she tells me I better start paying part of the rent or she'll evict me. And this time she'll toss out my Green Day posters, too, and turn that room into something called a craft room. I've never seen my mother do a craft in her life, but she'll take up popsicle stick construction if it means proving a point to me. Of that I have no doubt.

"But you loved that," Anika says, her mouth turning down in a frown. "I remember when you were coming up with the storyline and how much fun we had with it. I always thought one of your games could be made into a movie."

Because Hollywood is so much easier than Tech World. Or maybe it is. I'll never know.

The truth is I do love that work. I love it and it doesn't pay. It doesn't offer me the path I need to achieve my goals, the chief one being never having to live in that tiny apartment I grew up in again.

Actually, now that I think about it, Tech World is like a game. *Chutes and Ladders.* I work and work and none of it matters because I inevitably land on a chute, and not the golden parachute kind. The kind that deposits one back in the mud.

So it's time to clean myself up and start climbing again.

"Ani, it's not what I do now." I love my friends but sometimes I wonder if they even know who I am anymore. After college, they'd stayed here in New York. I'm pretty sure Harper hasn't left the city more than a handful of times. I'd moved to Austin for my first job, and then to San Francisco for most of my twenties. I've seen a lot of the world, and I know what it takes to make it.

Money.

Games are fun. Games might fill my soul, but they don't fill the bank account.

We made a promise years ago. We promised we would be friends forever and that we would make it all the way to Park Avenue. I'm not going to get there writing gaming apps, no matter how much I love them.

"Ani wants to find a project that will let her work with someone she likes." Harper sips her mimosa. "She's got terrible bosses."

"They're not all bad," Anika counters. "I've liked some of them. I think the boss I have right now is great. That's why I don't want to move."

This feels better. I greatly prefer talking about my friends' shitty existences rather than my own. "What did they do now?"

Anika started out as a production assistant. It's pretty much another term for being everyone's bitch. She's worked her way up to one rung below running her own shows. She keeps bringing her ideas to the table, but so far she hasn't gotten one through.

It's a little like everything in the world. She needs money to back her dreams.

Only Harper had been given a whole company, and I'm so glad it seems to be her dream. There's nothing my bestie loves more than taking a rundown piece of property and turning it into a gem.

Sometimes I wish she did the same for people. But then she tries and I get scared, so maybe she should stick to old brownstones.

"They want her to work as a PA on a reality show," Harper explains. "It's a huge step down."

"Not exactly," Anika hedges.

My cell buzzes, alerting me that I'm getting a text. I pray it isn't CeCe realizing she made a terrible mistake when she invited me. Anika is explaining her latest job and I glance down at my screen.

I don't recognize the number.

Hi, Ms. Jensen. My name is Heath Marino, and a mutual friend gave me your number. I was hoping to get some help with a piece of code I'm struggling with. I will be happy to pay for your expertise. If you're interested and have the time, please ring me back at this number.

I've never heard of this dude, and he seems way too polite to work in my world. Also, he didn't use a flurry of emoticons and acronyms only the hardest core of technophiles can decipher. I think about it because now the name does ring a very distant bell, but I can't pin it down. Who is the mutual friend? Who has my number? I'd given up my work phone that I'd had for so long, and only a couple of people have the new one. The list of suspects is short, and they're mostly here.

I look between the only two friends I have. "Heath Marino?"

I can tell immediately who has set me up with some dude who doesn't know this is a setup. Or maybe he does, and that's way worse. Anika's expression is one of pure curiosity while Harper has gone stone-cold poker face on me.

After a moment she shrugs, obviously giving up. "His cousin works on one of my crews. He fixed a bug in my estimation software, and now he's kind of my go-to guy when any of the tech goes down. He's such a nice guy, and he's working on this app."

I manage to not groan. Everyone is working on an app in my world. Every single person I meet. If they aren't actively working on an app, they have the idea for one, and hey, wouldn't I like to work with them on it? But I know this isn't really about work. "So you thought it would be cool to shove me into his arms or something?"

Harper sets down her fork. "He's a nice guy, and he could use some help. If you don't want to help him, I'll let him know to leave you alone.

See, I'm doing this thing where we're all friends and sometimes we help each other out."

There's another scenario I haven't considered. "If you like him, I'll do it. I'm sorry. I don't mind helping. I just don't want to meet some dude who thinks I'm desperate and looking."

Harper's high ponytail shakes. "No, I'm not interested in him like that." Anika sends her a look and they spend a couple of seconds communicating in a silent language of eyebrow raises and pursing lips. Finally, Harper sighs. "Fine. I did think you might like him, but he doesn't know that."

"He's super cute," Anika says with a nod. "I didn't know about the setup thing or I would have warned you, but I have met Heath. He's kind of adorable."

I'm back to wanting to spontaneously combust so I can avoid all of this. "No."

"You don't have to date him." Harper obviously gives up on me.

I'm cool with that. It's not that I want my friends to wash their hands of me. To the contrary. I need them now more than ever. But I can't even think about becoming involved with anything but my own looking-real-sad future.

You only get so many shots in my business, and fewer if you happen to have a vagina. If CeCe Foust had a penis, I doubt I would have gotten that invite. A man mentor would have already washed his hands of me and moved on to someone else.

I have to focus or I'll live the rest of my life in that six-hundred-square-foot apartment, and I've gotten used to having more than one bathroom. My place in San Fran had four of those suckers, and I would migrate between them, each with its own loving Japanese toilet…

"Where did she go?" Harper asks.

"She's probably thinking about bathrooms again," Anika says, getting back down to the business of brunch. She starts to work on her eggs Benedict. "That's the look she gets when she's thinking about her place in San Fran. She's got weird ideas about bathrooms now. I blame California."

I have news for Ani. There are some spectacular bathrooms right here in New York. We've simply never lived in a building that had them.

I thought we would be there by now. I thought we would all be living on Park Avenue building our businesses, and one of us would catch maternal yearnings so the two sane ones left could have a baby to love and send back home. It was going to be great.

I don't even have a dog.

When I'd had the money and space for a dog, I didn't have the time. Now I have the time but nothing else.

And just so we're clear, Park Avenue is a metaphor. We don't have to live there. It's simply the place we were when we realized there was more to the world than tiny apartments and parents who fought and bullies who made fun of us because we wore hand-me-downs.

Not that I would pass up Park. I wouldn't, but the key to all of those childhood dreams was being together and having financial stability.

Maybe that had been the problem in San Francisco. I hadn't had these two women with me. Maybe if I had, one of them would have said, *hey that Nick guy seems like a dick who's going to play around with the investment accounts and fuck you over.*

They probably wouldn't have said it like that. But they would have said something.

I need to make my stand here in New York this time. I need to rebuild here, and in the right way. Where my best friends can help me. Where we can watch out for each other.

I sit back as the revelation kind of flows over me.

Change has to start with me. And that sucks. I really wish it could start with someone else because I'm super tired.

"Will it help you out if I talk to this Heath guy?" I ask, already knowing the answer.

Honestly, I owe her because she's going to have to pick up the tab for this overpriced brunch she talked me into. Not that she knows it yet.

"Yes." Harper's lips turn up in a satisfied grin.

She really thinks I'm going to take one look at this dude and melt at his feet.

I don't melt anymore. I am Elsa, and the cold does not bother me. I quite like it. I would especially like it if we had an air conditioner that worked. It's getting hot in the city.

"Then I will call him back and help him with his app." I can suffer through for her. I'm sure I'll need her to return the favor at some point.

If things don't go well with CeCe tonight, I might need a job. I might be learning how to nail things into other things—a gross misrepresentation of what Harper does, but I know no technical terms when it comes to construction. She will have to teach me those too, so my fingers are crossed that tonight goes off without a hitch.

"Thank you so much, Ivy." Harper grins, and it's like the sun is back in the world.

I love my friends. How bad can this be?

"And thank you so much for this magnificent brunch." I lay down the bad news.

She waves me off. "I knew I was paying. And I knew I had to do this when I caught you double fisting tacos from the street vendor on 50th. I don't think it's healthy to eat that much meat."

They're tasty and two for three dollars. She will take those tacos from my cold, dead hands. But I do appreciate the brunch. More than that I appreciate sitting in a pretty place surrounded by pretty things and waiters who actually get tipped so they don't throw your food at you to save time because they're already dealing with the next customer.

I've gotten good at catching those tacos.

My cell buzzes as Anika starts talking about the new reality show they want her to work on. I hear her saying something about a king looking for a bride, which makes me want to vomit a little.

And then I read the text and want to vomit a lot.

Hey, babe. Heard you're going to be at the big party tonight. Maybe we can catch up.

Nick. Nick Stafford, the man who wrecked my life, is going to be at the party tonight.

Yeah, this could get real bad.

Chapter Two

The horrifying news that my ex is attending CeCe's party is still weighing heavily on my brain pan as I stride down the hall that I've been assured will lead me to Heath Marino's apartment. The building is a bit worn down, but compared to the one I live in it's a palace.

I'd been planning on wearing my very best dress to that party, and now I'm unsure. It's Chanel, and I bought it for the interview with *Code: The Magazine* that featured me as one of the thirty best minds under thirty. It's black and chic, and Nick has seen it about five hundred times. He calls it my armor.

If he sees me in that, it will let him know I'm feeling vulnerable, and I can't have that. I'm walking into a den of very well-dressed predators, and I'm going to be all alone. Even if Nick doesn't show up with a date, he'll be surrounded by the men I like to call the Bro Coders.

It's like the everyday, normal dumbass bro, complete with sports references and an actual "code" they claim to live by, but there's also physical coding, and let me tell you they think they are the smartest people in any room. These are the guys who fail up. I mean it. Nick devastated Jensen Medical Solutions to the point that we had to sell to simply pay off our creditors, but he's already been hired as CFO of an even bigger company.

While I scrape together quarters to pay for those tacos.

I'm pissed that I can't enjoy the day with my two best friends and the feeling of having a delightfully full belly, but no. Now I'm nauseous and wondering if I'm going to have a food baby tonight.

Maybe I should hire an escort. Like a really hot guy who smiles a lot and looks like he likes me. I could consider him an accessory.

I am contemplating how one goes about employing an escort when I find the apartment marked 9B and knock.

To top it all off, Heath Marino wants to meet in the middle of the afternoon, and I couldn't think of a good excuse to push this to next week, so here I am. I'm off my game because I am the queen of good excuses. I can put a guy off for years. Usually until he goes away. I call it ghosting via procrastination.

The door opens and a thin black man with glasses stands there, frowning. "Wow. That is the angriest face I've seen in a while. There is no manager here, lady."

Totally off my game because I usually don't scare people away until I actually want to. "Sorry. Shitty day. I'm looking for Heath."

Now the guy's eyes widen. He's wearing a Cornell T-shirt and sweatpants. "Holy shit. You're her. I didn't… You're not dressed the way you normally are."

So he's a techie. When Heath hadn't given any indication he knew who I was, I thought I'd maybe caught a break. "This is actually more normal than the power suits and stuff. I only dress up when I have to."

It's much more comfortable to write code in my pajamas, hair piled high on my head and fuzzy slippers on my feet. I would have worn that every day at the office except I'd been taught I have to look like the boss. Always.

I don't right now. I look like every other woman walking the streets of New York wondering where it all went wrong. Jeans. T-shirt. Sneakers. I hope I didn't get egg yolk on any of those three items, but it wouldn't surprise me. I hadn't gone home to change so I could help Heath Marino with whatever his damn app needed.

I'm pretty sure the dude in front of me must be his roommate. He's pretty cute in a nerdy way. I peg his age as mid to late twenties and would bet he's not currently a student at Cornell. It's probably his alma mater.

He opens the door wider, and I'm treated to the sight of a short hallway that leads into the living room, which is covered in computers and monitors.

"I'm Darnell. Darnell Green. Heath and I have been roommates since we met in college. Please come in," Darnell offers and turns his head toward the back of the apartment. "Heath, she's here."

I step inside, and it's obvious these two do not entertain. The living room is fairly big for a city apartment, but instead of seating, it's got four desks, each with a computer setup and several monitors.

"I take it you work from home." I slide my bag off my shoulder, but I'm not sure where to put it since there's no furniture that doesn't belong in an office. Oh, except the rocker game chair I spy pushed to the side.

Darnell nods, gesturing around the setup. "Yeah, we got sent home during the pandemic and haven't gone back to the office. So we work from here. It's so much nicer. I don't have to see people."

"I hear ya. People suck." That was one thing I did not miss. For the misanthrope, the pandemic was a time of great potential. The potential to hide from other people.

"They do. And I have everything I need here to be productive without some boss who doesn't remember shit about code breathing down my neck," Darnell continues. "I'm a full-stack developer for Dryson Inc. I'm on a team that handles all their web business."

So he knew all the languages. When I say that I don't mean he can ask for a beer in Spanish. In our world the languages are numerous and ever changing. Python, JavaScript, Go, Rust. Most people know what I mean when I say HTML, but the language of code is wide and varied. The man in front of me would have to know a whole lot of them because he would handle both front and back-end web development, including user interface.

He was probably developing an app on the side.

"I'll be right out," a masculine-sounding voice says.

"So what does Heath do?" I ask, curious.

"He's freelancing right now," Darnell says in a way that lets me know Heath is currently unemployed.

Awesome. Which should mean he could be out here with me and not taking up precious time I could use to figure out what I can do to change up a black sheath dress enough that my ex won't know it's my emotional support dress.

Maybe a scarf.

Anika knows how to sew. Maybe she could MacGyver a dress for me. I would borrow from her, but she is significantly smaller than me. Petite and sweet. That's our Ani. I'm more on the tall and not breakable side of the scale. I have a half foot on Harper, too, or I would try to raid her closet.

"Yeah, Nonna," I hear the man in the back say. "I gotta go. My friend is here. Yes, the one who's going to help me with my project." He rounds the corner, a cell phone to his ear, and I get my first look at Heath Marino.

There was a reason Anika said he was cute. Heath Marino looks like he walked off the set of a Taylor Swift video, and not in a bad way. This is the dude who did not take Tay's scarf and leave it in his sister's drawer as a reminder of his conquest. No. This is the one she wrote the happy songs about. He's the guy next door on the teen dramedy who's secretly way hotter than he seems, but it takes the heroine a couple of seasons to really get him.

Dark hair that's slightly shaggy, so it's got some curl to it. Superman-like jaw, but there's a softness to his face that's almost pretty. Soulful brown eyes, and I would bet that boy actually works out because his Marvel T-shirt fits really well, and I do not see evidence of a steady diet of Hot Pockets.

And he's taller than me. It can be hard to find a man who's taller than me. I could wear heels with this guy and not feel like a walking tree trunk from the Shire.

My mouth goes a little dry, and I have to remind myself.

I am Elsa.

I need to remember that Queen Taylor writes a whole lot of happy songs before she has to shred a man because he turns into a walking pile of garbage.

I'm sure I had these feelings about Nick before he ruined my life. Pretty sure. Sort of.

I realize Darnell is watching me, and his eyes are wide again. Like he knows what's going on in my head. He can't because I have a great poker face. But then he smiles and his head nods like he's saying *you go, girl*.

So. Off. My. Game.

"Yeah, the one that's a terrible idea and will never work," Heath says into the phone while giving me an apologetic look that causes a dimple on his right cheek make an appearance.

He is the perfect combination of adorable mess and sexy beast.

But I am Elsa, and I am frozen in all my parts. Including the ones Harper obviously wants to see if she can thaw out.

"Love you, too. I'll come by tomorrow. Yes, we loved the leftovers from dinner."

Darnell leans over. "They were excellent, Lydia. Thank you." He looks back at me. "His grandma can cook. It's all Italian, and she's not big on vegetables, but the woman makes some amazing pasta. It's one of the perks of living with Heath."

I never met my grandma, and my mom's version of cooking is heating up a frozen dinner.

"See, I told you I can share. Tell the nurse I want an update. I know. Bye." Heath hangs the cell up and slides it into his pocket. "Hey, Ms. Jensen. I'm sorry about the wait. My grandmother can talk."

Yep, he's simply another hot guy who loves his grandma and knows how to code.

Unemployed. I need to fixate on that word. "It's just Ivy. So Harper said you were having some trouble."

"Just Ivy." Darnell is still nodding and watching us like he's waiting for something to happen. "That's funny. You're not just Ivy. You're like an icon."

People throw that word around a lot. So much that it's lost all meaning. "I assure you I am not. I'm one more coder looking for my next gig."

"*Winter's End* is the best," Darnell proclaims. "I have played that game a hundred times. Your zombies are the coolest. I've been trying to get my man here to play with me. He's more into puzzle games than shooters. You know he put a game out a couple of years back. Maybe you've heard of it."

"She has not," Heath assures him. "No one has, hence the crappy apartment where we both live and work. It wasn't a hit."

"*Rain and Fury*," Darnell continues like Heath has said not a word. "I helped him with the storyline. See, what I really want to do is write. Speculative fiction. I'm not quite there yet, but I'm querying."

I turn Heath's way because I do know that game, and now it's my jaw dropping. "Are you serious? I bought that game as a Christmas present for all of my team. I mean, it was part of it. They also got bonuses. But I loved that game so much."

Heath blushes—an action that does not lessen his hotness in any way. "So you're the reason I sold a whole fifty copies in December two years back. You personally account for half my income off that game."

There's a reason it's a rough business. A game can be brilliant and utterly ignored because something else is popular at the time. App stores have made it easier to get products out in the public, so there's often a glut of games. Without a multimillion-dollar marketing campaign, good games get lost. "Sorry. It's really well done. I loved the puzzles, and the graphics were beautiful."

"Thanks. And I've filled out many a form that your work has made much easier," he assures me, thereby killing all my fantasies that he doesn't know my sad history. "Don't take that for faint praise. My grandmother had cancer last year. She's in remission and healthy now, but we've been in hospitals that use your system and ones that don't. Your system genuinely makes life better."

Those are not tears pulsing behind my eyes, threatening to spill over because it's been that freaking long since I felt like I was worth something. I manage to shake them off and swear I'm going to get down to business. "That's good to know. So, what is this app you're working on?"

Heath seems a bit flustered by the turn of conversation, but he quickly recovers. I wait for him to explain his new freemium game or how he's developed a better calculator app. "It's a matchmaking app. Not for like hookups. Tinder has that down. This is for predicting long-term, happy marriages."

"Ah, you're fucking with me. Good one, buddy." I wouldn't have said he was a joker, but that was funny. He's actually got me laughing. "So what's the real app?"

That's when I realize no one is laughing with me.

Spoiler alert—he was not, in fact, joking.

Chapter Three

Two hours later I'm a little in awe of what he's doing.

"So you're building an AI that can predict matches." I say the words slowly, trying them out. Not really believing them. He's not merely trying to match people up based on similar interests. It does more than that and matches more than people in relationships.

"Yes." Heath sits at his computer. He's been showing me some of his early work. He started with having the AI make simple choices based on input. He'd explained that he'd started with the basics—an app to help decide what to cook for dinner. "Like with the *What's for Dinner* app but on a grand scale. Your perfect dinner match along with a recipe and the information on where to buy the ingredients."

I like this. I'm not sure if it works for putting humans together, but my generation does not mind a screen telling them what to do. We are bombarded with choices every second of the day. Having them narrowed for us based on our needs can be a good thing. "This could be applicable to restaurants around the city, too. Like the user could answer simple questions. How far are they willing to go, what do they like, what level of service do they expect. This could be great when you're traveling."

My mind is racing with the possibilities. There are a couple of apps out there, but sometimes a popular app isn't merely about functionality. We could make this a social experience. That's another thing about my generation. We're always looking for a social experience that doesn't involve actual people. If we can post it online, we feel like we've done our duty and the memory is preserved for all of time.

Connect this app to reservation systems, review systems, and social media and we might have a gold mine.

"Sure." Heath's head is shaking. "But that's not the point. The point is a high-level matchmaking experience for people who want to look beyond hookups."

"His granny was considered one of Little Italy's greatest matchmakers back in the day," Darnell supplies helpfully. "That's what all this is about."

"Matchmakers? They still exist?" I ask. "I mean I know they do on *Netflix* and in other countries, but here? It seems so old-fashioned."

"Yes, here." Heath takes a swig of water and seems to decide how to handle me. "Okay, my great-grandmother came over from Sicily after the war. She'd been a matchmaker in the old country, and she took it up again here. She taught my grandmother. It's not as popular as it was once, but she still counsels the people of the neighborhood and beyond. Some clients come from as far away as Florida for her services."

"She puts people together?" I'm trying to wrap my head around that. See, this is one place where my generation does not want our choices narrowed down. We require many choices and want to be able to reject them all.

"Sometimes, or she gives you a list of what you should be looking for, what your red flags should be. Some red flags are universal. She makes her lists more personal. That's one of the things I'm trying to teach the AI to do. So if a person loves dogs, maybe it's better to not date a person with an allergy or one who's afraid of dogs," he offers. "Or if you love travel, you're probably not a good match with someone who hates to leave home."

There's only one problem with this. Well, more than one, but this is the big hurdle. "There are actual services who do this. A ton of them. There's Christian dating services. Apps for singles over fifty. Apps for people who don't want to date the poors. I'm pretty sure even farmers have their own app. It's a crowded field."

"No one is approaching the situation the way I am," he replies with surety. "I just have to refine my AI."

"How are you going to teach it?" For an AI to learn, it has to process data. A lot of data. Say you want an AI to be able to write a book. You would feed it as many books as you can so it learns what it means to write a book—thereby also maybe violating a whole lot of authors who don't want their work used that way. Trust me. They are very vocal about this, and no amount of promising them some cool future world will change their minds.

"I feed it information about couples with long-term relationships, and before you point out all the moral land mines, I have permission from each and every one," he replies. "I've been conducting interviews over the last couple of years. I started with my grandmother's clients. They make up the bulk of my research, but I've been trying to diversify so I'm going outside her work."

"He means he's interviewing gays and non-white people." Darnell seems to be a giver.

I like him.

"My grandma mostly works with people of Italian descent," Heath admits. "It's who she knows, but when I started this project I wanted it to be something more, to help more people."

It seems an odd quest for a man in his late twenties to be on, but I don't know him well enough to question him. What I do know is that his AI is looking good. For the restaurant app. Not the *Marry Me* app. I'm also interested in his framework, which I've learned he's been working on since he was in his teens.

But I've worked with guys like Heath for long enough that I know not to point that out now.

An idea is floating around in my head. I can take a couple of years and build my own or I can do what all smart businesspeople do and manipulate the cutie into a situation where he potentially makes a shit ton of cash and a real name for himself in the business.

Which means biding my time. And getting close to him. That sounds a little predatory, but when you really think about it, it's for his own good.

I sit back. At this point he's only asked me to look at a piece of code he's having trouble with. I need to be more involved. "So all you need from me is to smooth out your interface?"

I see the hesitation on his face. He wants to ask for more, but he's not sure he can trust me. Which proves he's smart.

You shouldn't trust anyone in our industry. There are a lot of sharks, and they often look harmless. They often present as fun nerds who wouldn't ever cut you. But they will, and sometimes that cut is deeper than you think.

I'm not going to do that to him. At this point I don't even know if his AI works the way he says it does. He wouldn't be the first dude to talk a good game with nothing to back him up.

"The truth of the matter is I'm going to have to find a job soon," he admits.

"You need funding." Didn't we all, but this explains why he was so interested in having me be the one to help out. He probably knows twenty programmers who could fix his interface. But he didn't know anyone who could navigate investor-filled waters the way I can.

The words seem to fluster him, and I feel a brief sympathy. That first move into the big bad business world can be hard. It's obvious he's been splashing around in the kiddie pool.

"Yeah. If I want to keep working on this, I need some funding. I'm going to be honest."

"That's always helpful."

He plunges on, completely ignoring my sarcasm. It's a point in his favor if we're going to work together, and that's where it seems like this thing is going. "I could use your help on the interface, but more than that I need advice on how to proceed. I've never done anything like this before. It requires more resources than I know how to get myself."

"He can't ask his nonna for a couple hundred bucks for this one." Darnell is the only one who doesn't seem to feel the weird tension in the room. Or he does and he's fascinated by it. I think he might be taking notes.

"What is your endgame? And buddy, it can't be helping people. I can't get you funding for helping people."

"I don't see why not. It's what Jensen Medical did," Heath points out.

He fundamentally misunderstands our business. How to explain to him? "I got the funding for Jensen Medical Solutions not because it helped sick people fill out less forms and streamlined their ability to gain access to services. That was a side effect. A bug, not a feature. The feature was allowing hospitals to run more efficiently, which meant they could cut back on everything from storing paperwork to employees who dealt with that paperwork. I know it sucks, but that's what investors will care about, so you need to show me how you plan to make money off this. You need to be able to talk to investors about why backing you will make them even more money than they already have."

He sits back, and I can see he doesn't like what I've said. I hate to disillusion him, but I've said nothing but the truth.

"So I can't get funding." He takes a steadying breath. "I'll look for grant money."

"That's not what she's saying, man." At least Darnell is keeping up.

"She's saying you gotta be sneaky about it."

"I wouldn't use that word. I would say he's got to be smart about it," I correct.

"But my purpose is to help people," he insists.

"Can't you help people and make money?" I'm not sure what the problem is. And then I kind of do.

He'd said something about a nurse. When he'd walked in he'd been talking to his grandmother and said he wanted an update.

Oh, I figure out what I'm dealing with. His grandmother recently had cancer. He loves his grandma. He's working on something close to her heart.

"I didn't start this project thinking I would become some millionaire," he says.

"Good, because you probably won't, but if you want it to work, you're going to have to find a way to focus on it. Unfortunately, that means having the money, and in order to get the money, you're going to have to bring people in, and that means working with them." And then I spring my trap. I don't know why this is suddenly so important, but I want this. I want to work with him. I want to see where this thing he's built can go and how far I can take it. "Of course, if you wanted me to, I could handle that part for you."

Darnell whistles. "That's some Faustian shit right there. I think you should do it."

"What do you mean?" Heath asks.

"I think she means she'll get you the money and deal with all the scary shark people and all you have to do is give her a tiny piece of your soul." Darnell proves he's probably a pretty good writer.

"I don't care about your soul," I admit. "But I would need a piece of whatever comes out of this. Say sixty percent."

I go high so we don't negotiate too low. I think I've figured this guy out a little and he'll want to be fair, but he'll still need to feel like he talked me down.

"Twenty," he replies, and that magnificent Captain America jaw of his has gone steely.

Now I have him. "Fifty."

"Forty."

I hold out my hand. "Done."

He shakes it and tries to act confident. I try to act like touching this man doesn't send a wave of heat through me. I am not this horny. It's nothing more than some static electricity.

But I move back from him as quickly as I can and tell myself this isn't a huge, impulsive, made-by-my-loins mistake. I'm sitting in a crappy apartment with a dude who is building an AI in honor of his granny, and I just promised to find him serious cash. I tied myself to him, and it cannot have anything to do with the fact that he's got dreamy eyes. Of course that doesn't mean I can't make use of them. It strikes me that he might be a solution to at least one of my problems. The man is hot. He'll make an excellent accessory for whatever I end up wearing. "All right. So do you have a suit?"

"Yes," he replies. "Somewhere."

That scares me. I turn to Darnell, who seems to know way more than his roommate. "Is it an acceptable suit?"

Darnell shrugs. "It's a boring white dude suit, but it'll pass in most business places. He could use some new shoes."

I don't care about his shoes. He's a creative and they can get away with a lot, but CeCe will want him in a suit. "If they're really bad, shove his feet in sneakers and we'll call him quirky. The party is at seven tonight. I'll text you where to meet me."

"I'm sorry. I'm confused," Heath admits.

"We need money, partner," I explain as I text him the address of CeCe's place. "This is one of the ways we get it. It's okay. All you have to do is look pretty and let me do all the talking. I'll see you at seven. Don't be late."

I walk out before he can argue.

And I would have settled for thirty. I definitely don't tell him that.

Chapter Four

I stare at myself in the mirror and wonder if anyone can see the tag I've hidden under my arm.

I cannot afford this dress. I could buy three hundred and sixty tacos with this dress. A year's worth of tacos. Well, not the way I eat them, but if I was a delicate princess, it would be a year's worth. For me it's more like a couple of months.

Harper is right. I need to work in a salad.

"Pretty dress," my mother says, glancing into my room. "Is it new?"

"I stopped by Bergdorf." I say that casually like it's on the way. It's not. I'm far from the Upper East Side.

"Why aren't you wearing that Chanel thing you're so proud of?" My mother frowns. That frown hasn't changed in the twenty-nine years I've been alive. Probably longer. I've seen pictures and my mom seems to have had that judgmental glare even as a child.

The only pictures I ever see of her smiling are ones with my dad. It seems like she was a different person for roughly twelve years. When he was gone, the frown returned.

"I need something new."

She stares as though she can see through me.

"Fine. I don't want to wear it because Nick is going to be there, and he knows I only wear it when I feel like I need armor to protect me."

The frown becomes a light snarl. Since I got back to New York my mom and I fight a lot, but we have one thing in common. My mother hates Nick Stafford. "Little bastard. So you think if he sees you in the dress he'll know you're feeling vulnerable and he'll pounce like the manipulative shit he is. Why is he going?"

I shrug. "He got invited. You know he moved here directly after he quit."

"Yes. I heard. He has a job. Shouldn't he be busy ruining someone else's business?"

Nick might be the only thing we're of one mind on. "I'm sure he's going with his bros. You know how they like to run in packs. And he's always looking to get ahead. He texted me."

My mother's gaze threatens to spew fire. "You didn't block him? Isn't that what you do to each other these days?"

I sigh. There's a reason I haven't blocked him. We still follow each other on socials because if I block his ass, I'll end up being labeled the crazy, takes-things-too-seriously ex. I am a woman in the world. I have to prove that nothing bothers me because the minute I show weakness, it will be used against me. "We work in the same circles. It's not like we're friends, but you know what they say. Keep your friends close and an eye on your enemy's Insta."

His is filled with what I like to call "Bro" shots. There are a lot of pictures of him at various hot spots around the world with his friends. #guytime #workhardpartyharder

He doesn't work very hard, so it's pretty easy for him to party harder.

I haven't posted anything interesting lately. I've been hiding. Which is probably why Nick thinks he can text me out of nowhere. He thinks he has the upper hand.

"In my day if a man treated me like that, I would have never spoken to him again," my mother announces.

Everything was easier back in her day. Until she needed things to be harder to prove I've had it easy. She's flexible about history and very good about putting me in Catch 22s. "I'm not planning on speaking to him. All I have to do is exist in the same space without murdering him. Can you see the tag?"

My mother eyes me critically. "Only if you lift your arm, but do you honestly think you can get through a whole cocktail party without spilling something on it? You should have picked black. I can get anything out of black."

The dress is a bold shade of pink. It's not a color I wear often, but I'd been drawn to it and when I'd put it on, I'd felt...pretty.

My mother stares at me for a moment. "I thought you never wore anything but black, white, or beige to these parties."

"I'm trying something new. I did the masculine femininity thing for years." Businesswomen do it all the time. They wear versions of dresses and suits that are really only women's wear because of a skirt or where the button is on the jacket.

There can be no doubt that the dress I'm wearing is meant to accentuate my curves. There's nothing utilitarian about the flouncy skirt or plunging neckline. It's a sexy dress, one meant to catch the eye of anyone who swung my particular way.

Had I bought this dress to show Nick Stafford what an idiot he is? I don't want to think about the other, far more dangerous possibility. I did not buy this dress to impress Heath Marino.

There's a knock at the door, but then I immediately hear a key in the lock and it opens.

"Hey, Mrs. Jensen. It's just me," Anika calls out.

When I'd first come home, I'd learned that Ani now has a key to my mom's apartment and has for a couple of years. Ani, it seems, checks up on my mom regularly and has dinner with her sometimes.

My mom smiles, a genuine expression I rarely see directed my way. "We're back here, Ani, darling."

I'm pretty sure my mom wishes Anika was her daughter instead of me. I shove that bit of psychological drama to the side. I'd asked Ani to come over for more than one reason.

"Come and look at Ivy. She's dressed like a bridesmaid."

Shit. Was I? "Maybe I should wear the Chanel. Who cares if he knows?"

Ani is suddenly standing beside my mom, and her eyes go wide. "Wow. You look great. That is totally not a bridesmaid dress. No bride would let your boobs look that good."

I have to admit, they do look good in this dress. "Is it professional? I'm not professional."

Ani shakes her head. "What will CeCe be wearing?"

Likely something worth a couple thousand tacos. Ani is right. Whatever CeCe is going to be wearing this evening wouldn't be boring. She wouldn't look like she could easily throw a jacket over her dress and walk into a board meeting. "Something wildly sexy. But she's CeCe Foust. She's kind of earned that right."

"How?" my mother asks. "From what I understand she married money and then he kicked it, and she married more money and he kicked it, too. Are we sure she didn't kill them?"

I'm sure CeCe would simply tell my mother she has very good instincts at telling when an old dude is on his way out and wants a younger wife to make that transition more fun. She would ignore the fact that my mom is completely rewriting history in favor of being sarcastic. "It was one husband. He left her with a hundred grand and a small investment firm. She built everything she has from there. She's now worth ten billion, and she will never remarry. Also, George was only twenty years older, and she loved him very much."

"All I'm saying is I don't think she's done anything beyond being luckier than you," my mom says.

It's almost the nicest thing she's said since I came home. "Wow. I don't agree with you, but thanks."

Mom shakes her head. "You misunderstand, child. Luck is everything. You should get a real job. I have to go back to the office for a couple of hours. Lock up when you go. And if you're not wearing that dress for a man, I'll be very surprised. Ani, convince her she has terrible taste in men and that you won't talk to her if she takes that fucker back."

"I am not wearing this dress for freaking Nick," I yell after her. At least not the way she thinks I am.

She does not look back. Mom knows how to make an exit.

"It is really pretty," Ani says as she sits on my bed. It's the same daybed my mom bought me at the age of twelve when I insisted on getting rid of the princess canopy bed I'd had since I was five.

It's one of the only memories I have of my father. He took me to a big-box furniture store in Newark and bought me a big-girl princess bed and we ate dinner at Olive Garden and my mom and dad talked about having another kid and how it would be fun to have a boy, but I wanted a sister.

He died from a heart attack three weeks later.

Sometimes I wonder if she was so upset about that bed because it felt like I was getting rid of a piece of him.

Spending time with Heath has me slightly unsettled. I'm not usually so introspective. I move forward, never looking back.

"So who are you wearing it for?" Ani asks, her tone breezy.

I'm not fooled. My parents might not have been able to have that other kid they'd wanted, but I'd found a sister. Two of them, and I knew them well. "I'm wearing it because I didn't like the other options. I've only got one dress that can pass for a cocktail dress, and it won't work."

"You met Heath," she says, her lips curling up.

The problem with sisters is they end up knowing you, too. "Yes, and now we're business partners, so you can forget about anything flirty happening between us."

Besides, the man hadn't flirted with me at all. He'd been all business. If anything, I would guess he's slightly afraid of me. He's interested in my skills and my ability to keep him in cheap food while he works on his precious.

"I'm sorry, what?" Ani sits up straight. "I thought you were helping him with…whatever it is you do."

I don't blame her for not knowing. I barely understand what goes into producing a TV show, and I'm cool with that. I will support my sisters-from-other-misters in whatever they want to pursue. "I was, and then I realized he was telling Harper a fib."

"Heath was lying? About what?"

"He doesn't need me to fix anything. Oh, I'm sure he'll be happy to have some help on the coding end, but what that man needs is financing."

Ani bites her bottom lip, a sure sign she's anxious. "Oh, Harper's going to be so upset."

"Why? He needs money. I need a project. I was lying this morning. I've got nothing. Not nothing, but a whole notebook of little ideas. Nothing that's going to make CeCe drool. He's got something that could be special." It just isn't the thing he thinks he has. That's a problem I plan to deal with later. "Harper did exactly what she set out to do. She managed to hook up two friends of hers, though not in the way she hoped. Or maybe it's not what she hoped. Does she like this guy? I know she said she didn't, but…"

I let the insinuation dangle, watching Ani carefully.

She shakes her head, her dark curls bouncing. "She's not into Heath that way. She met him. She liked him. He's into tech. You're into tech. There you go."

Not that it matters because I'm serious. I don't need a boyfriend. Not a real one anyway. If my ex takes one look at me with Heath and misinterprets our relationship, I have no problem with that. It would do him good to think I can find a man.

Even if I can't. Because I'm not looking for one.

The truth of the matter is I need to walk into that party tonight looking like the woman I want to be. Fake it 'til you make it. Even after you've already made it and lost it, so you fake it all over again.

"You weren't attracted to him at all?" Ani asks. "Are you wearing your hair that way?"

I am a great believer in multitasking. If Anika wants me to talk about my non love life, she can get to work. "Can you do an updo?"

She perks up. She takes any chance she can to make the world a prettier place. "Yes. I think that would be perfect with the dress. Sit."

I settle in at the vanity with its rhinestones and pink hearts that I hadn't wanted but my mother insisted I have because she found it at an estate sale for five dollars. Still, over the years it's become one of those memorable places. I'd sat here and let Anika do my hair for prom. Harper hadn't gone. Her father had been sick, and her mother needed too much help for her to do something as silly as prom, she'd claimed.

She'd sat here at the age of nineteen, and I'd helped her do her makeup for her dad's memorial service.

I stare at myself in that mirror now as Anika steps in behind me and picks up my brush.

"I know you're not wearing that dress because you want to entice Nick back, but have you considered you're wearing it as a revenge dress?" Anika asks as she starts to brush my hair. "I would bet anything you didn't plan on buying a new dress until after you found out Nick is going to be there."

"I just figure I've always played by the unwritten rules, and look where it got me. And I look good in this dress. The Chanel is pretty, but I don't stand out in it. That was kind of the point. I wanted to blend in. Now I need to stand out. CeCe will respect the gesture." I hope. CeCe was part grande dame, part barracuda who could eat a face off when she wanted.

"Why is he even going?" Anika asks. "He doesn't do what you do. I thought this was about connecting investors with people who need money for their business ideas. He doesn't have ideas."

He has plenty of ideas. All of them bad. "He's working for an associate of CeCe's."

I don't bother to tell her that pretty much everyone in tech is an associate of CeCe's.

"Okay. Let's make you gorgeous. One of the hairstylists on the set taught me some new tricks. And if Nick wonders what he's missing, well, he can keep on missing," Anika says. "Because you're done with him."

I was. I have to hope that he is done with me, too.

Chapter Five

I hurry up the steps and out of the subway station, the glow of the lights from the buildings all around illuminating the night. New York is never really dark. Not here in Manhattan. When we talk about the lights at night, we're not talking about the ones in the sky. Those are a distant thing, almost an afterthought in the great and grand nightly show that is New York.

Even here in the Upper East Side, the lights are all manmade. I walk along Fifth, the concrete and stone wall that separates the road from Central Park to my side, and wonder how long it's been since I went to the park to simply enjoy it. Not since I was a kid. I won't tonight either because I'm not looking to become a *Dateline* episode, but also because there's work to be done.

There's always work to be done.

It's not like I took advantage of the natural beauty of San Francisco. I can count on one hand the times I left the city proper to explore something beyond the office or other people's offices. If I went to a party, it was to network.

In the beginning it was fun. When Nick and I first got together we felt like we were building something. Then after a year we felt like roommates.

The truth of the matter is my mother doesn't have to worry I'll fall back into Nick's arms. What she doesn't know is that I hadn't felt anything like love for the man. I'd felt some attraction, and then he was comfortable. We wanted the same things. He didn't get upset when I canceled a date for work.

I guess when I think about it, Nick was an accessory. I'd used the phrase when thinking about Heath hours before, but it fit Nick to a T.

You know the old Coco Chanel saying? Something about before you go out, look in the mirror and take off one accessory.

He's the one I should have dumped before I ever walked out of the room.

He is also the one walking up the stairs to CeCe's magnificent brownstone as I turn the corner. CeCe lives in a building that looks like the Gilded Age happened inside it—the robber baron height of luxury and society version. Nick looks like he belongs there. Killer designer suit. A trendy haircut that probably cost two hundred dollars, and I happen to know those loafers are Ferragamos because I bought them. I don't like to think about how many tacos that cost me.

He's not alone. He's never alone. I've found that Bro Coders prefer to travel in packs. Whether they're the "Hot Pocket, never get out of a hoodie" kind, or the "look at how successful I am I have a Harry Styles haircut" kind. They like to move through the world like a school of high-tech fish, protecting each other and plotting the downfall of rival schools.

In this case, he's brought along two vaguely familiar figures. I say vaguely because honestly, they all look alike to me. They're almost always named Brad or Tad or something that makes them sound like they're still at a frat house living large off daddy's cash. I'm always surprised how in a community filled to the brim with super-talented immigrants and first-generation Americans, Nick manages to find the whitest of white dudes to hang with.

That should have been a big old red flag.

I stop, hoping he'll keep walking up those stairs. It's a big place, and CeCe will have several rooms open, so I might be able to completely avoid him if I'm careful.

All I really need to do is get about ten minutes with CeCe to lay out my plans and get on her radar. She might have a line on a job in case this whole thing with Heath goes nowhere. I'll show Heath around so investors know there's a guy behind the scenes and, sadly, feel more comfortable giving us money.

It's still a big old sexist world out there.

I'm about to try to hide behind a tree where a Goldendoodle is currently doing his business when disaster happens.

"Ivy?" Nick stops just short of ringing CeCe's bell.

Damn it. I blame the dog. He's overgrown and taking up all of the tree.

There's nothing to do except hold up a hand. "Hey."

"Is that his ex?" one of the bros asks.

So he's new. Or he could have been around for years and this is the amount of interest he has in a woman he's not actively trying to drag to bed. Not that I recognize him, but the other I do. Brad Langford the Third. Or Fourth. I don't know. His father owns one of the world's largest social media networks, not that he developed it. Rumor is he stole the idea from a group of coders who worked for him back in the nineties and then had their visas pulled so they couldn't sue him.

Brad is trying to grow up to be his daddy.

"Yeah, surely you've heard," he begins and then leans in, and I can't hear the rest.

Though I know what he's saying. She wrecked her company. She couldn't hack it.

It's not a thing I haven't heard before, but somehow it hits me differently, probably because I'm wearing this stupid pink dress and I did my makeup and I look like a girl on her way to prom.

"Wow." Nick jogs down the stairs, his brows raised as he looks me over. "I've never seen you wear pink."

"Hey, Elle Woods. How's it going?" Brad asks, checking out my boobs.

I frown up at him. "I'm not a blonde, and you do know she was the smart one in that film. The whole point of that film was how she brought down the asshole men around her."

Nick shakes his head. "Don't mind him. That's just the way he is. It's good to see you. I almost forgot you were here in New York until someone mentioned CeCe invited you."

He only knows CeCe because I introduced him. And he lived with me for two years so he should have known I came from here. "Well, I knew where you were since you sent out the announcement you took the CFO job with Golden Tech. Congratulations."

I happen to know Brad's dad got him that job, and I have to wonder if he's looking to take over Golden since it's highly likely Nick will drive them to the brink of bankruptcy.

His veneered teeth shine in the lamplight. "Thanks. It's a good place to land. I hear you're still looking for a gig. You know we've got some coding jobs. They're a little below your level, but I can get you an interview. You would be in management in no time at all."

Humiliation threatens to swamp me, but I keep my head high. "Thanks, but I'm working on something big."

"Ah, that's why you're here. I was surprised you were on the list," he admits. "Listen, Ivy, we didn't get much of a chance to talk."

"We don't need to talk."

He ignores me. "I know we were close, and that's why I should tell you I've been seeing Brad's sister, Veronica. I didn't want you to be surprised."

"Hey, babe. Who's the guy?" a deep voice asks.

I turn and Heath Marino is walking up the street. He's in a not-designer suit and sneakers and looks so adorable I kind of want to cry because he blows past Nick and stands in front of me. He leans in as though kissing my cheek.

"You need a save, partner?" he whispers.

I should be bigger than this. I should tell him I can save myself. I can. Hearing that Nick has moved on doesn't bother me. Good for him.

It's the idea that I haven't that bothers me.

"Please," I whisper back.

And he kisses me for the first time. He's a good head taller than me, even in the heels I forced myself to wear. It's not a passionate kiss. It's a brief brushing of lips.

And it is the most electric my body has ever felt.

He shifts to my side, one arm going around my shoulders as he holds the other out toward Nick. "Heath Marino. I'm Ivy's... What are we calling me? Sorry, it's pretty new and we've got a couple of things going. You know Ivy. She's a multitasker."

I wrinkle my nose at him because I don't love the way that sounds, but it's also fair.

Nick's expression has lost its placid "I've got the high ground" look in favor of studying Heath critically. "I've never heard of you."

"Marino?" The guy I don't know has joined us. "Man, aren't you the dude who developed *Rain and Fury*? I love that game. I always thought it should have been bigger. We met at South by Southwest a couple of years back."

Heath seems to search his brain. "Chad, right?"

It's always an -ad.

He nods enthusiastically and offers his hand, which Heath takes.

"I didn't hear you were seeing anyone," Nick murmurs as we all start making our way to the brownstone.

Piano music drifts out of one of the second story windows. I'm certain CeCe's brought in some Broadway star to impress her guests.

"It's not really anyone's business," I reply, ignoring the arm he offers to help me up the stairs.

I can make it up the stairs fine. Mostly.

"Still prickly as always," Nick says with a sigh. "You know that was always your problem, Ivy. You could never take good advice. You had to be the man."

"No, I had to be the boss. Because I was literally the boss," I reply, and I can hear my voice coming out louder than I expected.

He rings the bell, and I can see the inner doors opening. "When you're ready to be serious about getting back to work, give me a call. I'll help you out for old time's sake."

"She has a job." Heath is next to me again, and he frowns down at me, a confused cute-boy look. "Don't you?"

He looks like his heart could be broken with a few careless words, like he's hanging on to whatever I say next.

He's good at this. I wonder how many of his friends he's saved with this act.

"Of course. Why do you think we're here? For the excellent food? For the entertainment? For the massive amounts of gossip we're about to hear?" The doors open and there's a very CeCe Foust man there, ready to usher us in. By that I mean he can't be more than twenty-two and probably formerly worked as a stripper.

Nothing wrong with that. He's strictly there for show. She has a butler who is five hundred years old and knows all of New York's secrets. Harold runs the house while this guy opens the door and brings CeCe her coffee. It's a good gig. I've heard CeCe offers complete medical and dental, so good for him.

"We're here for the money," I announce as I put my arm through his and let him lead me right past my ex. Nick stares like he's trying to figure something out. It's not a look I like because a thoughtful Nick can be a troublesome Nick.

I ignore him. Heath has gotten me past the bad part, and I'm ready to move on.

"Nice dress," Heath whispers as we move into the inner sanctum. "You look great."

Yeah, Heath is proving good for my ego, but I need to put that aside.

It's time for the real performance to begin.

Chapter Six

"Sorry I was late." Heath grabs a shrimp tart off the very attractive cater waiter as he passes by. "I take it even though we aren't here for the excellent food, I can still eat it, right? Because I got caught up in this interview and forgot to eat. That's also why I was late."

I have no idea what he's talking about. "You were right on time."

He nods. "Which means I was late. Also, I'm sorry about the kissing you thing. I couldn't think of what else to do. He was being an asshole, and the other two were worse."

Ah, so he'd heard something I hadn't. I can guess it was something about me being the queen bitch of the world who tried to take Nick down with me. He'd been walking up from the opposite direction, coming in from behind the bros. I oddly don't like him apologizing for the kiss. "I was happy for the save. He was acting like I might cry at the thought of him with another woman. And you should absolutely eat everything here. It will all be spectacular. I've heard she's got the last winner of *Top Chef* chained to her kitchen island. You didn't seem surprised I had an ex here."

"I might have done a deep dive on you after you left." He refuses the wine he's offered. "Something I should have done before I gave you forty percent of my company."

"Forty percent of nothing is nothing." I do not let the gorgeous man with the red wine get away from me. I glance around the room and recognize most of the people here, the ones in the tech world. The rest of the party will be filled with actors and writers and singers and people who generally amuse CeCe.

She is not a woman who believes mixing business with pleasure is always a bad idea. Though I'm sure in my case she would argue about it.

CeCe can separate the two. I'm still learning.

"When you think about it, it's less than nothing because I actually do have some debt associated with the project, and you took that on, too," Heath points out.

I take a sip of the wine. I need it. I also should have done a deep dive, but we have Harper between us, and that's very likely why we ignored everything we knew about business. "That's why we need cash."

This place is swimming in it. I recognize three billionaires within twenty feet of me.

"Yeah, I get that. The question is why do you need me? Like I said, I did some research after you left. I knew your name and that you've been pretty high up in the tech world, but I guess I didn't know how high up. You've made some big deals. You could have stayed in Silicon Valley. Why come back here?"

"It's always easiest to lick one's wounds in the comfort of one's home," I reply, wishing we would get off this subject. I haven't seen CeCe yet, but she will make her grand entrance at some point. I'd heard the whispers, though, as we'd walked in. The investors here are definitely surprised to see me.

"I guess I can understand that, though I never left," he admits, snagging what looks like a gougère. "After the game debuted, I was called one of the hottest up-and-coming game designers. And then I was cold."

"You could have gotten on at one of the big game companies." They were always looking for good coders, and his experience would have made him very attractive even if the game hadn't lit the world on fire.

"I've always wanted to work for myself," he murmurs as he looks around the place. "I'm afraid I'm lost here. Should I know these people?"

Oh, he should, and the fact that he doesn't know several of them on sight makes me think he isn't truly interested in going big. That's okay. I prefer it that way. He can handle the creative parts while I deal with the big picture. And the big picture is cash flow. There were rivers of cash in this room.

I get close because despite how big CeCe's space is, there's always someone listening. "See the guy in the navy suit over there?"

"Yeah," Heath says, and he doesn't directly stare at the man proving he's got some discretion.

"That's Ishaan Lagarhi. They call him the Marauder, a name he wears with relish," I explain. "He is a vegetarian in his private life, but he eats people for lunch in the professional one."

"I know the name," Heath replies. "I didn't know he invested. I kind of think we should avoid partnering with anyone called the Marauder. I don't particularly want to be marauded, if that's a word."

I understand the sentiment. "He's not here for the reason the others are. He's a shark scenting the water. He's looking for any hint that there's a company he can gobble up and sell for parts. And I've heard he does like his whiskey, and CeCe promised a tasting this evening."

"That's good to know." Heath suddenly has a pastry-wrapped something in his hand. I have zero idea how he manages to catch every server who walks through. "How about that guy? He looks interesting."

I glance over and see he's talking about an Asian man wearing comfy sneakers and a linen suit that looks casual, but I would bet the price tag is tons of tacos. He's got a heavy gold chain and a ready smile that seems to light up the room around him. "Kenzo Ito. He recently inherited his father's megacorporation. Multigenerational wealth, but they deal mostly with real estate and shipping in Southeast Asia. Kenzo's always wanted to get into the high-tech game. He's a pretty good coder, but what he's excellent at is really getting behind a project. I'll ask CeCe if he's looking to invest. What was it?"

Heath finishes chewing and seems to understand what I'm talking about. "Mini Beef Wellington. It was excellent. You're right. Whoever she's got in the kitchen is amazing."

And yet I can't seem to find a single server. "Grab me something the next time you see a waiter. And get a couple of those Wellingtons. I bet they travel well."

Shrimp is not something I'm willing to shove into my bag to eat later when I'm banished from Cinderella's castle again. But I bet those Wellingtons will hold up well in last year's Prada bag.

"So that's what an angel investor looks like." Heath is glancing over at Kenzo, who honestly seems like he should be in a boy band.

"He's kind of on the angelic side of angel," I explain quietly. "If you want to meet the devil, he's over by the door. What a surprise, he's talking to Nick."

Lance Norfolk. He's tall and thin, proof that he spends an

enormous amount of time at CrossFit gyms across the country. He could afford to go private but he likes to show off, and he loves his own celebrity. He's also a litigious motherfucker. The only thing he loves more than his washboard abs is a good lawsuit.

"Yeah, I know him. Hasn't he been on that investor show?" Heath asks. "He's kind of mean."

"He's the dude most likely to one day buy a private island, start a weird sex cult, and get his own dedicated Netflix documentary. We'll steer clear of him." I see someone I don't want to steer clear of. "Hey, give me a minute. I'll be right back. Do not give anyone a percentage of our company."

Heath's eyes widen like how dare I, but I dare because he gave me forty percent without a deep dive, so I can only imagine what will happen if Lance or Ishaan get hold of him.

Or they might take one look at his work and let him swim right by. That's what I need to figure out, and the man in the tux at the back of the room by the stairs is exactly the one to tell me.

Benjamin Johnson. He's a stately-looking gentleman. I joke about how old he is because he often does, too. He's told me he's been around since the Gilded Age, and that's how he knows every family in New York. The truth is Benjamin—I would never call him Ben—was born in Harlem in 1951, and he's a living, breathing history of the civil rights movement. He was friends with CeCe's older brother, who joined him on a bridge in Montgomery, Alabama, and then a hospital afterward. I often wonder if they were more than friends, but I don't ask. Craig died in the eighties, and shortly after that CeCe's husband passed as well. After George died, Benjamin and CeCe figured out how to turn a small inheritance into billions. He was her CFO for a long time but now has his own firm, though they often work together.

He's one of my favorite humans in the world, and that is a very short list.

His normally placid look is replaced with a smile as I approach. "Look who's come home to grace us with her presence. How are you, Ivy?"

I give him a hug. I'm not naturally a huggy person, but Benjamin has been almost like a father to me. Or a very kind uncle. He's the one who suggested I use the framework I'd already put so much effort into for medical forms. Benjamin believes in coding once and modifying forever.

I hate that I'm getting teary, and not in just a nice to see him way.

In a shame way.

Such a useless emotion, and yet it rears up at the most inopportune times. You can try to banish it, logic telling you how wasteful it is, but it's etched on our souls. Thanks, Puritans.

"Well, I'm back with my tail between my legs." I'm never going to pretend with this man. I might with CeCe because there's an odd social contract between us, but not Benjamin.

"You should definitely keep that tail there. It would ruin the line of your dress," Benjamin says, looking me over.

"You know what I mean."

"I do, but I also know that you're here and that's the first step at getting back off the ground," he says in that deep, soothing voice of his. "If you're here, then you're ready to try again, and I for one am damn glad to see that, Ivy. What happened to you in California does not have to define your life."

"Are you the reason I got the invite?" I hadn't considered the possibility that CeCe hadn't invited me herself.

Benjamin shakes his head. He went bald long before I met him, the hair left in an elegant semicircle of pure silver, like a crown he wears. "Absolutely not, but she's not happy with you. The only reason she didn't reach out sooner was she was waiting for you to inform her you were in town. She knew, of course, but thought you might need a bit of space. You took months of space and she got tired of waiting."

I feel my gut tighten. Shame had won that time, too. "I didn't know how to reach out."

"There's phones and emails, and I've heard one can even walk up to a door and knock on it." Benjamin's version of sarcasm comes with an enormous amount of old-school judgment.

"It's not that easy. You know she funded that project."

A brow rises over his dark eyes. "And she very likely would have funded getting you out of trouble, but you didn't ask. She'd already made her money back on you."

"And then I lost it all because I trusted the wrong person. Though she doesn't seem to have a problem with him." I take a deep breath. "I'm sorry. Please don't tell her I said that. I know he's got deep connections with this world, and I would never put her in a position where she would have to choose."

His lips curl up in a slight smile. "And that is why she would have backed you even knowing she might lose." He sighs as he looks at me. "Who is the new kid? I take it he's yours and you didn't bring him here to feed to CeCe."

Benjamin is well aware of CeCe's proclivities, though he claims he stays out of that part of her life. "His name is Heath Marino. I brought him here to meet CeCe, but not because I think she would find him amusing. He's built an interesting AI."

That brow is back up, but I read Benjamin pretty well. This is his "I'm listening" brow.

"I find the methodology behind it very intriguing."

"Then I'm sure CeCe will, too." Benjamin looks down at his watch. "She's got another twenty minutes before she's planning to make her grand entrance. I'll be sure to put you on her schedule. And do not try to stuff a bunch of food in that bag."

He knows my tricks. "But it looks so good."

"I've already had Chef make a whole bag for you," he offers. "Consider it a party favor. It'll be in the kitchen when you're ready to leave. Should I make another? That new boy of yours seems to be hungry."

Sure enough, Heath is standing to the side of the grand salon, and he's double fisting canapés. "I think it's a state a lot of us are in these days. Thank you, Benjamin. And I promise I won't stay away again."

Unless CeCe took one look at me and decided I was a bad bet.

"And Ivy? CeCe didn't invite Nick," Benjamin says. "I did."

Okay, that hurts more than I thought it would. "It's all right. I can handle being in the same room. Big girl here."

"I thought I could connect him with Lance Norfolk," Benjamin explains, his expression regaining that utter calm he normally sports. He looks out over the crowd, studying them with his practiced eye. "I know a man like Nick Stafford is always looking to move up in this world. Lance turns over staff quite regularly."

And sues them regularly, too. No one with a lick of sense would work for the man.

Nick doesn't have a lot of that. What he probably sees is a bro with a lot of cash and entrée into all the best gyms and a hundred thousand followers on social media.

Lance would be friendly right up until Nick did something to offend him, and then the man would pick his bones clean. Nick would think he was special, that it couldn't happen to him. Like the leopard eating faces meme. He could help the evil guy because Lance would never eat his face.

"I love you, Benjamin," I say.

"Karma sometimes needs a little push and a bit of patience." He gives me a wink. "Now go out there and shine like you do, dear. Don't let them see you sweat. Not even for a second."

I nod and join the party again.

But that is going to be one tall order.

Chapter Seven

"Yes, I'm working on something kind of interesting," Heath is saying to a woman who's worth more than a billion. Teresa Fleishman. She's from money that spans back to old Europe. Her family's been in New York for generations.

I like how he handles her. He's charming, but not in a skeevy way. He's good at presenting an authentic front.

Or maybe he's simply an authentic guy.

"It's a matchmaking program," he says.

And the light in Teresa's eyes dies, but she nods politely. "Ah, yes. That's interesting."

She is so not interested.

"The AI behind it certainly is." I need to find a way to save this. Teresa likes to talk, and if she hates an idea, it's pretty much dead with this group, and that includes CeCe. "There are so many ways to use what Heath is building. I think it's innovative far beyond its first-use intentions."

"Well, it's first-use intentions were to tell me what I wanted for dinner without me having to make the decision," Heath allows.

Teresa's hand reaches up to touch the Van Cleef necklace she's wearing. "Well, see *that* I might be interested in." She studies Heath for a moment, and I see the light of recognition in her eyes. "Marino? I know it's a fairly common name, but the whole matchmaking thing makes me think of Lydia Marino. You don't happen to be related, do you?"

I'm surprised Teresa knows the woman's name. No matter what

Heath says, I find it hard to believe that old-school matchmaking services are still a thing in modern New York.

Heath's lips kick up and his shoulders square like he's proud. "Yeah, she's my grandmother."

Teresa seems to think for a moment. "Is she behind this project? Is she working with you?"

"Of course. She always supports me," Heath replies. "I like to say I'm her favorite grandchild, but the truth is I'm her only grandchild. I've got a very big family on my mother's side, but on my father's side it's down to me and my grandmother. We have to stick together."

I don't believe him. Something about the way he hesitated makes me wonder. It's like he's convincing himself. I know I've only known him for a few hours, but he's an open book. I would say this man can't lie to save his life. He's not doing a good job of it now.

However, I'm interested in the fact that his grandmother's name piqued Teresa's interest.

"Why don't you give me a call next week and we'll talk." She turns my way. "I take it you're the lead on this."

"We're partners." Of course I'm the lead, but I know how to stroke a man's ego.

She hands me her card, though I don't need it. She's in my contacts, but this is proof that she's interested.

"That was good, right?" Heath manages to ask the question in between bites of meatball that likely has a much fancier name and is probably made with some hella expensive Japanese beef. I hope there's a Tupperware container of those in my future.

"That was good. And now we need to shut down on the talk because we've got some interest, but I don't want the idea everywhere. Teresa won't talk if she's interested. CeCe won't talk. I'm not sure about anyone else, so from here out all we talk about is your interesting approach to artificial intelligence. When we start presenting we can have investors sign NDAs." I'm feeling more positive. If I can get enough out of CeCe tonight, then we can have a couple of weeks to make a real business plan worthy of serious cash.

If CeCe opens the cash flow, then we find a workspace and hire some people to help write the code we need, some staff to back us up.

If that happens, we're a start-up. I'm a start-up.

Again.

I let that truth wash over me in the middle of this wildly decadent party. Let it bubble up and pop over and try to come to some sort of peace with it. I'm back at the bottom. I have to prove myself all over again.

This, of course, is the moment the lights dim slightly, and I hear the sound of piano music swelling. Benjamin is standing by the stairs as CeCe makes her entrance.

"Is she an investor or a rock star?" Heath asks, though he's smart enough to whisper the question.

All heads have turned and all eyes are on the queen of the Manhattan investor world.

"Can't she be both?" I whisper back.

CeCe Foust is a force of nature. Sometimes it's hard to believe she came from Brownsville in Brooklyn. I've heard the tales of George Foust meeting her at a diner she worked at, falling immediately in love, and carrying her back to Manhattan.

CeCe looks far younger than whatever her actual age is. I don't know her real age. I'm pretty sure she paid someone to change her birthdate because she was absolutely not born in 1992. Though I also don't believe the rumor that she was spawned from Satan sometime in the Middle Ages and has been working his will ever since. She's really not that bad. But she does look good for whatever her age happens to be, and she gives all that glory to her plastic surgeon, a woman named Candace who I swear can deliver Botox with one hand while holding an overly full martini in the other.

Still, CeCe looks fabulous in her designer gown and sky-high heels. She towers over many of the men here, but that doesn't faze her at all. CeCe Foust has been intimidating men for her whole adult life, and she doesn't mean to stop now. She waves with one hand while holding a tiny white puff ball in the other. She always keeps a gorgeously groomed Maltese with her. That dog fits beautifully into her every handbag, and I swear it knows how pretty it is. I catch the gleam of diamonds around the dog's neck and am reminded that CeCe buys her puppy's collars from Tiffany.

CeCe is my role model in life, and I'm worried I failed her.

"Welcome, my darlings." CeCe allows Benjamin to help her down the last step, and she graciously accepts the martini that has been waiting for her. No frou frou drinks for CeCe. She likes her martinis with ridiculously expensive gin and the barest hint of vermouth. I swear she has the bartender brush it over the glass. In a closed bottle. "It's so good to see you all here again, both new faces and old. And Ronald, you fit into both. The facelift looks wonderful on you, dear. And the very tight fit gives you a smile at last. Welcome to all our new creatives. It's lovely to meet you. Now let's get to know each other, shall we?"

She steps into the crowd but doesn't disappear into it. It's hard to when you top out at six foot three in stilettos and are wearing an elegant mirror ball as a dress. She gives air kisses and takes compliments.

"Wow, she is a lot," Heath whispers. "And is that a dog?"

"Yes, it's a dog, and if the dog doesn't like you CeCe will take it as a bad sign. She believes all dogs are psychic and can tell when a person is not good to do business with. The dog's name is Lady Buttercup, and you better make her like you. If she growls at you, we're dead in the water." Now that I think about it, Her Ladyship had growled at Nick, and I didn't listen to her.

"Now I'm afraid of the dog," Heath admits. "What if I'm more of a cat person?"

"Then she will know," I warn as I realize the crowd is parting and all eyes are turning our way.

I should have guessed it. This is the dramatic moment these people have been waiting for. They all know she is my mentor and I'd fucked up big time. Will the queen take back her wayward handmaiden? Or will she give me the cut direct? It's a phrase from super-old times, but the cut direct never really went out of style in Manhattan society. It's kind of like ghosting someone except in person, and it feels like someone is actually stabbing you.

It's a scenario I haven't included in my seemingly never-ending roster of how this will go, and suddenly I'm nervous about it.

Sometimes I can be a glass is half empty and probably has hidden cracks and will disintegrate when I try to drink from it person.

"Hey, you okay?" Heath seems to have picked up on my sudden anxiety.

Which means everyone likely can, and I'm screwing this up.

CeCe stops in front of me and studies me from head to toe, critically dissecting every part of me. Though there's still music playing, I swear it's faded into the background as the queen passes her judgment.

Will I be a diamond? Or the piece of coal that didn't quite make it?

"Ivy, that dress is lovely on you. Which of your friends knocked you out and dressed you?"

Relief floods through me. If she's insulting my fashion sense, we're okay. "I got it myself at Bergdorf this afternoon, thank you very much."

She looks me over again, but her expression is softer. "Then maybe you've learned a thing or two. Though you can do better than kitten heels, Ivy. That dress needs some height. I would send you to my surgeon, but Candace hasn't figured out how to lengthen her clients' legs without scars and pain and whatnot. Though she could do your breasts, dear. They're not getting any younger."

"Well, yours did," I shoot back, and I hear Heath gasp.

CeCe merely smiles, an expression that moves her forehead not a centimeter. "I've been assured they're eighteen and my face is thirty-five."

"Your liver is still in its nineties, and it got there the hard way." This is what we do. Sometimes I think she took a liking to me because I was willing to spar with her. In a weird way, it's how she shows affection.

"My liver is eternal." She raises her glass and then her gaze catches on Heath. And laser focuses in.

We're in the danger zone now. Oh, yes, we've moved into that place where the world can explode because she's caught the scent of something. I can see it in her eyes. She's not sure what it is, but she senses something about the young man in front of her.

She looks back at me. "Is he yours?"

I feel the moment Heath's hand finds my shoulder. It's a plea. *Save me from the sexual barracuda who has entered the pool.*

As he saved me before, it's a request I cannot refuse. I don't even want to. I don't want to think about the implications, but I don't like the idea of Heath being one of CeCe's pretty-boy conquests.

"Yes, he's mine." I say the words that will assure CeCe stays hands-off around Heath. CeCe plays by a set of very strict rules. *Thou shalt not poach* being one of them. I have tried to argue that one can't poach a human being capable of making their own choices, but she doesn't listen and honestly, in this case I think she's right. "CeCe, this is Heath Marino. He's a developer, and we're working on something together. Heath, this is Cecelia Foust."

"Darling, I'll never remember his name," CeCe assures me. "He's your project. If he's still around in a year or so, reintroduce us."

"Hello, I'm right here," Heath says.

"Thank you." CeCe holds up Lady Buttercup. "Since you are here, hold my baby while I take Ivy on a walk around the garden, won't you, dear? So many eyes here. There you go, baby. Is he all right or do you want to chew his face off?"

Heath is suddenly holding six pounds of judgmental show dog, and he looks super awkward doing it. "Uhm, I don't really know a lot about dogs."

CeCe is already threading her arm through mine and turning me toward the garden. "That's all right. She'll show you. It seems she likes you, Mr. Whatever Ivy Called You. We'll return soon."

I glance back to see Heath pull the dog against his chest. He puts his hand up to her little mouth, and I realize why she hadn't tried to bite his face off. The pup could smell the meatball in his hand.

And that is the moment I decide this partnership of ours just might work.

Chapter Eight

A tuxedoed man opens the door that leads us to the garden. Some New York City brownstones have green spaces, quaint little courts where the owners can place a bistro table and a couple of plants and pretend they're in a private park.

CeCe's *is* a private park.

I take in the elegant patio and the garden just past the soft lights. It's one of those that looks like a wild jumble of plants, but it's actually carefully curated and landscaped by the young man she lovingly calls Gardener. Harper would love this space, but then she'd always wanted to come along with me. I didn't think CeCe would appreciate Harper taking pictures and measurements and asking questions about the craftsmanship that CeCe would likely have zero idea how to answer.

CeCe stops at the edge of the elegant stone patio and stares out at the garden. I wait because she's figuring out how to handle me, and the fact that she doesn't have a prepared speech means I'm a mystery to her. It's a good thing. CeCe likes a mystery. After a moment she turns, her arms crossing her chest. "You didn't call me."

Here is the dressing down I've been expecting, but at least it didn't start with the actual business. "I was ashamed to, and you know why."

"Well of course I know why, darling," she replies. "You let yourself think with your pussy and it got you in trouble, but I've also taught you that shame has no place in your life. Shame is nothing but a social construct meant to drag you down. Especially in this. You hurt no one but yourself."

That's where she's wrong. "My former employees would disagree."

I still think about them every night. I had promised a lot to get them to go on a journey with me, and I'd crashed and burned.

"Your employees were given all the tools they needed to find other jobs," she points out in a firm tone. "I know you took as good care of them as you could. Your board has gone on to find new positions. You're the only one wearing a hair shirt and hiding in Hell's Kitchen."

I don't know what a hair shirt is, but it sounds terrible, so I get what she means. "It was my company."

She points an elegantly manicured finger my way. "And you should have used every resource you had."

I sigh because I knew what had gone down. She hadn't been there. "You couldn't have saved it. I was too heavily leveraged. You would have looked at the books and what we were bringing in and decided to let it go the same way I did. There is no use throwing money into a sinking ship."

She's the one who'd taught me that lesson long ago.

"I would have liked to have had the chance to make that decision myself." She goes silent, the moment lengthening and weighing between us. "I understand that I have a certain reputation, but not all of my decisions are made with my pocketbook. I reserve the right to throw my money away on people I care about. The good news for my bank account is I don't care about many people. You and Benjamin have been my real family the last decade, and you've been gone for half of that. When you come home, you don't even bother to call me. I have to throw this lavish party simply to get you to talk to me."

She might not appreciate shame, but the woman is good with guilt. "I'm sorry. I feel like I was the biggest disappointment. You trusted me and I failed."

She sighs, a long-suffering sound. "Everyone fails, Ivy. It's *how* you fail that counts. Men in our business tend to fail up. They don't allow shame to drag them down, even when they wreck and ruin lives. They pull the ripcord on that golden parachute and find the next position of power they'll be handed."

"It's different for us." Women aren't allowed the same amount of chances men are. It's just a fact of life.

"Then we need to change that, and you won't change a damn thing hiding in your mother's apartment. Have you ever wondered if we don't get those chances because we don't demand them? Because we play by rules the men never have to." Her hand moves, gesturing to my dress.

"This is an excellent first step. You've always dressed like a stuffy old man. You have tits. Use them. I assure you if it was acceptable for men to wear codpieces in this century, every one of the men in that room would be stuffing theirs, showing off like peacocks. No more business suits. Dress to flatter yourself. Now who is Heath Marino?"

She pounces with that question. It is the one she's absolutely wanted to ask since the minute I introduced him, and I knew very well she would remember his name. CeCe forgets nothing except the year she was born. That always changes. Still, I feel like teasing her. "I thought you weren't going to remember his name."

"You know me better," she chides. "I'll not only remember his name, I'll have a dossier on him by morning. Benjamin has likely already submitted his name to Private Investigator."

This is a surprise. I have not heard of this PI who almost certainly has a name that CeCe remembers but will not use. "You have a private investigator?"

"Of course. My staff is wide and varied, and despite being very lovely, they're also excellent at their jobs. Well, the little one who cleans is not that good, but he's got the bluest eyes, you see." She frowns. "I genuinely don't remember *his* name. But I do remember the name of the new man in your life. He looks like a gamer boy."

"But I put him in a suit." I was trying to avoid the gamer boy look.

She shakes her head. "You can put a gamer in a suit, but you can't make him comfortable in it. That young man owns a gaming laptop and one of those headsets I despise, and likely one of those chairs that has speakers in it." She shudders in distaste. "Please tell me you're not going into game development. I know it was your first love, but…"

If there's one space in our world that CeCe can't stand, it's gaming. She's the one who taught me my creativity could work past MMORPGs. "He's working on an AI."

CeCe snorts, but it's an oddly elegant sound. "Well isn't everyone?"

She has a point. In the last decade AI has taken off in multiple directions, but I still think Heath might have something. "He's got some interesting protocols, and there's a great deal of innovation in how he's attempting to train the AI. I want to see how it works."

"If you're interested, I'm interested," she says. "Is there money to be made?"

"I wouldn't be here if I didn't think so."

"There's something you're not telling me." She always seems to know.

I think about hedging, but she'll find out. "He thinks he's working on a matchmaking app."

She throws her head back, throaty laughter filling the garden. Then it stops. "Oh, dear. You're serious."

"His grandmother was something of a matchmaker in Little Italy, and he thinks he can make it work for him, too. But it's not the app I'm interested in. I've played around with the AI, and I think it's got a lot going for it. I think it's a starting point for any number of applications," I explain.

"Does he know that's what you're interested in?"

This is the part that makes me feel a bit queasy. I'd been clear with him that I didn't think a matchmaking app is the best idea. He wants the chance to prove to me it is. Still, I don't think he understands how much I hate the idea. "I need some time to work on him."

She considers me for a moment, her eyes narrowing in the soft glow from the twinkle lights above. They function much the same way a filter on a social media app works. They give her softness she doesn't have in the harsh daylight. "You like him."

"Yes, but we don't have anything serious. This is not the same in any way." I need her to understand I won't make the same mistakes I made with Nick. I should tell her we only met today and the only kiss we've shared was meant to spare me the embarrassment of being single—which shouldn't be an embarrassment at all. "The truth is I think he's an overgrown golden retriever with some very good ideas. He'll be incredibly loyal, and I won't have to worry about him making huge mistakes because all I intend to trust him with is the product."

"Excellent. Then you learned something in California, and it was worth it." CeCe nods approvingly. "You need to figure out why he's working on this particular project. If he's in it for the money, you'll be able to steer him in the right direction fairly easily once he sees the potential cash."

"And if he's not?" I worry this is some way to connect with his grandmother, and I have zero idea how to deal with that.

"Then you'll need leverage, and I can give that to you in the form of cash. How much do you need to get started?"

The offer threatens to floor me. I thought I would have to talk more, have to beg a little maybe. "Why?"

"Why what?"

"Why would you give me money again? Without a single meeting about the concept."

An elegant shoulder shrugs. "Because I know what you don't. I know that you are stronger for having failed. You see this as weakness, and I see a woman who got kicked hard and is doing the only thing life requires of us. We are not guaranteed success, Ivy. In fact we're almost sure to find the opposite. You climbed the mountain at a very young age. Your failures were minor things that barely registered as anything beyond inconveniences. This gutted you."

"Yes." Even as I reply, I can feel the humiliation threaten to sweep me under again. I realize I've been holding it together all day. It took a lot to walk into this party, to let all these people see me again when I want to be hiding under a rock somewhere. "I'm still wounded, CeCe."

"I know, but you're not showing it on the outside. Feel all your young woman feelings and then get a bottle of wine and a reasonable amount of comfort food and in the morning, you get on the treadmill again. You start climbing again. You do it every single night until one morning you wake up and you don't need it anymore because you're climbing again and you know you can make it. That's the difference between the people who achieve their goals and the people who don't. The people who make it believe they can. It's why there are so many successful men. Testosterone is a magnificent deceiver. It makes a man feel confident and so he does the thing and even when it's half assed, he presents it as extraordinary. Not all of them, of course. But it certainly works for your Nick."

I'm not sure a hormone is responsible for the success of most men, but I can buy it with Nick. I also can't wait to see if that particular leopard eats his face. "I need fifty thousand seed money, and I'm going to be honest, that's only going to hold me a month maybe two, but I should have enough for a proof of concept meeting then."

"I'll have a transfer for you in the morning, and I'll see you back here in two months," CeCe says and starts for the doors again. "Now run along, my darling. The party will get harder the more they drink. I'd like you out of the line of fire. Put on your blinders and run your race."

She'd often called me a thoroughbred. I'd often laughed.

But I know she's right about one thing. The race is on.

Chapter Nine

I'm still thinking about what CeCe said to me an hour later as I sit on the fire escape of my childhood home and look out at the people walking around. It's closing in on midnight, but that means nothing in the city.

"You want another?" Heath sits next to me and offers me another tiny tart.

We've gotten to the dessert portion of the bag Benjamin had made for me. The man knew me well. He'd gathered up a feast because he'd known I wouldn't be able to eat until I'd seen CeCe and once I'd seen her I would run back to my hidey-hole.

There is only so much a girl can do in one night.

I hadn't planned on Heath coming up with me.

"You don't know me so you can't know how odd it is for me to say these words, but I'm full." The moon hangs low in the sky, and I'm happy to have changed into yoga pants and a sweatshirt. It reminds me I'm not usually the woman who wears sexy dresses and gets kissed by guys. I shouldn't have worn the sexy dress at all because it now has a red wine stain that means I own that sucker and I'll be eating more cheap tacos. Maybe less of them since it was so expensive.

Anyway, I feel more like me now, but that also means I'm feeling the weight of what happened tonight.

Heath pops the tart in his mouth and leans back against the brick wall. He dumped his jacket the minute we walked in. "That was a lot."

We've been talking about innocuous things up until now. I found out he went to Cornell. That had surprised me, but I was starting to get the feeling that there was some family money in his background. After that he'd worked for several big tech firms before going off on his own. We hadn't talked much about me, but I liked it that way.

"CeCe is always over the top," I say, my legs dangling over the edge. I like to sit out here and think. The building is quiet, filled with mostly older people like my mom. "It's kind of her thing. I think in the beginning she used her outrageousness to help her climb the ladder. She needed something beyond money to get people to notice her. Our world likes a performer."

"What do you mean?" Heath asks. "I would think the over-the-top thing would hurt her."

"It didn't hurt Jobs," I point out. "He held court like a king."

"Huh," Heath says. "I guess I never thought about it that way. And now I feel super sexist because I'm thinking of all the over-the-top billionaire tech gods who I would never have said that about. Bezos rode a giant dick into space."

He had. "CeCe would do the same if she had any interest in leaving the earth. She would say a dick is most likely to get you extremely high before it brings you right back down."

Heath laughs, and I like the sound. "You seem to be really close to her. I've got to know how you met her. You grew up here, right? You didn't grow up in her world."

"Exactly here. This very apartment," I agree. I'm barely three miles away from CeCe's mansion, but there's a massive world between us. "When I was in high school, she came to my school to talk about going into STEM. The girls, that is. One of the teachers at my school was her husband's cousin's daughter, and she would do anything for anyone connected to George."

"He's been gone for a long time, right?"

"Far longer than they were married, but she says he was the love of her life, and now she's happy living out the rest of it, having fun." Sometimes I wonder if her lush lifestyle isn't an odd way of grieving. I know in the beginning building a business with what George left her had been. "Anyway, she came in and talked about how the future was in the code, and whoever wrote that code controlled the future. She was very intense, and there was a lot of talk about not depending on anyone to take care of you. There was the 'money protects you' talk. I'm pretty sure she scared most of the girls."

"But not you."

I remember being in awe of her. Harper had pretty much ignored her, and Anika had been one of the ones who wouldn't look her in the eyes. But I'd seen someone with confidence. Someone I wanted to be. "I was already a complete nerd. I was a mathlete, and I'd been playing around with robotics and game theory. I started hacking around that time."

He grins, his eyes shining in the low light. "Seriously?"

I stare at him. "Like you never hacked a system?"

His hands come up as though to show me how innocent he is. "I'm a good Catholic boy. I stay away from the illegal stuff. Though I can get through a password. I have to be able to. No one remembers their passwords. I've got an aunt and uncle who run a restaurant and they password protect their systems, but no one writes it down. Not anywhere. They're paranoid someone will find it and steal their recipe for caponata, because they do write that down even though they've made exactly the same thing for fifty years. But the password they have to change every two months they think they'll remember. So I have to break in."

I know how it feels to be everyone's tech support. "When I was running Jensen Medical, my mom would call me in the middle of board meetings to ask me how to get on Google."

Heath snorts. "It's fun to be the only tech savvy person in a family of Luddites." He seems to remember he had started this line of questioning for a reason. "So you met her there, but how did we get from high school to her giving you fifty grand because you showed up at a party?"

"Simple. I emailed her and asked her some questions," I reply. It had taken a lot for me to get the courage to write to CeCe. "I wanted to know what she thought I should study in college and what I needed to learn to become successful. I never expected her to write me back, but she asked if I would like to take tea with her. I did not know what that entailed at the time, but, unlike my mom, I was pretty good with Google even back then."

I had dressed in my very nicest skirt and borrowed a silk blouse my mom wore when we went to church every Christmas or Easter, and I'd made my way to the Upper East Side where I met with CeCe and tried to pretend like I knew what teas to drink and how to sit in the big, luxurious wingback chairs and that I was perfectly comfortable with the white-gloved waiters who gracefully poured from silver pots.

She'd had two martinis and none of the tea cakes or elegant

sandwiches I'd inhaled, but when it had come time to go, she'd had them pack up everything left and sent it home with me.

I've been in love with her on some level ever since. "She asked me to meet with her and offered me an internship that summer. Paid because she told me I should never work for someone else with no pay. While my friends were doing volunteer work at the hospital or helping with their family business, I was learning how to navigate the world of angel investors and getting paid to do it. The next summer I came to her with my first business plan. I'd written my first game. It was a version of chess with the teachers at my school as the pieces. She gave me a four-hundred-dollar loan for marketing, and I paid her back within a month. Within a year I had adapted it so you could easily change out the pieces with your own characters, and that is how I partially paid for MIT. The rest was scholarships and work study programs. And yes, one of the scholarships was from the Foust Foundation."

"So she's been your mentor for years."

"Over a decade." It's more than a mentorship. I spent most of my summers with CeCe until I graduated and took a job with a tech firm in Austin. Then I'd moved out to Silicon Valley and the worst had happened and I hadn't called her in over a year.

I'm kind of an asshole.

When I'd pulled away, Anika and Harper had shown up on my doorstep. CeCe didn't work that way. She'd called and left a message, and then the ball had been in my court.

"Since I graduated, I've worked for three start-ups, two corporations, and a nonprofit. Six jobs in seven years, and most of them I didn't walk away from," Heath says with a sigh. "I was either laid off or the company went under. I've never had time anywhere to find a mentor like that."

"Is that why you decided to work for yourself? I've seen what you can do. You could get a job," I point out. I'm not surprised to hear his story. I've heard it a thousand times. Businesses start-up and then nose-dive, and the employees keep riding the wave.

"I'm tired of moving around, tired of always being the new guy. I want to build something for myself, something that can last."

But our world moves so fast that nothing lasts for long. What's the highest of tech today will be antiquated in a few years. It's why I never get too invested in any project. If what Heath is working on had only one application, I would not be sitting here with him.

Because I'm all business. I wouldn't be sitting here with him because I like him, because he moves me in a way I haven't felt in a long time.

Heath turns my way. "So that was an incredible place. I don't think I've ever been in a brownstone that big. Was your place in San Francisco that nice?"

I laugh at the thought, happy to be able to veer away from thinking about how he's probably going to fail and I'm going to be there when it happens. "No. Not even close, but it was nice. I liked having more than one bathroom."

"Growing up we had a place with two and a half baths," Heath says with a sigh. "I had my own. My parents had their own, and there was a place for guests, too. I miss that. I share with Darnell. I think he wants to kill me sometimes. I'm probably the messier one."

"Because you're a princess who had your own bathroom." There's a lot we haven't talked about yet, and I've been hesitant because I've enjoyed the easy conversation we've found, but I can't let the night end without knowing a few things. "So you said you did more research this afternoon. Were you upset by what you found out? Were you upset to find out you'd hitched yourself to someone who had to sell her company? I did, you know. And the house. That was how in debt we were at the end."

He seems to think about that for a moment. "I think we all have our ups and downs, and we fail until we succeed. Yours happened to be really big and covered by a bunch of media outlets. Mine were small and no one noticed. Mine felt very lonely."

"And mine felt like the world was ending and everyone was watching me. Still are." I know they're talking about me back at CeCe's. The party will be going to the wee hours of the morning, and I will be the center of gossip whether or not I'm there.

"That's a mark of success," he argues. "You know the old 'no publicity is bad publicity' saying."

"Well, it feels bad." Now it felt like a healing wound—itchy at times, like the skin isn't really mine and fits too tight. At the time it had felt like the end of the world.

"To answer your question, no. It didn't upset me. Look, I meant what I said earlier. You did good work. You made a product that genuinely helped people. You can say that wasn't what you meant to do, that all you were doing when you created it was filling a need for cash. But the end result helped people." He's quiet for a moment. "I'm going to assume that guy was an ex."

I groan. Of all the things we need to discuss, this is the one I don't want to. "I'm sorry you were put in that position tonight. I promise I'll be perfectly professional from now on."

He seems to think about his next question. "Did you invite me so you didn't have to go alone?"

I want to lie to him, but the truth is the truth. He hadn't been necessary to this evening's task. In fact, having CeCe meet him put me in the bad position of having to explain why he was there. "I was fine attending alone until I found out Nick was going to be there. I knew he'd either have a pack of bros with him or a new girlfriend. He never goes anywhere alone."

"Were you planning on introducing me as your boyfriend?"

I shake my head. "No, but I wasn't going to correct anyone if they got that impression, and now that I'm saying the words, I feel like an idiot. I'm not some sad chick who always needs a boyfriend. Nick was actually only my second long-term relationship. I'm perfectly content on my own. I don't know what came over me. I can tell him the truth."

"And waste my knight riding in moves? That feels harsh. Was the kiss that bad?"

"You know it was not. It was a perfectly fine kiss."

"It was a pretty good kiss." There's a wealth of masculine arrogance in his tone, and I wish I didn't find that charming coming from him.

It had been my only kiss in the last six months, and probably the most passion I'd had from a guy in a couple of years, and that was so sad. "It was a kiss we both need to forget because we're going to be working very closely together for the next couple of months. We've got to hire at least one, maybe two contractors."

"Where are we going to put them? I don't know if you noticed, but neither one of us has a whole lot of space. I was worried about where I was going to put you."

"They can work remotely if we can't find someplace cheap." The remote work might be a necessary thing since I intend to have one of the coders working on what I want them to work on—an interface for a social media/commerce app. I can give Heath a little, but I know what CeCe wants. The AI and Heath's unique framework is what will sell this project.

"And if we get full funding?"

I like that he's an optimist. One of us needs to be. "Then we find a small office probably somewhere in Jersey because that's what we'll be able to afford and we spend the next three or four years working our asses off only to fail because some asshole swoops in two months ahead of our launch date with something too similar. Then we can decide if we want to spend the money on the inevitable lawsuits, but that's only if we get the choice. There's also the possibility that someone out there gets word of what we're doing and preemptively files for a patent that will block us even though the fucker doesn't have enough to prove concept. Then, it's back to the lawyers and we decide if we have deep enough pockets to fight, and that answer is almost always no."

Heath stands, and I can't help but notice how tall and fit he is. I need to take some me time because my brain is spending too much energy on how hot he is. He starts to lift one long leg over the railing.

I pop up. "What are you doing?"

His head turns slightly, lips curling in a mischievous grin. "Ending it all. I've seen the future, Ivy. It's not worth it."

He's teasing me. I'm not sure why it rankles. Or maybe I am. "It can happen, and it does all the time. This is the big leagues, and it's a battle every single day."

He looms over me, so close I can practically feel the warmth of his skin. "Is it war or baseball? I need to know because you are the queen of mixed metaphors, and I want to be sure I'm all kitted up. So glove or rifle?"

He's really not ready for this. "Both."

"All right, then." He glances down at his watch. "I should go. Apparently I've got both a game and a war to prepare for. I'm going to need some sleep. Now I know you said we shouldn't kiss again, but we already went there so…"

I take a big old coward's step back. If I let him kiss me now, it won't be because someone's watching and we need to keep up our "cover." It will be because I want him to, and I can't want him to. I just can't.

I'm lying to him. Oh, it's for his own naïve good, but I'm still lying.

"I think we should keep this professional," I say, but the words come out all breathy.

One brow cocks over those warm eyes of his. "I'm not sure that's going to work for us. I don't know if you've noticed, but we've got this crazy chemistry thing going on."

I shake my head. I don't believe in chemistry things. What's going on is nothing more than horniness and the availability of an attractive partner of the right persuasion. That's all it is. There's not some mystical thing that happens between men and women. "And we have a business going on."

"And you learned your lesson," he says, the words an obvious reluctant acceptance. He backs off. "I've learned these things tend to fall into place. So I'll be patient. I think you should help me on one of my interviews. I'll pick you up at ten tomorrow morning."

A light comes on in the background, and I realize my mother is staring out at us. She's still in jeans and a sweater, her purse on her shoulder because she's just walked in.

I climb through the window, feeling like a teen who's gotten caught with a forbidden boyfriend. He's forbidden all right, and that's why he's not going to be my boyfriend. "Hey, Ma. This is Heath. He went with me to the party tonight. We're going to be working together. Heath, this is my mother, Diane Jensen."

Heath has to bend in two to get through, but he's smiling when he makes it. He holds out an overly large hand. "Mrs. Jensen. I'm Heath Marino. Nice to meet you."

My mother shakes it, but her eyes are narrowed on him. "Are you planning on screwing my daughter over?"

Heath takes that question with a cool I wouldn't have thought he had. "Not at all. I'm entirely in her hands. She's already stolen forty percent of my company and held the first investor meeting without me, while I was left in a pool of sharks holding a flatulent… I don't know. It was a dog of some kind, or a really big rodent with excellent hair. I mean it was shiny like someone loved it. And I'm pretty sure that collar had actual diamonds on it. My point is if anyone is being taken advantage of, it's me."

My mother's smile is reluctant but genuine. "See that it stays that way. Now off with you. It's after midnight. Nothing good happens after midnight."

"Good night, Mrs. Jensen. Good night, Ivy." He gives a jaunty salute. "I'll see you in the morning. Bring a box of tissues. These usually get emotional."

I'm not sure why we need emotions to train an AI, but I watch him go, and then my mother is locking the door behind him, turning every dead bolt and finishing with the chain that would keep absolutely no one out.

In her mind, we're locked away from the rest of the world now and it's safe.

I know it's not. I know the world is here with us every second of the day.

"How much did CeCe give you?" My mother wastes no time.

This again. I hate this. My mother loathes CeCe, and I don't get it. "None of your business. I'm going to bed."

I turn because I can see she's had a couple of glasses of wine or a few beers, and that's usually when she wants to argue. My mother is not a drunk by any definition, but on the infrequent occasions when she's tipsy, she veers to the aggressive.

"Can't you see this is how she controls you?"

I whirl around. "She doesn't control me at all. That's what you don't understand. You're the one who wants control. CeCe only wants what's best for me."

"Turning you into another her is what's best for you? Turning you into a person who lives to do nothing but grab money from hardworking people?"

"It's called building a business, and I never grabbed a dime of your money, Ma. If you recall, I worked my way through school."

"No, you got lucky," she argues.

I'm so tired of this. She believes because I don't work with my hands or have an MD or a career she sees on TV, that I don't really work. She can't conceive of coding as building something. "Good. I got lucky. I'll get lucky again."

Her face flushes. "Or you'll ruin everything again. Do you have any idea how your father would feel about his daughter constantly taking handouts from some rich bitch? He would be so ashamed."

The words punch me right in the gut. So hard I swear it takes me a moment to breathe again, and I realize why. Because deep down I've asked the question and wondered about the answer.

My mom's hand slaps over her mouth, but it's too late. "Ivy, I'm so sorry. I shouldn't have said that."

Not *I didn't mean that. I shouldn't have said that.*

She did mean it, and an ache opens inside me. I turn and go to bed.

I'm pretty sure I won't be sleeping much tonight.

Chapter Ten

I'm still thinking about the fight with my mother the next day as Heath sets up the video and sound equipment. It isn't some crazy professional setup, but I've been assured he can get the job done.

We're in a small apartment looking over Rockaway Beach. It took an hour via subway to get out here, and Heath had chatted much of the time. At first with me, and then when he realized I wasn't talking back, with the various other travelers around us. He was a chatty motherfucker. He now knew the basic histories of a ninety-two-year-old woman on her way home from visiting a friend at a nursing home, a twenty-three-year-old grad student who was totally hitting on him, and a tourist who thought he was heading to MOMA. He is in for a treat because he gets to see Queens instead.

I am the dour center of the universe. The black hole everyone tries to avoid getting sucked into.

Not even the sight of the beach calms me today.

"Do you know Mrs. Marino?"

I look up, and one of the interviewees stands there in her brilliantly colored housedress, a full gray helmet of tight curls around her head. "No."

Anna Maria Brambilla is a sixty-eight-year-old retired nurse. From the file I read on her while Heath charmed the A train, she's been married to her husband, Phil, for forty-eight years. He's seventy and worked for the Port Authority most of his life.

For some reason Heath believes their story will help train his AI to better match people.

"Well, she's the loveliest lady I ever met." Anna Maria takes this time to sit across the bistro table from me. She does not seem to understand that I came out on the balcony to be alone. "I was barely nineteen when my mother took me to her."

Through the haze of my misery—and lack of sleep—I find something interesting in her words. "You went to a matchmaker?"

Heath likely mentioned all of this in his long explanation of his methods, which I nodded through and heard very little of because I was thinking about the fact that my father would be ashamed of me.

"I went to *the* matchmaker." Anna sits up, shoulders back. "My mother scrimped and saved, and she was so excited when Mrs. Marino took us on. She didn't take on every client she met with, you know."

I do not know, and I am curious. I have to admit to being cynical about things like matchmaking. I put it in the same basket as the mystical arts. I don't think anyone can know how two people are going to work in a relationship. It's a money grab, like most things. It's precisely why I feel okay doing what I'm doing. Heath is full of enthusiasm and says all the right things, but at the end of the day, he's creating something that will potentially build up vulnerable people's hopes, take their money, and still leave them divorced a few years down the road.

"I would think she would take the clients who could pay," I reply.

Anna shakes her head. "Oh, she's not like that. I mean, obviously, she got paid and paid well, but she also took on clients who couldn't pay her a dime. I heard a very prominent member of our city once went to her and asked to be matched and she said 'Mr. Mayor, I wouldn't match you with a goat, and I don't like goats.'"

I snort at that one. "So she took you on and matched you with Phil?"

"For me it was very quick. I spent a day with her and then filled out all her forms and answered all the questions and she did her research on me."

I feel the need to interrupt her. "What kind of research?"

"Oh, she talked to my friends and former teachers. I know she had tea with my priest. And of course she interviewed my whole family extensively. All my sisters and cousins. She even went to prison to talk to my brother. Now he was in prison because he got too involved in Gino Rossi's business, which was too involved in Sicilian business around the area."

I could make that leap. "He was in the mob."

"He was mob adjacent," Anna corrected. "Until he went to prison, and then he was totally a mafia man after that. But the point is how thorough Mrs. Marino is."

"Did she tell Phil's family you had a mafioso brother?"

A shoulder shrugged. "Honey, we all do. There's always that one bad apple. Phil's second cousin believes the world is flat. Give me a made man over a moron any day of the week. Anyway, like I said, it was quick for me. Within three months she'd given me three different men to date, and after I went on one date I knew he was the guy for me and I didn't have to meet anyone else. But Phil had been waiting almost three years."

"Why so long?" That sounded like a long time.

"She said she hadn't found the right woman for him. She told him he had to be patient. So he waited."

"I told everyone who tried to set me up that I was a taken man. I just didn't know by who yet," a deep voice says. I turn and Phil Brambilla is standing in the doorway. He's short and bald. The only hair on his head is a moustache. He has kind eyes that beam when he looks at his wife. "I would have waited another three years for you. Now come in here. Mrs. Marino's grandson needs something called a sound check."

I follow her back in the two-bedroom apartment. This, I've been told, is their retirement place. They raised their three kids in Little Italy and moved out here when they retired. The wall in their living room is covered with pictures, snapshots of a family history. A girl on a bike, her hair in pigtails, surrounded by two boys wearing Yankees T-shirts. A big family around the table, all smiling for the camera. Three of the pictures are of the kids grown and in their caps and gowns. And there were so many grandkids.

I don't have these things where I live. Time stopped when my father died. My mother didn't take many pictures, and she didn't have siblings to back her up. All our pictures end shortly after the millennium. The ones we do have are on our phones now or stashed away in slowly disintegrating albums. I tried to look through one of them a few years back, an old one, and the glue was so sticky I couldn't get the pages to move.

"Hey, you okay?"

Heath startles me but I manage to quash the weird emotion running through me and the questions.

If his grandmother really did have some skill, what would it feel like to know she'd helped create more than a couple? She'd created a family.

"I'm fine. So do you have questions you start with?" I ask, hoping the emotions don't show on my face.

"Yes, and the first one is for you. Do you need a hug?"

I roll my eyes.

He shrugs. "Hey, I've been told I'm an excellent hugger. I'm not one of those zero percent body fatters who feel like a rock. I'm squishy in all the right places."

He's ridiculous, and it's exactly what I need to get out of that terrible headspace. I laugh because he's not squishy anywhere but in his head. "I'm fine. No hugs needed. Now answer me."

He seems like he doesn't quite believe me, but he moves on. "We're going to sit and ask them about their lives."

"Should we ask about how they're compatible?"

"Most of that is in the data my grandmother compiled," Heath points out. "You looked through it, right?"

I'd sifted. It had been lots of questions about normal things a couple should know. Do you want children? What religion do you follow? How important is it your children are raised in your faith?

And then there were weird ones like what's your favorite color.

"Yeah. I didn't read the essays though."

He grimaces. "Then you missed the best parts. She asks everyone to write an essay on what they want their marriage to look like in five years. Those are the best. For Anna and Phil, they both saw Anna staying home to raise the kids while he took care of them all financially. And there was a bunch of stuff about dogs and picket fences and moving to the suburbs."

I'm confused because I did know enough to know some of their basic history. "But she worked the whole time. And they didn't leave the city."

"Yeah, but they both wanted the same things," he points out. "It doesn't mean they got them. It simply means they were willing to work toward a goal. When that goal had to change, so did they. My grandmother always tells me the only way to have a successful relationship is to be willing to grow together. Change will always come. It's how a couple handles the change that makes or breaks them. Anna and Phil didn't get the house they wanted, but I think they would say they got the family they wanted."

And I'm back to emotional. I shove that aside in favor of something I do understand. Business. "And how is this going to teach the AI?"

Heath seems to think about how to explain this to me. He leans in. "Think of it as stories. You know AIs can write whole books now."

"But should they?" Somehow I don't think I want to read a romance written by HAL.

"That is above my pay grade. Anyway, I feed them these successful stories and the AI puts together people who could potentially be more successful stories," Heath explains. "I'm trying to teach it how to balance what people say they want with what actually helps build a healthy relationship."

"And you think you know how to do this?"

His big shoulders shrug. "I think I've been around many of them. I learned a lot from my grandmother."

"Who gets paid to put people together." It wasn't like she did it out of the kindness of her heart.

"Yes. It's a job like a lot of others, but if you talked to clients like Anna, you would know my grandmother also did it for less or free sometimes." He studies me for a moment. "You don't like this project, do you?"

We are in dangerous water here. He's not ready to hear what I really think. "I'm skeptical. Call me Scully to your happily-ever-after believing Mulder."

"Love is out there," he promises me. "Come on. Let's get started."

Two hours later I think I understand these people more. Or I don't but I want to.

They survived so much together. They got through their youngest being born with a heart problem. They got through taking care of Anna's parents in their old age. They survived 9-11 and the aftermath. Thirty-seven Port Authority officers died that day, and Phil had known most of them. Anna had taken care of some who suffered from ailments caused by that day. It had taken a massive toll on them, but they'd held on and gotten through it.

"How do you solve disputes?" Heath is looking down at his notebook.

"We don't have that many anymore," Anna admits.

"I learned to do what my wife says." Phil gives me a wink.

See, this is what I don't get. "But then you never get your way?"

Phil seems to think about that for a moment. "I get my way all the time. I get it when she cooks my favorite meals or when she makes sure I have coffee in the morning. She's worked all these years, too, you know. And in the beginning I wasn't good at helping with the housework."

"He's gotten better over the years," Anna assures us. "He's a whiz with the slow cooker, and the man knows how to use the washing machine."

"But I didn't in the beginning, and that was a struggle. She had so much on her," Phil says. "So if she wanted to see a movie instead of going to the ballpark, we did that. Compromise is important in a marriage. I suppose I should put it better. I guess the youth would say I was being a little misogynistic. I don't just do what my wife tells me to. We've learned enough about each other that we compromise on the big things and give way on the things that don't matter as much."

"Some people can't compromise." I know many of them. I worry I'm one of them. I hadn't really compromised with Nick. I gave in because I got tired of arguing. I let him wear me down to the point that we did what he wanted. We'd seen his friends and not mine. We ate at the restaurants he chose. Is there a difference between compromising and giving in?

"Everyone can compromise," Anna corrects. "It comes down to how much love and respect you have for your partner as to whether you do or don't."

"But how do we teach the AI that?" I try to wrap my head around the only thing I can—how does this help the business?

"The AI will learn which people value compromise and which don't," Heath replies. "At least that's the plan. Once it knows how to pair people—those who are more reluctant to compromise with those who prefer to let someone else take the lead—it can make logical decisions."

I can think of a problem with that. A big one. "So you want to pair people who rule with an iron fist with their next victims?"

"I didn't say that, Ivy." It's the first time I've seen him get irritated.

But I have a point. "It feels like we're setting people up for domestic abuse."

"I don't think that's what Heath wants to do," Phil says, obviously uncomfortable.

"No system is perfect." Heath ignores everyone but me.

"I don't know if a computer is ever going to be able to do what your grandmother does." Anna's head shakes as she stands. "She's got the touch, that one. You can't get that from a computer. But as for Ivy's worry, I think that can happen anywhere. A computer program might be able to catch a potential abuser better than a normal dating app."

Heath stands, and it seems this interview is over now. He holds a hand out, and his game face smile is back on. "Anna, Phil, thank you so much for your time."

I get the feeling he's highly annoyed with me. I don't like how that sits in my chest. Like it's too tight, and I want to go back to when he was feeding me mini tarts on the fire escape the night before.

He packs up and before I know it I'm walking down the street, the ocean to one side. We're making our way back to the train. He's walking ahead of me, his long legs eating the distance.

I can't keep up with him without jogging, and I'm not going to do that. I can find my own way back if he's butthurt and won't talk about it.

I'm butthurt, too.

I find a bench and sit while he gets farther from me.

We're not friends. We barely know each other. Sure he kissed me, but we're on proper footing now and this feels better, honestly. For a couple of hours there I thought he was beyond human annoyance. I'm really good at annoying people. It's how I get things done, but it also means I don't have a ton of men rushing to spend time with me.

I wonder how much the tacos cost around here. It's lunchtime, and I don't do well when I'm hangry.

"Ivy?"

I look up and he's staring down at me. He moves so he's blocking the sun and I can see him. Yep. There it is. Pure annoyance. This feels familiar, and I know how to deal with it. "I'm fine. You can head back to the city. I'll take the next train."

He frowns down at me. "What is going on with you?"

With me? Yes, this feels far more familiar to me than his nice-guy routine. "You're the one who was practically running away. I don't jog, Heath. And I don't have long legs, so if you want me to keep up with you, you need to slow down. Isn't that compromise?"

"I thought you didn't do that," he counters.

"I don't often, hence me finding this nice bench and letting you continue on your way," I reply. "We should meet again tomorrow. I'll have some résumés for you to look over. I want to hire the coders by the end of the week."

He's quiet for a moment, and then he shifts that big body of his, sitting on the bench beside me. "All right. I'm sorry. I was upset, and I didn't think about you."

"Oh, I think you were definitely thinking about me."

"Maybe." He settles his bag beside him and turns my way. "I hoped that showing you my methods would warm you up to the idea of matchmaking. Instead you accused me of setting up a domestic violence victim ring."

That's taking it a bit far. "I pointed out what I thought might be a flaw in the system. I thought that was what I'm here for. If you want to work in a bubble, don't take on a partner."

"You said it in front of friends of my grandmother," he points out. "And I've already got a solution. Like Anna said, an AI is probably going to be better at picking up red flags then letting a human vet an applicant. That's all anyone can do."

He's right about that. But it's one more layer of additional cost that makes my case for selling it as a restaurant app. He's not ready to hear that yet. "I'm sorry. I will hold my comments for private from now on."

He's not done with me. "You were very cold, and I don't get the feeling you got anything out of Anna and Phil's story except you think they're some old couple who don't have any meaning in the world today."

"That's not true." I don't mean to be cold. "They seem lovely, but I guess I don't understand them. They talk about compromise, but I think that just means everyone loses." Never compromise is one of CeCe's highest laws of business. She doesn't mean minor things. Of course there will always be negotiations, but on the big things there's no room for anything beyond one's personal vision. That's where I screwed up with Nick. I let him wear me down to the point I was willing to do anything not to fight anymore.

"It's not about winning. Not in a relationship. Where would you get that?" Heath seems genuinely confused, and I wonder if he'd spent his childhood in some Disney film.

"From life. I don't know. I guess I didn't grow up around a bunch of happy families. My dad died before I could start processing what their marriage was like. Anika's parents divorced when we were in junior high, and let me tell you they fought before the divorce, but it was all-out war after. She got shipped back and forth like a prize of battle. You know about Harper's family."

"Yeah, a little. They seemed fine."

Which goes to show he didn't know them at all. "Her mom is a doormat. She did anything her dad wanted. Now she mostly follows Harper around like she needs someone to take care of."

"Some people do," he counters. "There's nothing wrong with that. It's how she's wired. Not everyone is an independent, take-on-the-world person like you. We would be in trouble if they were. Believe it or not what really upset me was that if you don't appreciate what I'm doing professionally, there's no way you will respect me personally, and that bugs me."

He's totally wrong about that. I worry I respect him as a person far more than I have anyone I've met in a long time. "That's not true. I think Anika has the weirdest, most useless job in the world and I adore her."

"You've been upset all day, and I wonder if you're regretting going into business with me."

"No." I don't want him to think that at all. I'm so interested in his business I'm planning to gently shift his focus so I can make him as successful as I think he can be. I'm putting my all into his business, and I realize it's as much about the man as anything else. I kind of believe in Heath Marino, and that's a scary feeling. "I don't regret it. I don't understand all of it. And while I promise to do it in private from now on, you can't take me asking questions as an affront."

He gives me those soulful eyes again. "I won't. I'm sorry."

But he's not the only one who didn't talk about what was bothering him. "But I probably didn't go into that meeting in the right mindset. After you left last night, I had this fight with my mom, and it got intense."

"Fight? About what?"

"About CeCe, of course."

"Ah." He nods as though this is not surprising information. "I wondered about that. I can see where she might not have liked the influence when you were a kid, but she has to see how helpful it is to have a woman like CeCe Foust in your corner now."

That's the way a logical person thinks. "Oh, very much the opposite. She thinks I got into the trouble I did because CeCe put delusions of grandeur in my head. My mom didn't see the point in me going to college, much less studying computer science. She doesn't understand it therefore it's not really work, and CeCe stole me or something like that." I don't like to think about how many fights we've had over the years. "The funny thing is that first summer I worked for CeCe she barely noticed I was gone. I told her I had a job, and she was happy I was making money and not hanging around the apartment so much. I think my mom wishes I'd been the one who died instead of my dad."

The words come out before I can think to not say them. They come out because they've been bubbling in my soul for a very long time, a kind of soundtrack my life has been lived to. It's there in the background, always threatening to poke a hole in any happiness I find.

"That can't be true." Heath has obviously never had to ask a similar question. "Ivy, why would you say such a thing?"

For so many reasons, but I give him the most recent one. "Last night she told me my father would be ashamed of me."

"What?"

I look at him, the outrage I see on his face a balm to the wound. "Yeah, she said he wouldn't be proud of me, and I'm letting that affect my whole day. So I questioned you. It's what I do. I feel backed into a corner, and I try to fight my way out. You're not the one who put me there, so I'm sorry. I don't understand your work entirely, but I shouldn't have questioned you in front of friends of your family."

He sighs and sits back. "Well, Anna doesn't think it's going to work either. That bugs me, too."

"Because she said your grandmother had the touch?" I hadn't completely understood what she'd meant.

He shrugs. "It's a family myth. The way the story goes, women in the family have some mystical sight that helps them put people together. It's an old myth spanning generations, all the way back to long before we left Sicily. My grandmother is the last. She only had my dad, and he and my mom only had me. So it dies with her."

Holy crap. Heath thinks he let everyone down by being born with a penis. He's trying to keep his family business alive the only way he knows how. He has the weight of his family on him, and I have the unbearable lightness of mine.

We are a pair, and I don't see how either of us fixes it. Good family. Bad family. It seems to all lead to the same place. We are worried we will let them down.

I know I let mine down, but I've never been able to reconcile having the kind of life I want, the kind I think will make me happy, with pleasing my mother. She's lived in misery for so long I worry she doesn't believe happiness is possible.

I worry I'm going to go the same way eventually.

"I think I'll take that hug now."

"Jeez, I think I can use one, too. This is a mutual comfort hug." He stands. "So you have to put something in it."

He is the weirdest guy. Most guys would use it as an excuse to touch my butt, but no, Heath Marino has to put something mystical behind it. "I have to put something in a hug?"

He nods. "I'm going to hug you and wish the best for you, and you're going to do the same for me."

It strikes me suddenly that this might have been what Anna and Phil had meant—that their version of compromise is to always have the other in mind when they make decisions, to always wish the very best for the person they love.

When he wraps those big arms around me, I do what he asked. I wish the best for him.

And somehow in doing it, I feel lighter.

I just wish the best for him could be me.

Chapter Eleven

"It's the last one on the right." Heath is once more practically running away from me, but I don't blame him this time.

After our overly long hug that was also over way too fast, we'd made our way to the train. He'd been talking about the project when he'd gotten the call from his grandmother's nurse.

I'm still not sure what's happened, but I'm not going to leave him alone. Or maybe I like being with him enough I'm willing to put us both in an awkward position since I'm about to meet his grandma and she's probably hurt.

I do jog this time. I'm not a great believer in running, but this is an emergency. At least it feels like one.

He has his key out as I catch up to him. He opens the door and I follow him into a foyer that leads me into what looks like a sitting area. This is a nice building, and I would bet it's not rent controlled. Heath might live in a dump like the rest of us, but someone in the family has cash. This is the kind of place one buys, and the building fees are more than most people's rent.

An older woman in scrubs arrives. She shakes her head. "It's nothing serious. She took a little spill."

Heath drops his bag on the coffee table. "What was she doing?"

The nurse frowns. "She was practicing her line dancing. There's a party next week."

The groan that comes out of Heath's mouth is pure frustration. "Line dancing? I thought we talked about her taking it easy."

"You should mind your business, *nipote*." A short woman in a wildly colorful caftan walks in, leaning on her cane. "I'm not sick anymore, and I can take it easy when I'm dead. Which is not going to be today. Oh, look, it's lunchtime, Maggie, and my grandson is here. I'm glad I made enough." She sees me and stops, her eyes widening, and for a moment I think seriously about running. "You brought a friend."

There is a wealth of expectation in those words. Friend does not mean friend to this woman. Friend means potential mother of a whole new generation. She's already planning out how many babies I can give her.

"Nonna, did you have Maggie call and freak me out because you wanted me to have lunch with you?" Heath is giving her the sternest look I've seen from him so far.

"Yes," Maggie says as she grabs her sweater. "That's exactly what she did, and I'm going to leave now. I have two more clients to see today. You are a menace, Lydia Marino. Have a nice lunch."

"Love you, too," Lydia says with a wave. She moves into Heath's space, putting a hand on his arm and tilting her head. "And I did fall. It was terrible. I was in the middle of a perfectly good Tush Push when I rolled my ankle."

"I do not want to know what that is," Heath says as he dips his head down and gives her a kiss on the cheek.

My curious nature gets the best of me. I know I should probably be sneaking out right behind Maggie, but I stand there. "I do."

Lydia Marino gives me the biggest smile. "It's a song my friends and I line dance to. It's a bit older. I can also do an excellent *Save a Horse Ride a Cowboy*."

"Nonna got into line dancing a few years back." Heath is smiling but his teeth are clenched. "At the local rec center."

"For exercise," Lydia assures me.

"Now she and a pack of her friends hit up country dive bars, and I have to listen to songs about dogs and love gone wrong and whiskey," Heath finishes. "Thanks, rec center."

I like how annoyed he is. Mostly because he's still ridiculously cute and he's normally the chillest dude I've ever met. I like that this one tiny old lady can set him off his calm.

Also, she mentioned lunch and I'm hungry, and most people who go by names like Nonna know how to cook. I mean I could be wrong, but I'm betting I might've hit the jackpot here.

"So come along, children. I've got everything ready for lunch. I'll set another place, and you can tell me all about this beautiful young woman you've brought with you to see your nonna." She turns and starts toward what I suspect is a formal dining room.

"We can't. We have to work," Heath announces. "Ivy is my business partner, so stop eyeing her like she's the future mother of your grandchildren."

I knew I called that one right.

She turns and looks hurt. "But I made lasagna."

Oh, we are not taking a moral stand here. I get it. He doesn't want his grandmother to think she can trick him into visiting, but I have no such qualms. No one makes me lasagna. I'm lucky if my mom stocks the kitchen with pizza rolls, and at CeCe's version of a weekday lunch, she usually just passes me a martini.

"And we would love to join you," I say.

Lydia beams my way. "Excellent. I'll have a place for you in a moment, my dear."

The minute she's gone Heath turns my way. "Are you kidding? You do know that she's not going to buy the whole business partner thing. She's going to view you as a potential romantic partner for me. She's already wondering if we're compatible and how soon she could have us married off with two point five kids. My grandmother will ask you all kinds of invasive questions and probably try to turn this lunch of hers into a matchmaking session."

I shrug because he's seriously underestimating how much I'll do for decent food. I spent years in California eating sushi and tofu and fish tacos. I'm back in New York and I've barely had street food, much less something cooked by the expert hand of a Sicilian woman who raised a family. "I think we should name the first one Alex." I start for the dining room. "We slap an -er or -dra on the end and voila. Or just leave it Alex, and that way we're not gendering the kid. Very trendy. Oh, that smells delicious."

He hurries after me as though he can stave off the impending disaster. "Fine. Apparently we're staying for lunch, but Nonna, she really is a business partner."

The dining room is cozy with a six-seater table that looks midcentury modern and a matching china cabinet complete with old-school dishes and plates and probably silver. I settle into the seat Lydia gestures to and there's a real napkin someone has to launder. "I am. I own forty percent of your grandson's company."

Now Lydia's eyes narrow. "Forty percent?"

I nod. She should know everything. "Yup. Of course, I've brought in one hundred percent of our seed money."

Lydia nods Heath's way, and he begins the process of passing a basket of garlic bread around. "Why do you need seed money? From what I understood Heath has everything he needs to get the job done."

I wonder what stories he's been telling his grandmother. I should totally back him up on everything, but then the smell of the garlic bread hits me. It's like truth serum, and I can't lie to the woman who baked this bit of deliciousness. I put two slices on my plate and wonder how little salad I can take and still look like a normal vegetable-eating human. I don't want to fill up on lettuce. I need room for pasta and cheese and…oh, that is Italian sausage in there. Jackpot. "Well, he needed someone to fix his code, and he's going to need a couple of people to work on the base and ancillary codes. Building an AI with the capability to do what he wants it to do could take years on his own. We've got to do training and testing and come up with a business plan. It's a lot of work, and not the kind we're going to find unpaid interns for, if you know what I mean."

I manage to get a big old serving of lasagna on my plate. It's gooey and cheesy, and I might work for this food. I wonder if we can get coders willing to work for Lydia's pasta dishes.

"I don't," she replies, taking a large helping of salad. "I don't understand anything except the fact that he's trying to replace me with a computer."

Only the faintest stain on his cheeks lets me know I've managed to step on a land mine.

"I'm not trying to replace you. I'm trying to build something even bigger off all that knowledge you have," he says. "It's really a project to honor your work."

"You are not naming that robot after me," she replies, a worried expression coming over her face.

I can fix this. And I will after I eat this big heaping bite of heaven. It is exactly that. Freaking heaven in my mouth. And I want to live here in this pretty place with a nonna who worries about me and feeds me.

I am still a child in the world looking for a mommy.

"There's no robot involved," I assure her. "And the matchmaking aspect is only part of what Heath's AI can do. He really is working on it as a way to honor you, and he's got so much data that might help future couples. Isn't that what we all want someday? For our stories to inform the next generations?"

She stares at me like she's got a bullshit detector, and it's going off. It might be. The woman spends a lot of time in country bars. "There is more to matchmaking than data."

I hope Heath takes this one because I'm eating, and I am serious about that.

He does not. He gives me a look that tells me I started this and I better finish it.

"Like I said, it's not merely matchmaking. That's only one aspect of the AI's potential, and I think you can help us decide if it's worthwhile to pursue," I offer.

Heath sends me a death stare. Probably because I invited his nonna to join us at our non-office and meddle as she pleases. Well, he'd let me answer her.

"All right. What else is interesting about it?" she asks. "I don't understand all the terms, but I've heard Heath talk about the framework. His roommate Darnell comes for dinner sometimes, and he says the framework is lovely. Also, you should ask Darnell to let you read his novel. It's very exciting but it's not finished."

I'm betting Lydia Marino isn't very tech savvy. I'm sure she can use her phone and the Internet and a smart TV, but she likely doesn't write a lot of her own code. It's clear to me no one has explained this to her. I understand Darnell. He's a writer. He wants to find a reader. But Heath should have informed her of what he does. "It's like a base. So most people when they start writing a program use some kind of framework as a base. Like Ruby on Rails, AppMaster, Flask. There are tons of good ones out there. It basically puts you a bunch of steps ahead in the program, and then all the real programming work you have to do is to customize it."

"So it's a cheat?" Lydia asks.

Wow, she's a little judgey there. "It's a base." I search for something she can understand. "Like when you make soup. You don't make your own stock."

"Of course I do," she insists.

I'm not going to fault her for that. I hope I get to eat that soup someday. "Well, the rest of the world is lazy, and they need a little help and don't want to spend a year building a base they don't have to. Except for your grandson, who I would bet has been building this framework for a long time. Years, probably."

Heath takes a sip of his water. He's already halfway through the massive piece of lasagna he took, so I don't feel so bad. "I've been working on it since I was fifteen. I like to do things my own way."

"And from what I've seen his way is super innovative and can help many coders in the future. And that's what the business part is about. That and the AI he's building. They could both be very popular once they're out there in the marketplace." It actually feels kind of good to tell the truth. Even if I'm telling the truth to the goddess of a woman at the head of the table, and her grandbaby thinks I'm saving him.

I'm not joking, this shit melts in my mouth, and I feel it in my soul.

I'm already wondering if she's made dessert. She feels like a dessert-making person.

"Well, I'm sure it's all very technical," Lydia declares, and Heath seems to relax, the danger of what is probably a lecture he's heard many times before passing. "But I'm more interested in you, dear. I already like you more than Heath's usual dates. The last one was on some kind of diet. Kettle or something."

"Keto," Heath corrects and sits back, a smirk coming over his face. "She was on keto and wouldn't eat pasta. I don't think you'll have the same trouble feeding Ivy. She is very food focused."

"Well, I like a young woman with a healthy appetite." Lydia leans toward me. "Tell me about your family, dear. Where are they from?"

"Hell's Kitchen." Crap. We've gotten to the interrogative portion of the meal. The one Heath warned me about. "I mean that's where we've lived my whole life. My dad was from Queens, though. He died when I was a kid, so it's just me and my mom."

"What about your grandparents and uncles and aunts and cousins?" Lydia asks the question like she can't think of anything worse than not having a large group of nosy relatives hanging around all the time.

Maybe the only thing worse is having one relative who is mostly disinterested. "I don't have those. Mom and Dad were only children, and I only met my mom's mom a couple of times. She moved to Boca Raton to retire and didn't visit much. She died a couple of years back, but she had a great tan."

Lydia seems to take this information with a steady resolve to dig deeper. "And your mother? What does she do?"

"Mostly complain," I reply.

Heath snorts and shakes his head. "Her mom is a legal secretary for a big law firm here in the city."

Well, someone has been listening to me. I would bet Nick couldn't tell me what my mom did for a living, and we were together for three years. "That's my mom. She helps people get divorced and screw each other over."

Lydia nods like I've given her important information.

I suddenly feel like a bad guest. I'm being more honest than polite. "This is very delicious. Thank you so much. I'm enjoying it immensely."

Heath sends me an oddly approving look. "Told you. Highly food motivated. Your kind of girl, Nonna."

She winks his way. "I knew one day you would bring one home. Well, eat up, my dear, but save some room. I made a cheesecake."

I close my eyes and thank the universe for bringing me here.

Forty minutes later, I sit on the balcony with Lydia, a tray of tea between us and Heath somewhere in the living room trying to fix the TV because the Netflix has gone out. I offered to delete and reinstall the app—which usually fixes things—but she'd insisted Heath was the only one in the world who knows how to deal with her old television.

It didn't look that old to me. I'd gotten a tour of the apartment, and it did nothing to change my mind about the family money. The whole place is lovely and I would bet it's gone through a renovation in the last couple of years because everything is modern.

It makes me wonder why Heath came to me.

Except I know some of it. His grandmother isn't fully behind the project. She might not want to sink her money into something she doesn't believe in. Or she might know it's best for family to stay family and not go into business together.

"So you and Heath met via a mutual friend." Lydia sips her tea. "Which friend?"

Ah, so my interview is not over. I wonder if she futzed with the TV to buy herself more time. She seems crafty that way. "Harper Ross. One of his cousins works for her construction company."

She nods. "Yes, the one on his mother's side. So Harper is a woman and she runs a construction company. That's very interesting. Such a man's world."

"She inherited it from her dad. He built a lot of the buildings here in the city," I explain. It's easier to talk about my friends. "She oversees those constructions, but she herself specializes in renovations. I've often thought she should have her own home improvement show. It would be better than what Ani's working on."

"Ani is your other friend?"

"Yes. Anika. She works in television production. She's not the money behind it. She helps run the shows. She's a production assistant, but they're talking about giving her more responsibility. I don't know exactly what she does, but she might be doing it for a show called *The King Takes a Bride*. And saying the name makes me vomit a little in my mouth."

"Is it one of those *Bachelor* shows?" Lydia looks properly horrified.

I nod. "Except with the king of a small European country, so some skinny model wannabe is going to be a queen and Anika will likely be getting them all coffee. Or whatever the king drinks. As a professional matchmaker, what is your opinion of a dude dating fifteen women at the same time and slowly dropping them off one by one?"

"That it sounds rather like a murder show," she muses. "At least it would turn me into a murderer. No. That is not the way to find a life partner. I think the best way is to spend a lot of time with one person, to see how it feels to have that person in your life. If you're building something at the same time, that's simply a plus."

And we're back. "I really am just a business associate. I think the world of your grandson, but I'm not involved with him in any emotional way."

She stares at me for a moment. "Aren't you? You certainly didn't have to come with him to see his injured grandmother. I assume you were together when he got the call. You came with him when you easily could have stayed behind."

She's got me there. "Okay. I can't be emotionally involved with him. We're working together, and I don't date where I work."

Her eyes feel like they're piercing through me as she studies me. "Because you did once and it went wrong."

That's not much of a stretch. I'm lucky she's not in the tech world or she wouldn't have had to guess. "Spectacularly wrong. Possible career-ending wrong. So wrong I really won't make the same mistake again. Heath and I are going to be friends and I'm going to take his work and make him a lot of money. He'll be set up so he can do whatever he wants, though I'm looking around here and wondering if he's not already there."

She glances into the room behind us. "The apartment? This place has been in the family for years. I have enough to stay here and be comfortable, but I'm afraid medical bills ate up much of what I could have left Heath. First my husband and then me. I had a bout with breast cancer last year. I'm perfectly healthy now, but Heath insists on bringing

Maggie in a few times a week. And there's a lovely woman who cleans my house and helps with the groceries. Doris. Such a nice lady. But the point is a lot of money goes into making sure Heath doesn't have to worry. I don't know how much there will be at the end because my goal is to live a long time. Long enough to see my great grandchildren. I suppose he'll sell this place when I'm gone. It will bring in some money, but not enough for him to build a company from. Odd. I never saw Heath building a company as such. He liked programming his games. I didn't understand them, but they were beautiful to look at."

"They're fun to play," I admit. "I did some game programming in my time. I enjoyed it. It felt like storytelling to me."

"You liked being creative in that way?"

"Oh, yes. I liked a lot about those days. I worked for a game design firm in Austin and it was just…fun. It was cool when the work was done and we got to watch people play. Don't get me wrong. Some people suck, but most liked it. I went to conventions and met fans, and they would tell me how I took their mind off the world for a while. That was a good feeling."

"I think that Heath liked that part, too," she replies. "See, so much in common."

She smiles and it's the kind of smile that makes me nervous. "You know the cancer was so hard on me. In some ways, I'm still recovering. Not physically, of course, but mentally. I still think about what could have happened. Do you know? I need a distraction. Ivy, would you be so kind as to indulge an old woman?"

"Indulge?" I'm not sure if she's going to ask me to write a game for her or marry her grandson here and now so the babymaking can begin, and I'm not ready for Alex or -er or -dra.

"Yes." She sits back with the surety of a woman who is going to get her way. "I don't matchmake much anymore. I've only got a handful of clientele. I'd like you to fill out my questionnaires."

I shake my head. "I'm not looking for a boyfriend. I'm concentrating on my career."

Which is on the rocks and needs all the attention it can get.

She waves that bit of information off. "It's more than matching you with one person. I can tell you what you should look for in a partner. Think of it as one of those frameworks you were talking about. I can build a list of what you need in a partner, and you use it or don't. It's just something I do for fun."

I seriously doubt that.

"You're looking for an office." Her eyes narrow, and there's such ruthless intelligence behind them. I'm surprised at the turn. "How much space do you need?"

"I'm thinking an efficiency if I can find it. I need a couple of desks, space for me and Heath. We need white boards." I've been thinking about this all day. "The truth is we can probably work at Heath's and have the coders work remotely, but if we ever have to get the team together, we'll be meeting at the library or something. Also, I'd really like to get to know the coders, but I don't think Darnell is giving up his half of the living room."

She gestures around her balcony. "You can work here at my place."

Now I get it. "If I fill out your forms."

She shrugs a slim shoulder. "It's a few forms and maybe an interview or two. Nothing more. It wouldn't be inconvenient. You would be here, after all. All I would need is a few moments of your day."

It would be so much more because I didn't buy the whole "I'm just doing this for fun" thing. "I don't…"

"I, of course, would provide lunch, and if you happen to work late, well, I have to eat dinner, too."

She is the devil tempting me with food I don't have to eat from a paper wrapper. And having a beautiful place to work where we won't be cramped and Darnell won't get so mad he eventually writes me into one of his books as the bad guy.

It solves so many problems. Any place I can actually afford will likely have crappy Wi-Fi I will have to pay through the nose for, and then there's the problem of the commute because I was serious about Jersey. Lydia's place is so much closer.

She leans forward. "I've got several rooms no one uses. You can take the furniture out and turn them into offices. Or you can use my office. It's already got a desk. I don't need it these days. You can use the formal dining room as a conference room when you need it. All the bathrooms are clean, and you don't have to worry about rent. You can come and go as you please."

It is far too good to be true. "All for me filling out a couple of forms?"

"All because I want to see my grandson more often, and this is a way to do it. Ivy, dear, I don't know how much time I have left. That is the lesson I learned from cancer. None of us knows, and I don't want to waste the time I have. I want to spend it looking after my grandson and his…friends. I'm lonely. You would be doing me a big favor," she says quietly.

"We accept."

I close my eyes in utter relief because it was Heath who said the words. I turn and he's standing there in the doorway.

Lydia uses her cane to stand and holds her arms out. "I'm so glad."

She hugs him and I now know where he learned to hug with his whole being. It's lovely to see people who care about each other so much.

And nice to know I'm off the hook.

Heath steps back, an arm around his grandmother. "But Ivy still has to fill out the forms."

He's got a shit-eating grin on his face.

Yep, back on the hook.

Chapter Twelve

"I'm sorry. I'm still trying to wrap my head around the fact that you now own forty percent of Heath's company." Harper stares at me over the table.

We're sitting in a restaurant in Grand Central known for its oysters, but it looks like I'm the one who's about to get shucked.

It's been a full week since we decided to move our business into Lydia Marino's upscale apartment. Heath and I have spent pretty much every waking hour together looking through résumés and doing interviews. Come Monday morning we will have two brand spanking new contractors to work with, and I happen to know Lydia was planning fabulous lunches most days of the week.

For the first time in a long time I'm excited to go to work. I realize now how much I'd dreaded the last year at Jensen Med. It had been a slog, and this feels fresh and new, and god I hope it's not because I'm falling for Heath Marino.

I take a sip of the Chardonnay the menu assured me paired well with the salty richness of the oysters we're sharing. I wasn't sure why everyone was so surprised that as a partner I would own part of the project. "Well, right now that forty percent is worth negative fifty thousand dollars."

This particular conversation had been initiated by Harper. She'd asked how the work with Heath was going. She apparently hadn't realized how entwined we've become businesswise, though I talk about him a lot. It's been a busy week, and we'd skipped our normal Tuesday brunch plans. This dinner is our first real catch-up session.

"What?" Harper looks horrified.

Anika sits back as though resigned that this dinner is not going the way she hoped it would. "Harper, you know how this works. You often put your own money into a project."

"But she's not putting her money in the project. She's putting CeCe's money in the project." Harper is wearing a chic black dress that shows off how toned her arms are. We're supposed to go to a party thrown by one of her clients after we finish dinner, so we're all dressed to impress. I was sure it would be a fabulous affair since it was being held in an Upper West Side penthouse Harper had been renovating for the last six months.

I'm wearing one of my sheath dresses. It's one I normally would wear with a jacket, but I'm hoping it looks cocktaily this evening and not like part of a power suit. It's a little tight, and I'm not moving as gracefully as I should.

I blame Lydia. Not only does she feed me lunch, she sends home whatever's left for my dinner.

Lydia is a sweet counterpoint to my relationship with my mother, which is icy at best. She woke up the next day and instead of apologizing, she asked when I would start paying rent since CeCe had opened the money valve again. Those exact words.

I tried to explain that the money was for the business, but she did not care.

I have to find a new place to stay and fast, and dear god it looks like it won't be with Harper because she's obviously annoyed with me. I don't understand it. I thought she wanted me to help him.

"I think it's fun that you're working at his grandma's." Anika always likes to turn the conversation away from conflict. It's kind of her job in this sisterhood of ours. Harper and I have big personalities, and Anika often finds herself playing referee. It's been better the last few years, but I wonder if that's because I've been in San Francisco.

I worry I've come back and the place I used to have in this little found family changed while I was gone. I worry I changed so much I no longer fit and I'm trying to hammer myself back in.

I have no idea what I will do if I lose them, too.

"Lydia seems to be having the time of her life," I say, grateful to move away from money and into happier parts of what I'm doing right now. "At first she listened in on us talking about hiring, but now she walks right in and tells us what she thinks. She does not care about a person's skill set. She's more interested in kind faces."

She claims she can tell from a person's smile whether they're kind or not. It's funny because this one guy had a gorgeous smile and she rejected him immediately. Her ways are mysterious. I'm going with it for now.

Anika smiles at this. "I bet that annoys the hell out of you."

Oddly not. I like Lydia. I find her a deeply calming presence in my life. A bit like her grandson. "I hired the people she told me to. Now they also have the skills we need, but after interviewing them I realized I was looking at them in different ways. I've always thought I could work with anyone who can do the job. I realize now that people kind of suck, and I'll take a slightly less talented coder over one I will want to murder within thirty minutes of hiring."

It might have been one of the mistakes I made back when I was starting up Jensen Med. I hired what I thought of as the best of the best, never considering how they would fit into their roles. People like Nick, who came with stellar recommendations but wasn't anything close to a team player.

"Are you serious?" Harper asks, setting her empty oyster shell down. "You're letting an eighty-year-old woman tell you who to hire?"

"She's a matchmaker. I'm letting her make me some matches." It's not exactly true, but it sounds cute. Though Lydia does seem to know people and how they fit together. She's given us insight on how she thought the team will work, and Heath has complete confidence in her.

The good news is that if she's wrong, I'm excellent at firing people.

"I thought you didn't believe in stuff like that," Harper counters.

"Do you?" I'm not sure why she's all over me tonight, but I'm incapable of not handing it back to her.

She sits back and seems to think for a moment. "I don't know. I know the way Heath talks about her she's made a lot of people happy over the years, so there's probably something to her method."

"Well, I've met a bunch of people who swear she's the reason they're happily married," I say. Over the course of the last week, I'd gone out with Heath on two more interviews. They went much more smoothly because I went in with a more open mind. One was an older couple, very wealthy. The other was a couple in their thirties with a small apartment that smelled a little like curdled milk, a highly gassy baby, and an exhaustion that permeated everything around them.

I'd been told they were one of the last professional matches Lydia had made, and despite all the tiredness they passed the baby between them and held hands during the interview. They were in the middle of the hurricane of new parenthood and holding on to each other with everything they had.

"I don't know if I believe anyone can predict how a couple is going to be ten or twenty years down the road," Harper says.

"I would love for her to find me a guy," Anika says with enthusiasm. "All the ones I meet are terrible. I know this is going to shock you, but people who desperately want to be on TV are often not great people to date."

"Especially when they want to date a whole bunch of women at the same time and in the same hot tub." I can't help but tease her, too.

Anika blushes, and I immediately feel bad. "It's just a job. I don't even start for a couple of weeks, so who knows. Maybe they'll find someone else."

"Or you could say no," Harper insists. "This is a big step down for you. I don't understand why you're sitting back and accepting a demotion."

The pink in Anika's cheeks deepens, a sure sign she's getting emotional, and I wonder how hard this is for her. She changes the subject when it's brought up. "Well, I guess you know more than I do about my job. Except you know absolutely nothing about it and I wish you would keep your opinions to yourself, Harper. You've made it plain. You don't like my decisions. You don't like Ivy's. We get it."

Well, that escalated quickly. It's not often I find myself playing the mediator. Like I said, Anika is usually the peacemaker, so I have to wonder what's going on. "It's your career, Ani. We know you know what you're doing."

Anika pushes her seat back and tosses her napkin down. Her sequined dress sparkles in a happy way that runs counter to our current vibe. "Oh, I don't think Harper believes that in any way. I'm going to the bathroom. I do not need company."

I watch her walk away and wish I had something stronger than the wine. "What was that about?"

Harper sighs, toying with the whiskey sour she ordered. "She's mad that I expressed an opinion about her letting her bosses push her around. This show she's going to start work on is beneath her. She should be running her own show by now. She needs to stand up for herself." Harper looks a bit defeated. "I know I sound like a bitch, but I'm really trying to help her."

"I think it's dumb, too," I admit. "But we can't know what she's going through. I think you've made your statement and it's time to support her unconditionally the same way she would support you. You don't know how hard it is to build something from nothing."

Her eyes narrow. "I do it every day."

She's so literal. "I meant a business. And before you get your back up, I know I don't understand how hard it is to step into someone else's shoes. Can we agree it's all crappy and we should support each other even if we don't completely understand the whys and hows?"

She's quiet for a moment and then takes a long drink of the whiskey as though she's steeling herself. "It's hard because I worry that supporting you might mean I contribute to something bad happening to Heath."

We're back to me, and my gut takes a deep dive. "What do you mean?"

"Forty percent, Ivy?"

I can't help but feel exasperated. "He needs seed money. I'm not sure what you expected me to do."

"I expected you to date him, not take almost half the man's company," Harper replies.

That hurts more than I expected. "So this *was* a setup."

"Of course it was a setup. I told you that a week ago," Harper replies, obviously exasperated. "I hoped you would help him out with his code and realize what a great guy he is. I thought Heath would…"

"Would what?" I ask, not sure I want the answer. But I'm a "pull the bandage off in one painful swoop" kind of girl.

She stops, seeming to understand she's walked onto a big old minefield. "I don't know, smooth out your rough edges. I thought he would make you happy."

"Rough edges?" I know I'm not some polished gem of a woman, but I don't think I'm that terrible.

"You can't be unaware of how irritable you've been since you got back. You're crabby all the time and you won't let anyone except CeCe help you, and the only way she helps is giving you cash so you feel obligated to spend time with her."

I feel my jaw drop. I've never heard this kind of crap come out of Harper's mouth. "Have you been spending time with my mother, too? Because you suddenly sound a lot like her."

"Maybe she makes some sense," Harper insists. "Ivy, she's your mom. Don't you think she wants the best for you? I have to ask. How much of Heath's business does CeCe now own? Are you two going to take the whole thing away from him?"

She can't know how she's just sliced my heart into ribbons. I've always had Harper on my side. Yes, she's often the voice of doom when it comes to business because she's not a risk taker, but she's still on my side. "The initial investment we'll have to pay back, but we did not sign a contract with her. Honestly, we have no legal requirement to pay it back, but she knows if we start showing a profit I'll do it. Once we have a good business plan if she chooses to fund us, we'll negotiate her part. It would be great if we could fund ourselves because we're super wealthy or if we could find people who didn't need to get paid, but this is the reality of our business."

"I'm not saying you mean to hurt him."

It feels like she's saying something far worse. "No, what you're saying is that it's my nature to."

"It's not your nature. That's the whole point. CeCe taught you to be this way."

"To be a businessperson? To be tough? To ask for what I'm worth?" Harper does all of those things, too. I can't help but think the word *hypocrite*.

"To not care about anything but money." She sits back, and her eyes close for a moment. "Ivy, I didn't mean that."

It's my turn to push my chair back. "I think you did. We're disappointing the hell out of you, aren't we? Me and Ani."

Her hands are flat on the table as if she's ready to pop up if she has to. "I just want you to be happy."

"Are you happy? You seem to be the supreme ruler on everyone else's choices and yet I don't see you dating anyone. I don't see you doing anything but working like the rest of us. I'm sorry we're not successful enough for you, but we also didn't have everything handed to us."

"CeCe handed you a whole lot," Harper counters. "I'm so sick of hearing your 'woe is me, I started from the bottom' story. You didn't start from the bottom. You started from CeCe's mountain of cash, and you started at the top of it. She wanted a daughter because she's never had one and you're her freaking heir."

I'm not her heir. That's a Jewish charity organization, but I get Harper's point. I don't see why being CeCe's selected daughter is such a bad thing. "I have worked hard for everything I have. I am well aware that CeCe's backing acts as privilege, but don't think I didn't work to build every business I've been associated with, and I'll work my ass off to make Heath as much money as I can. Money is freedom in tech. Money means we get to work on anything we want to work on even when it's completely off the rails. And if you think I'm such a bad bet, why don't you talk to Heath and get him to dump me. We haven't signed anything yet. We've got a handshake. You still might be able to save him if you try real hard."

She's quiet, and her eyes are firmly on the table.

The betrayal hits me like a slap to the face. I swear I can feel it. "You already did."

She bites her bottom lip. "I just want him to be careful."

Somewhere along the way I became the enemy here. I stare at the woman I think of as a sister and realize that even sisters break.

"What's going on?" Anika is back, and it looks like she's touched up her eye makeup which means she's likely been crying.

I turn her way. "Do you think I'm going to screw Heath over?"

She hesitates. "No. I don't think you mean to."

But they think I'm the bad guy. They think I'm going to drag him down. I wonder how much further this goes. "Like I dragged Nick down?"

Harper's head shakes. "That's a completely different situation. I know what happened with him. He screwed you over and all you've talked about since is never letting it happen again. I don't want Heath to get caught in your crossfire."

"You do talk about revenge a lot," Anika agrees.

"On Nick, not the whole male population. And I haven't even thought about Nick in a week." Honestly, tonight is the first time he popped into my head, and it's all because they're dredging up my old business. This is ridiculous, and we're gathering an audience.

"You haven't?" Harper's gaze sharpens. "Now why is that?"

"Because I'm building a business," I reply. "Or maybe it's because I'm having so much fun coming up with ways to fuck Heath over. Apparently in your head it's what I think about always."

"I didn't say that," Harper insists. "I don't think you'll mean to hurt him."

"No. You think everyone around me gets hurt." It wasn't anything I hadn't thought while I'd been forced to shut down a company that should have been in business for years. I screwed up. I trusted the wrong people.

"That's not true," Anika says quietly. "Look, we're all under pressure right now. All three of us. Harper isn't telling you that she's got money flow problems and it's put her on edge."

"No, I only told you that," Harper says, her mouth a firm line.

"She's not going to judge you for it, but it might explain why you're acting like some holier than thou bitch," Anika shoots back. "We're all under pressure, and I don't want us to break over it."

So Harper isn't perfect, and she's taking it out on me. Great. I'm everyone's punching bag these days, and I'm tired of it. "I think we already have. Look, I've already dealt with my mom telling me how ashamed my dad would be of me. I don't need this."

Anika's eyes go sympathetic. "Ivy, she didn't mean that."

A lot of people didn't mean what they said lately.

"Can we sit down and talk this out?" Harper offers. "Ani's right. We're all in high-tension situations right now, and I'm not handling it well. I put a lot of money into a project that is turning into a nightmare. Maybe you can help me figure out how to save it."

It's all nice and conciliatory, but I can't forget what she said before. I can't forget the fact that she went behind my back and warned Heath about me. I can't help but wonder if Heath believed her.

I can't be okay right now, and I'm feeling mean.

"Or I would steal it out from under you. You never know with someone like me," I reply, reaching into my bag and pulling out the last of my cash because I can't be pathetic and let her pay for my food again. I throw forty dollars on the table and grab my bag. "Can't trust me with a business, you know. Have fun at your party."

I start to leave, hearing them call out for me, but I'm done.

I walk up the long ramp that leads me out of the station. I would take the subway but my MetroCard is empty, and I left my cash behind in a gesture of pure pride. And I didn't even eat my share of the oysters, and the fries hadn't come out yet.

Frustration wells inside me as I step up and see the rain coming down. I also don't have an umbrella. Or money for a cab.

The frustration is really sorrow. I don't want it to be, but that's the truth.

They don't come running after me. My cell isn't blowing up with requests to come back.

I'm on my own.

I step out and let the rain hit me. I have no place to go so I just begin walking.

Chapter Thirteen

Somehow I end up at Heath's. Not somehow. I walked all those blocks in the rain, and my feet knew exactly where they were going. It certainly wasn't going to be home. I don't even know if I should use that word in connection to my mother's apartment anymore.

I'm feeling wiped out and yet oddly energized. I can't explain it. As I press the buzzer to let Heath know I'm here, I want the confrontation that's about to come. I didn't come here to get comfort from this man. I came here to let him know he's safe from me.

And then I can be done with all of them and I can talk to CeCe and she'll help me find a job far away from here and I'll sit at a desk and slowly disintegrate. That sounds good right now.

I expect Heath's voice to come over the line, but I merely hear the buzz that lets me know he's opened the door. I don't think he has a camera, so I worry he might be expecting someone.

A date?

I've been with him pretty constantly over the last week, and he's never mentioned he's seeing someone, but I could be overestimating the level of our friendship.

I think about leaving but decide if he has a woman he's waiting for, that will be damn good for me to know. I stride through, not caring a bit that I'm literally dripping water. I take the stairs instead of the elevator. It's only three flights and it gives me a chance to get the words straight in my head.

This is not a breakup because we're not together. So why does it feel like I'm about to lose something precious?

By the time I get to his door, I'm forcing my teeth to stop chattering. I probably look like a drowned rat. I very likely look as pathetic as I feel. Still, I knock on that door, ready to get it all over with. I'll head to CeCe's from here to explain my latest debacle. I believe Heath will honor the handshake agreement I have with her. He's a stand-up guy, but I know this is going to disappoint the hell out of CeCe. Again.

Maybe I should throw a dart at a map and move wherever that sucker lands. Completely start over somewhere new. Somewhere no one knows what a screw-up I am.

The door opens and it's Darnell, who looks surprised and then deeply disturbed. "I thought you were Jerry. You are not Jerry, and you probably didn't bring the subs."

I don't have time for Darnell's verbal game play. I don't think about the relief I feel that they're waiting for someone named Jerry to bring them dinner and not a pretty woman Heath's entertaining. "I need to talk to Heath."

"You need to…" He gestures up and down my body. "…do a lot with that. I can't even begin to list the things you need to do. I don't like to sound like my mother, but you are going to catch pneumonia and die, and you will die looking exactly like that. Is that really how you want to go out?"

Yep, he confirms all of my nasty suspicions. I do not look romantic walking in the rain. No Jane Austen-heroine look for me. "Is he here? If you'll let me talk to him, you won't have to see me again."

He frowns. "Why would I want that? You know I'm teasing you because I like you. It's one of my love languages. I'm excellent at ignoring the people I don't like. Come in. You obviously have some serious drama to play out. Heath, your business partner is here, and she looks like she walked off the pages of a Dickens novel. We might need to get her some gruel."

He steps back, allowing me into the apartment.

It's set up for some kind of gathering. They've brought in extra chairs, and it looks like the bar in the kitchen has been turned into a mini buffet with chips and crackers and store-bought cookies.

He's having a party and didn't invite me. I'm surprised he didn't invite Harper. Unless he did and she chose to go to the big client party. Hypocrite.

He walks out wearing sweats and a tank top that shows off the fact that he understands the term arm day. He has a smile on his face until he gets a look at me. "Hey, what's going on? Are you okay?"

He's not going to make this easy on me. Maybe some hard truth will get him in the mood to be mean. I don't know that I can walk away from gorgeous, warm, affectionate Heath. I need him to reject me so I can get on with my life.

"I just came by to let you know that I'm going to pull out of the project and give you back my forty percent. You now are the sole owner of your company, which still does not have a name." It's something I've been talking to him about. He'd published his game under H Marino LLC, but I think he needs a better name. Something catchy.

But with me out, he can be boring now.

Darnell opens the bag of chips and sits down, crossing one leg over the other. "See, told you. Drama. Could you wait and hash this out in front of my writing group? Some of the fuckers do not understand how to write tension, and you two are the perfect illustration. They don't get sexual vibes. They're sci-fi writers. Well, most of them. One of the women is writing a series about her heroine being used as breeding stock by space pirates. Guess which one of us sold."

Heath frowns his way. "No." He looks back at me. "What is going on? You can't pull out of the project. You brought in all the money."

"No one's taking the money back. It's yours." I would talk to CeCe about finding someone else who could shepherd him through the process. Maybe Benjamin would be a better business mentor. "You need to follow the schedule I set up. CeCe will need to see a solid business plan. If she rejects you, I'll leave a list of other investors you can talk to."

He pales a bit at that news. "That is not what I do. That's your job, Ivy. I don't understand what's going on here."

I don't want a long sit-down. I'm ready to move on to the me leaving portion of the evening. I'll go back home, hole up in my tiny bedroom, and figure out what to do now. I still have connections on the West Coast. I need a job. It won't be what I want to do, but I can find a place on a programming team. "You don't have to. I'm going to be in town for a couple of days if you have questions. Text me."

He reaches out and puts a hand on my shoulder. "Now I'm really worried. The project is going great. You were happy when you left this afternoon. You were excited about starting with the new hires on Monday. This isn't about the project. You were supposed to go to a party with Harper and Anika. What happened?"

It's his hand on me that flusters me enough I blurt out the truth.

"Why didn't you tell me Harper tried to warn you off me?"

An "ooooo" from Darnell reminds us that he's watching and has Heath taking my hand and leading me back toward his bedroom.

"Spoilsports," Darnell says, and I hear the buzzer go off again. It looked like Jerry would be bringing up the subs, and for once my stomach doesn't care.

I allow Heath to lead me back to his bedroom. I haven't been in it, but I'm not surprised to find it neat and organized, like the man himself. He's got a full bed and another desk that has yet another system on it, and I spy a VR rig. He's got a bookshelf that looks to be half books on code and half high fantasy.

I'm so curious, but I'm not indulging at this point. I'm leaving. Or at least I'm supposed to be. I'm further from the door than I should be.

He turns, his expression grim. "I didn't mention Harper talking to me because it wasn't important. And it wasn't like she was warning me off you. She was talking about business connections. I think she was more concerned about CeCe Foust than you. You have to know Harper loves you."

I am no longer certain of that. She loved the me I'd been in high school and college. She doesn't seem impressed with the me I am now. "It doesn't matter. She's right. Not about me screwing you out of money, but I'm not interested in the project you want to sell, and neither is CeCe."

He stops, his expression going blank as he obviously thinks the problem through. "Then what are you… The framework and the AI. Okay. You pretty much told me that in the beginning. So instead of coding the app I want to build, you want to use the coders to showcase how easily adaptable the AI is to any number of applications."

It's good that he understands. Though I had meant to give him one of the coders for his app. I'd been planning on working with the other one on the part of the project that will really sell. "Yeah. I was going to sell it right out from under you."

He seems a bit startled by that, but not in the way I would have thought. He gives me a half grin. "Baby, I still own sixty percent. You can't sell it out from under me. I suspect you were going to use this time to gently maneuver me to the place you think is the best bet to get us the most money."

I don't want to think about the fact that he called me baby. "Yeah. I was only thinking about the money."

He sighs. "It's a language for you. That's what Harper doesn't get.

You view money as security, and you want that for me, too. When you think about it, it's kind of sweet."

Tears spring to my eyes because he is not understanding me. "Heath, I knew I didn't want your matchmaking program and I still talked you into giving me half the company."

"Forty percent. You could have had half if you'd worked harder," he admits. "And as for the matchmaking program, I'll prove it to you. That's on me. I've got some time."

"No, you don't. We need a business plan," I explain.

"Can't the matchmaking app be one of the many apps one can create with the AI I've built?" He sounds so damn reasonable it's making me crazy. "Also, you do realize the AI wouldn't be working properly if you hadn't come in and fixed it. It's not like you do nothing but bring in cash. You are crazy talented, and not merely with putting together a start-up business. So forget about all this noise, and Monday we'll go back to work. Nonna told me she's making pasta al timballo. It's going to be delicious, and then you can spend a bunch of time trying to make me understand the business plan."

"You aren't hearing me," I insist.

His gaze is soft as he stares down at me. "I think I hear you better than your friends do. There's a lot of history between the three of you. They remember the you in high school. I only know the Ivy I see in front of me, and she seems to be hard on the outside, but that's because her life has been a roller coaster lately, and she's a little traumatized. But even while she's processing all the pain of failure, she finds ways to be genuinely kind. My grandmother adores you."

I feel my expression go stubborn. Why won't he fight with me? "She offered me a way to cut back on rent."

"Yes. That's why you spend long hours talking to her and explaining how you work." His tone has gone soothing, like I'm some beast he needs to ease.

Or a friend he's showing sympathy to. It's getting to me, and I'm not any closer to the door. "She's a nice lady. I find her interesting."

"And I thank you for that. Did you think I didn't see you give her that new murder mystery she's been wanting to read?" he asks.

"I found it for half price. When she's done, I'll read it, too."

His eyes roll slightly, and he huffs. "Yes, you're a monster. But you're a monster I'm happy to be in business with. I need you to understand something. I don't care what Harper thinks. I'm happy I met you, and I'm not willing to let you off my hook. Maybe I'm the bad guy here. Maybe I'm the one who's using you. Have you thought about that?"

A little in the beginning, but it's hard to think of Heath as a user. I should, though. "Maybe."

I can see he doesn't believe me, but he plows forward anyway. "Good. Then we're both in the same boat, and we should carefully watch the other. I can think of no better way to ensure neither of us is hatching terrible plots than we spend more time together. So get in my shower and get warm. I'll order us a pizza. You're obviously hungry."

How had we gotten here? I was seriously considering taking that shower because I was so cold, and it would feel good to be warm and comfortable. Still, I'm stubborn. "I'm not hungry."

His eyes widen. "Then that is the problem. You've been body snatched."

"Heath, I'm serious. I am leaving. I'm leaving the city and the freaking business."

"I'm going to ask you not to go," he says quietly, his voice a low rumble, and I hear the emotion in him. "Stay with me, Ivy. It's barely been a week, and I don't want to do this without you. The one thing Harper isn't thinking about is the fact that I believe you have my best interest at heart, and if I tell you no, you'll honor it."

He was so confusing. "I can't promise you that. There's money on the line, money we'll have to pay back if we can't bring CeCe on."

"We'll cross that bridge when we get there. It's way in the distance."

"I won't honor what you want," I say stubbornly. "Not if I know I'm right."

He shrugs. "Then we'll do it your way, but we don't know what you'll do until you're faced with the actual problem. The only thing I do know is I will be very bad at dealing with CeCe. I'm scared of her dog, much less the woman herself. You cannot be so cruel as to leave me alone with her. She doesn't even know my name. She calls me Ivy's Side Piece. I don't think she understands what that means."

CeCe often heard some phrase she thought was funny and used it in a totally bizarre way. What the hell was happening? "I'm not good for you."

"And I'm not a side piece. I'm the whole piece," he assures me. His hands come up, cupping my cheeks. "You had a shit night, and someone backed you up against the wall so you're fighting. You feel alone, so you're fighting. I suspect that person was Harper, so you feel like someone else you love is ready to abandon you so…"

"I'm fighting." It's what I do.

"You don't need to fight me," Heath says, and he's so close to me now. So close I can see how warm his eyes are, how there's gold in the deep brown of his irises. "And I'm getting really tired of fighting my every instinct."

"Your instinct?" I feel rooted in place, still in the face of coming disaster because if he kisses me this time, it's not to help me out. It's because he wants to.

He nods. "This one."

He leans in and his lips meet mine, and I'm suddenly not cold.

I'm suddenly not alone.

He's right. I'm fighting and being dramatic and veering wildly when I should sit and think the problem through. Although I can't think now. All I can do is feel the way his mouth moves over mine, how his hands find my waist and bring our bodies close. My arms go up to his shoulders, and that's when I realize how wet I am and I'm going to make him cold and wet, too.

I step back. "I should…"

He looks disappointed. "Take a shower. I'll grab some clothes that will be way too big for you and order a pizza, and when you're done, we'll do one of two things. We'll talk this through or we'll watch a bunch of crappy TikTok videos and make fun of people because you'll realize you're not going anywhere tonight." His lips turn up in the most delicious smirk. "Or you can pick door number three."

"Number three?" I shake my head because I'm being obtuse. "I don't think that's a good idea."

"Then pick one or two because you're not leaving. You would miss me."

God, I would, and that's the best reason of all to leave.

He moves to the small dresser and pulls out a Cornell sweatshirt and a pair of sweats with a draw string at the waist. "I know you feel like you're cursed, but you are not, Ivy Jensen. You are going through a rough patch, but the end of that dark tunnel is coming up fast. Don't make a U-turn and stay in the dark."

He leans forward and kisses my forehead, the gesture making my heart squeeze.

"I…I've given you every reason to push me away."

He winks. "And still I didn't. And that's why you should seriously consider door number three." He sobers. "I can handle your damage. All this drama, it doesn't scare me off at all. The truth is my life was a little boring until you showed up." He walks to the door. "Now wash the pretty gross rainwater off and find your appetite, woman. I do not know what to do with an appetite-less Ivy. I'm used to being able to manipulate you with food."

I stand there and realize just how much trouble I'm in.

Chapter Fourteen

The water goes cold far too soon and I turn it off, wondering if I should try to sneak out. It's not that I think Heath would ever try to make me do something I don't want to do. It's simply the fact that door number three is so tempting.

I don't know if I can walk out there and eat pizza and watch dumb videos with him and not end up entwined with that gorgeous man who seems to understand me in a way no one else does.

Who seems to fit with me. I spent the time in the shower going over all the ways he could be saying these things to manipulate me. I've had every bad scenario play out through my head in the last fifteen minutes.

He just wants the money and he's right. He owns the majority of the company so he can use me and lose me whenever he wants.

He's upset that I don't want to use his app as the main focus of our business plan, and he thinks he can use sex to manipulate me. He thinks if he pleases me in bed, I'll do whatever he wants.

He's been sent in by someone who hates me to humiliate me.

As I stand at the mirror and accept that I am completely paranoid, I also think about the one scenario I usually don't consider.

He's a good thing.

He's being honest and he cares about me and wants to take this thing between us to the next level. He's dumb and thinks it can work, and maybe he's so dumb he's smart and I'm the dumb one and if I just let it, it could work.

I use his very utilitarian hair dryer and then braid my hair because if I don't put a million pounds of product on it, it kind of goes in all different directions. He has neither flat iron nor curling iron. He's iron free, so this is my only choice.

He was right about the clothes. I'm lost in them, and that weirdly does something for me. I like wearing his clothes. It's like he's hugging me.

I am not this girl. I am not.

I never once put on Nick's clothes and cuddled with him. I'm not the girl who moons over some guy and sits around writing our names on notepads like it's some plea to the universe that we end up together. I hadn't done it in school. I hadn't done it as a young adult.

Maybe you didn't do it because most guys suck and he's the right one.

I don't believe in the right one.

And still I open the door and step outside with no real thought to leaving.

He looks up from his computer. He's got glasses on. He wears these blue light blockers when he's working that make him look super nerdy and adorable, and I'm freaking done for.

"I found an entire profile made up of nothing but dogs doing stupid things," he announces. "That should put you in a happier mood."

I'm not watching videos with this man. It's been a day, and all the good parts of it revolved around him. He's told me what he wants. I tried to talk him out of it but he's still here, and he's far too tempting for me to walk away from.

I move into his space and see the minute he realizes I've changed my mind. His expression goes from amused to slightly predatory in a heartbeat, and he turns his chair so I can straddle him. It's a bold move, but I'm going all in.

I settle myself on his lap, and his hands move to hold me to him. Those big hands I watch all day are right above my backside. Another inch or two and he'll be cupping my cheeks. I study him for a minute. I've never been this girl either—the one who needs to take her time so she remembers. Sex is very much a biological function. It's an itch to scratch.

He doesn't feel like an itch. He feels like a blanket that soothes me, that warms and surrounds me, so I look at him, really look at him. I let myself do something I've wanted to from pretty much the minute I'd seen him. I run my hands through his hair and let myself feel how soft and silky it is despite the fact the man has no conditioner.

His eyes close as though he deeply appreciates the physical contact. "What made you change your mind?"

"I decided maybe you're not playing me."

His eyes open again, a brow rising. "Baby, I don't know how to play anything but games, and I mean the video and board game kind. I will screw you over if we ever play *Ticket to Ride*, but otherwise you're safe with me. I know this is going to come as a shock, but I don't have a string of exes across the city wishing I would come back. I've had two serious girlfriends—one in college and one right after I started my first job. I haven't dated anyone in over a year, and that also means I haven't had sex in over a year. You seem to have some misconceptions."

I put a finger over those gorgeous lips of his. "No misconceptions. Just a whole bunch of baggage that you have recently promised me you can handle."

His hands move more confidently now, molding my hips as his lips curl up. "I am absolutely capable of handling all your baggage, Ivy. Trust me."

I shouldn't, but I do. That trust is precisely why I'm risking everything on him. Harper would think I'm dragging him further into my web. This is the opposite of what I should do, but I can't stop myself. I can't not lean forward and let my forehead rest against his. I can't not breathe him in.

His forehead rubs gently against mine as his hands move, shifting over my thighs to my waist and almost up to my breasts. Like he's learning that part of my body.

It's been so long since I let my brain shut down and my body take over. Even the last year with Nick had been fairly sex deficient. We'd worked and fought, and then he'd started traveling more and more. I hadn't even realized he was using the travel to interview.

"Hey, stay here with me." Heath gently tugs on the braid, getting my attention. "You're here with me. No one else."

He pulls me away from the insecurity that's plagued me for almost a year. He's right. I don't have to think about anything but him and the way he makes me feel.

One of those big hands finds the back of my neck, drawing me down to him. Our lips meet and then all thoughts beyond him are gone. I need this. I need the rest of the world to fall away.

When I feel his mouth open, I let him in, let his tongue find mine, the caress sending shots of arousal through my body. They feel like lightning flashes, waking me up from a long slumber. He kisses me over and over, taking his time. His hands slip under the big sweatshirt, and I shiver at the sensation of him touching me.

His fingertips trace my spine as his tongue plays with mine.

It's intimate in a way I don't know I've experienced before.

When he starts to pull the sweatshirt over my head, I lift my arms and feel the cool air on my breasts. His eyes are warm and filled with desire as he looks down and palms a breast.

"Do you have any idea how much I've thought about you?" he whispers. "Twenty-four seven since the minute I met you."

I'm not entirely sure if he's talking to me or my breasts. It could be either, but I smile anyway. "The minute you met me?"

He leans over and nuzzles my neck, like a big, affectionate lion. "I told you. We have chemistry, and yes, I was attracted to you the minute I saw you. Why do you think I gave you half my company?"

"Forty percent," I whisper back because he's kissing his way down my chest, his lips seeming to brand me wherever they touch. "And I thought that was about my business acumen."

"You are the whole package, baby." The words skim over my skin as he continues moving down my body. "That's why I've been lying in wait for you. I'm a patient predator, but I knew I wanted to make a meal out of you."

I'm about to argue with his metaphors, but that's the moment he captures a nipple in his mouth and I forget to breathe. The sensation causes a wave of arousal that's piercing and sweet. I hold on as he licks and sucks one nipple and then the other.

His hands finally fully cup my ass, and he stands up like I don't weigh a thing. He's kissing me again as he moves over to the bed. I can hear people chatting in the living room, but it doesn't really register because my world is all about him for now.

He lays me down on the soft comforter that covers his probably going to be a tight fit bed and pulls the tank over his head and tosses it aside. His chest is a thing of beauty, made of lean muscle and graceful lines. There's the faintest dusting of hair there that tickles my breasts when he lowers himself down.

When he's on top of me, the bed suddenly doesn't seem small. It seems just right. I love his weight on me as he presses me down. His mouth finds mine again, and I'm infused with heat. I wrap myself around him, loving every inch of skin I can touch.

He kisses his way down my throat and over my chest. When I feel him kissing the curve of my belly, a deep sense of anticipation hits my system, knocking through all the walls I've built up recently. I realize I've spent the last year so focused on getting back to the top that I haven't let myself want anything else.

I want him. I want everything he can give me. Pleasure. Security. Affection. They might be temporary, but I want them.

He gets to his knees and unties the string holding the sweats on me. He's staring down as he drags them off my body and I'm naked. There's nothing but appreciation in those eyes of his, and I don't even think about being insecure. He makes me feel sexy, like my body has a purpose beyond hauling me around to business meetings and typing out line after line of code.

He lowers himself down again, and those kisses of his turn ravenous as he spreads my legs and makes good on his threat to make a meal of me.

It's beyond anything. The intimacy, the sensations have me clawing at the blanket beneath me. I have to hold on because I'm riding this magnificent wave he's created with his lips and tongue, and I don't ever want it to stop.

He eases one finger inside me, teasing at my core, and I'm done for. I can't help the shout that comes out of my throat as he sends me right over the edge and into complete pleasure. I feel the blood pounding through my body as every muscle seems to tense and then blissfully release.

He's on his feet then, shoving his pants off, and I get a look at him. Heath is beautiful inside and out. I can't imagine how I ever thought he was nerdy, except I kind of like a nerd. He's a hot nerd. Exactly my type, and I can't help but smile as he fumbles with the condom.

He grins at me. "I'm suddenly not good with my hands."

I push off the bed and take the condom. "I'll help you."

His eyes close as I take him in hand, loving the feel of him. I paid attention in sex ed. I know how to roll a condom on, but I have to admit to taking my time. I watch his chest hitch as I stroke him.

"You're going to kill me," he whispers.

"Never." He's kind of the only person I like in the world right now. I intend to be very careful with him.

I finally stop teasing him and get the condom on and then he's easing me onto the bed again. His weight comes down on me and when he kisses me this time, I can taste my own arousal on his lips.

I feel him, his cock sliding over me as he makes a place for himself between my legs. It makes my breath catch.

"I need you to know I'm not playing around with you," he says.

I stop him because the last thing I want right now is a Heath speech. He's the good guy. I get it. He's the one who won't hurt me. He needs to be the one who makes me forget everything but how good he can make me feel. I know how to get to him though. I bring my head up and kiss him while I tilt my hips and wrap my legs around his waist.

"Fuck," he whispers against my lips, and then I feel him inside me.

This is what I need. I've needed it for so long I forgot how good it can feel to be deeply connected to someone I like.

I don't even let myself think that other word. That other word is dangerous, and I'm not expecting anything out of this beyond adding a physical aspect to our friendship.

His hips move and he starts to thrust in and drag out, and it's so perfect it can't last. He works over me until I can't hold back, and that wave hits me for the second time tonight. I cling to him as he grinds against me, giving me everything he has.

When he falls on top of me, a sense of peace flows over me.

We lay there, wrapped in each other, and it's such a sweet moment.

"That is what we call a release of sexual tension," I hear Darnell say. "You want to avoid that in a book for as long as you can."

"But in real life, it's what you're looking for," an unfamiliar feminine-sounding voice says.

Embarrassment flashes through my system. "Oh, shit."

"And there's the regret." Darnell definitely knows we can hear him. "See, I told you putting some sex in your book can lead to a plethora of emotional conflict. Not all of your conflict has to come from aliens plundering our planet. They can plunder our women, too. Or men. I'm all for equal-opportunity plundering. And I think they're done. Hey, Heath, your pizza's here."

Heath chuckles and kisses my cheek as he rolls off me. "Do you want to ignore him and wait until the group leaves for the night?"

There's only one problem with that. "I'm a little hungry."

"And she's back." He reaches for his clothes. "Get under the covers, baby. I won't be long."

I ignore the applause that comes when Heath walks out. I am all about the pizza.

It feels good to be hungry again.

Chapter Fifteen

I'm feeling infinitely better now that Heath's properly fed me and we're cuddled up on his bed. I'm in another of his overly large shirts as we'd hopped back in the shower, this time together. The sounds of Darnell's writer group have faded, and I think he went with them to get a drink at the bar downstairs and probably talk about us. I'm cool with that. I would do the same, so it's fair.

"Do you need to call anyone to let them know where you are?" Heath asks, brushing back my hair.

I've got my head on his chest as we lie in bed. "I should probably go home."

"Do you want to go home?"

It's not home anymore. "Not really, but it's getting late."

"And your clothes aren't dry yet," he points out. "Stay with me. I promise I will get you donuts in the morning, and Darnell will make fun of us. Doesn't that sound like a great way to start your day?"

The idea of spending a lazy weekend with him is too much temptation. There's only one problem with it. "I've got to work. If I don't, I won't have things in place for the new hires."

"We'll get your laptop in the morning. You can work here, and I'll help you so we can find time to do something that is not work. See there's this thing called leisure."

My insecurity is starting up again as I realize the ramifications of what happened tonight. I sit up. We need to talk. "You don't have to entertain me, Heath."

He frowns up at me. "You're going to be difficult, aren't you?"

I don't think I'm difficult at all. I need to let him know this doesn't have to change anything between us. "Not at all. I don't want this to change our working relationship."

"So when you're all stressed I should tell you to meditate instead of sneaking you into a room for a quickie?"

Actually, that didn't sound bad at all. I do get stressed, and an orgasm is way better than meditation. I can't get my head empty enough to meditate, but all thought tends to flee when this man touches me. "I mean, if it's affecting work…"

He laughs and sits up, his chest on glorious display. "Okay. Let me get this straight. So you accept that we're sleeping together now?"

"I'm not going to deny it." Though there hasn't been any sleeping yet, and that feels like a whole other thing.

"But you're also not going to pretend like this won't happen again," he prompts.

I should, but I know me. I won't be able to stay away from him. "I think it probably will."

"Yes," he agrees. "And likely very soon. So are we going to define this relationship or pretend that it's all the same except every now and then we have sex?"

I don't like the way he's phrased it. He means something to me, but definitions are hard. "I think we're friends who now have a physical aspect to our relationship."

He nods like I've said something smart and true. "And that is called?"

"I don't like the term *friends with benefits*." I think it cheapens the relationship, and besides, I have some parameters. "Because that feels like we're open to sleeping with other people, and I don't think we should do that."

He nods as though I've said something wise. "I'm glad we agree. So we're friends who exclusively sleep together and have very warm feelings for each other and want to spend time together away from other friends."

I like being alone with him, so I don't see a problem with that. "Yes."

I can see he's amused with me. "All right then. That's what we're calling it."

I know what he wants me to say, but that feels like too much right now. I can't be his girlfriend. I'm not sure I can be anyone's girlfriend ever again. It would be so easy to fall into a relationship with Heath. It would be warm and comforting, and I have to remember that if we don't get funding for this project, it will likely all fall apart. The work is the base for the relationship, and I know all too well how quickly that can change.

"I think so. Do we have to call it anything at all?" I ask.

His expression goes serious, and he reaches over to grab my hand, lacing our fingers together. "We don't have to call us anything at all beyond friends and business partners. The rest of it is our business. Though I'm going to warn you my grandmother will know."

The thought of Lydia knowing we've had sex kind of freaks me out. I hadn't thought about that. "She won't. We'll be very careful around her. We'll maintain a professional demeanor at work."

"She'll know, and we haven't kept much of a professional demeanor up to this point." He leans over and brings my hand up, kissing it. "She's got a sex radar you won't believe. I lost my virginity to Veronica Garcia my senior year of high school at band camp. My grandmother took one look at me when I got back and asked if I'd at least been smart enough to wear a condom."

I snort at the thought. "She was playing the odds there. Was Veronica your girlfriend?"

He shrugs. "Yeah, but she had been for over a year at that time. How did Nonna know we'd done the deed?"

He was giving her too much mystical power. "Because you were dumb teens, and that's what dumbass teens do at band camp. Although mine was a robotics competition in Chicago. He was on the opposing team, so it was an enemies-to-lovers tale. We were running high on the adrenaline of creating robots that did very limited tasks, and then suddenly I was a woman."

He's back to smiling. "Was that your first long-distance relationship?"

"Oh, no. See, I'd actually been thinking about sex for a long time, and like everything I do I read up and studied and I had a few notes for him," I admit.

He chuckles. "Oh, baby, did you ruin him for life?"

It had not been my finest moment, but I think a little critical input is important to every successful endeavor, and that one was not so much on the successful side. "Probably not. Maybe. Although I did hear a couple of years later that he spends a lot of time on 4chan."

Heath's head drops back as he laughs and tugs me close. "You got any notes for me?"

Not a single one. I cuddle close. I like the sound of his heartbeat. "You get an A plus from me. I think you're ready to move to beta testing. We should really practice so we get it just right."

"You'll have to stay if you want to practice," he whispers.

I'm too tired to pretend that doesn't sound like the best idea ever. "Okay."

There's a knock on the door and then Darnell is talking. "Heath, your drama has yet another player. I do not know what is happening, but you have to start charging for crying white chicks."

Heath frowns and eases out of bed. He goes to the door, opening it slightly. "Who would come by... Hey, Harper. Anika."

Now I'm the one sitting up, and I realize it's been hours since I checked my phone. I scramble across the bed. I'd turned it off earlier because I didn't want to think about calling either one of them. Now I turn it back on and sure enough, there's twenty messages between the two of them. Crap. I'd thought they would go to the party and we'd likely talk about the fight sometime in the future, if ever.

"Heath, I know this is a long shot, but have you seen Ivy?" Harper asks. "We had a fight earlier, and she's not at home. I'm worried about her."

It's nice that she's worried about me because earlier she'd seemed like she didn't care at all. But I'm not sure catching me in Heath's bedroom is going to fix our situation.

"Ivy?" Heath is blocking her view from the door. "Have I seen Ivy?"

Darnell snorts. "Yes. That is the question she asked. If I had known this was going to happen, I wouldn't have let the group leave so soon. This is some reality TV shit right here. Anyone want a beer?"

I would take one.

"We've been everywhere," Anika says. "We called CeCe and all her other friends. No one's seen her."

"We tried the taco vendor, but he hasn't seen her all night," Harper says like this is information that absolutely points to me being dead in a ditch somewhere.

"We talked to all the street food guys in a three-block radius," Anika continues, and I hear her sniffle. "She hasn't gone to any of them."

I really need a better thing I'm known for than being every food truck's best customer.

I quickly text them back, glancing through the increasingly frantic messages they sent.

Don't worry about it. We'll talk in the morning. I'm fine. Hanging with some friends.

And I add a heart emoji and send.

I hear the ping from their phones.

"It's her," Harper says, her relief obvious. "Thank god. Though she says she's with friends. I thought I'd talked to all her friends. Hell, I called Nick looking for her."

I bite back a groan. The last thing I need is Nick to think I'm walking the streets of Manhattan crying over the debacle of my life.

"See," Heath says. "She's good. I bet it's some of the people we met over the last week. They seemed cool."

"Well, she could have told us," Harper says with a huff. "We've been worried sick about her."

"Her mom hasn't heard from her either," Anika adds.

"I'm sure she'll text her mom soon," Heath promises. "I bet she got caught up in something and didn't look at her phone for a while. Or maybe she had to charge it."

"Ivy is never without her phone." Harper's tone has gone from worried to slightly annoyed. Or maybe the better word is suspicious. "She's hyper vigilant about keeping it charged. So she was ignoring my texts."

"You keep going, girl." Darnell urges her on. "You're almost there."

"Well, you made her feel like crap, Harper." At least Anika's on my side.

"This isn't about the fight," Harper counters, suspicion creeping into her tone. "This is about what would keep Ivy Jensen from reading her texts. Because she hadn't even read them until a minute ago, and that is not the Ivy I know. I can see her ignoring the texts. I can see her sending me a bunch of flaming poop emojis to properly express her feelings. What I can't see is her hanging with a bunch of randos she recently met and not picking up her phone even once."

"Well, I guess she could be somewhere else." Heath is not good at this.

And then Harper does the one thing that is sure to let her know where I am. She texts me, and my phone trills with the unique harp sound I assigned to her years ago.

Damn it. I really should have silenced my damn phone.

There's a gasp from Anika. "That was her phone. Is she here?"

"She shoots, she scores," Darnell announces, and I can practically see his hands over his head like he's at a game. "And there's a damn fine reason she wasn't looking at her phone, if you know what I mean."

I slide out of bed because there's nothing more to do.

Heath opens the door and gives me a grimace. "Sorry. I'm not ever going to be the guy who covers up a conspiracy."

"Hey," I say as I walk out into the hall. "I was hanging out here with Heath and lost track of time."

"And your pants," Harper points out.

"They got wet because someone made me walk in the rain," I shoot back.

"She looked like a drowned rat," Darnell explains. "It was all very pathetic. So, Ivy, when you wonder if Heath is into you only for your looks, remember this day."

"I did not make you walk in the rain, you drama llama." Harper has a hand on her hip and looks ready to pick things right back up. "That was pure Ivy Jensen theatrics right there."

"And this is pure Harper can't give an inch," Anika replies. "You swore if we found her you would be nice, and here we are."

"Well, that was when I thought I would find her in a hospital or a ditch, not warm and cozy with the very man we were fighting over," Harper replies.

"I came here to tell Heath I was giving him back his business," I explain.

Heath moves to the couch, sitting down beside Darnell. I notice he has not put his shirt on. It's distracting. "I didn't want it back. She's done all this stuff I don't understand and now there are employees, and I've never really wanted to manage anyone."

"He's bad at it," Darnell agrees.

"I did not tell you to do that." Harper keeps her focus on me, ignoring our superhot peanut gallery.

I point Heath's way. "You told him to dump me."

"Not exactly," Heath hedges.

"I did not," Harper insists. "I asked him if everything was going okay and to be very sure that he was covered. I told you I'm more worried about CeCe than you. I think CeCe can be ruthless when it comes to business, and I don't want either of you getting steamrolled."

I'm not letting her out of this. "That's not what you said at dinner. You worried I was becoming too much like CeCe."

"In Ivy's defense, she did tell me my matchmaking app is a dumb idea, and she thinks the framework and AI I'm working on are way more valuable," Heath explains.

"She did," Darnell agrees. "She was all teary and shit. Like she was the bad guy in a Bond film. Oh, and hey, then she slept with him like she was the good girl in a Bond film."

"I don't think the bad guys cry." Anika finally gives up and plops on the couch next to Darnell. "She was doing the martyr thing. This is not the first time I've lived through an Ivy-Harper showdown. Harper can't see shades of gray."

"I see shades of gray just fine," Harper insists.

Anika's eyes roll. "And the minute Ivy feels judged by someone she cares about, she goes into martyr mode and swings wildly the other way. I was worried she would be on a Greyhound bus going to like Maine or something to live out the rest of her life in the solitude she deserves in her head."

"Nah," Heath corrects. "I got her naked pretty fast and now we're friends… Let me see if I can keep this straight. We're friends who sleep together exclusively and hang out and have warm feelings for each other. Right, babe?"

"I was never going to Maine." I've lost all control of this conversation.

"You know you're the one most likely to *Grey Gardens* on us," Harper says, her arms crossed over her chest.

I should never have watched that documentary with her. "I am not going to end up in a rambling mansion eating cat food." The truth is I can't afford a mansion. If that's how my life ends up, I'll be eating my cat food in a small apartment, thank you very much. "But she's right about you not being able to see shades of gray. I did not go into this agreement with Heath to hurt him."

"I know you didn't. I worry that you're so determined to get back to the top you won't see a good thing sitting in front of you," Harper says. "I'm sorry. I'm sorry to both of you. You guys are my sisters. Do you have any idea how hard it is to see you guys doing things I think will hurt you?"

"What did you do?" Darnell asks Anika. "I thought Ivy was the only fuckup."

"I never said that either." Harper looks worse for the wear. The rain got to her in a way it hadn't with Anika's high ponytail. Harper's hair had been stick straight, and now it looks like she'd spent some time in

Florida. Maybe wrestling a gator.

"I have taken a job on a reality TV dating show Harper thinks is beneath me," Anika announces. "I start in a couple of weeks, and she's trying to get me to battle with my bosses when she doesn't even understand what's going on."

"Then explain it to me," Harper counters.

Anika stands, facing off with her. She's still wearing the glittery dress she'd worn for the party. "I would but I signed an NDA, so back off."

This is tea she has not spilled to this point.

"Heath, I think the little disco ball and Wednesday Addams are going to fight," Darnell whispers.

I need to take control. If Anika's signed some kind of NDA, then we don't know what's going on and we can't. "Everyone's going to their respective corners. Harper, you can't control the world. I know you want to. I know you would be a benevolent wicked queen, but we don't live in a fantasy world, and you're pushing us away with this crap."

Tears shine in Harper's eyes. "I don't mean to. I want everyone to be happy. You can't imagine how much I envied you when I thought you were living the dream out in San Francisco. I was so proud of you, and then I realized it was all a lie and you never told us."

"I didn't tell anyone."

"I knew you built walls to protect yourself. But I didn't think I was on the other side of one." Harper takes a long breath, seeming to steel herself for something. "Fuck it. I'm doing the same thing. Ani's right. I've run into some trouble. I'm overleveraged, and I could lose the company if I'm not careful. Ivy, could you please help me? I need someone to talk to about it."

All of my anger washes away in the face of her plea.

The years I spent away did build a wall between us, and I don't want this particular wall.

"Are they going to do a girl cry thing?" Darnell is whispering.

Heath hushes him.

"Of course I'll help you." I move close to her and wrap my arms around the woman who's been my family since we were children.

Anika completes our circle. "And I'm fine, guys. I can't talk about it, but my career is perfectly on track."

"I'm sorry," Harper says, squeezing us tight.

Emotion wells inside me. I'm sorry, too. I kept things from them. I didn't allow them to help me or take care of me, and I'm starting to learn that is not fair to the people we love, to the ones who love us. "I won't keep things from you again. I was just so ashamed."

Harper's head shakes. "You have nothing to be ashamed of."

And then we're a mass of crying women, hugging and promising things are going to be fine because we won't ever leave each other.

"I liked it better when I thought they were going to fight." Darnell stands. "This is…this is a lot of estrogen, man. You wanna play some *Call of Duty* while they do whatever rituals they need to do?"

Heath looks my way, and it's so clear that's exactly what he wants to do. I've put him through a lot of roiling emotional turmoil this evening, so I nod and he and Darnell are in Darnell's room shooting people before I know it.

"We ran off the guys," Anika says with a laugh.

"Do you want to go somewhere and talk?" Harper asks. "Or should we stay here at Ivy's friend who she's sleeping exclusively with and has warm feelings for's place. That's a lot."

"Let's just call him Heath." I move to the kitchen. "And we're going to steal his beer, too."

I grab three cold bottles and realize the night has been a good one.

Chapter Sixteen

It's early the next morning when I quietly let myself into my mother's apartment.

"I was wondering if you would come home." Mom is sitting in her favorite chair, a mug of coffee to her side. "Your friends are worried about you. Whose shirt are you wearing? I wasn't aware you were seeing anyone."

"It's mine." Heath has slipped in behind me. I'd thought we'd agreed he would stay outside while I grabbed a few things, but I should have known he would stay close. He moves toward her, a hand out like the polite man he'd been raised to be. "Ivy got caught in the rain yesterday and needed to borrow something. Hello again, Mrs. Jensen."

She gets to her feet. She's dressed but hasn't put on the makeup she wears most days even if she doesn't go out. "Hello, young man from my fire escape. Ivy didn't mention you were seeing each other in that fashion. I believe she told me you were business partners."

He nods. "Yeah. She struggles when it comes to defining relationships. I think any way you look at it you'll probably be seeing more of me."

"Well, I hope you're nothing like the last one. He should be in jail."

"Mom," I whisper under my breath.

Heath gives her a bright smile guaranteed to melt the heart of any woman in a two-mile radius. "She's right. He was an asshole. Now if you don't mind, I'll use your bathroom if that's okay. I took Ivy out for donuts and drank way too much coffee."

She nods and shows him which hall to go down. It's the only hall, really, so he shouldn't have too much trouble.

She looks tired in the early morning light, and I don't really want to fight with her. Talking things through with my friends last night made me realize how often in the last few years I'd gone into fight-or-flight mode.

"I'm picking up some things and then we're going back to his place, so don't worry. I won't bother you this weekend. I'll send you money on Monday for the month. Is it only rent you want? I know I ate some stuff you bought last week. And drank some of the milk."

She's watching the hall, studying Heath as he disappears. "Just the rent is fine. I suspect you'll be out of the place more than in it now that you're…working again."

I do not understand her, and I'm worried I never will. I don't know how everyone else in my life can be supportive and she simply can't. But I'm tired of fighting her, and I told Heath I wouldn't be long. "All right then."

She looks my way. "You're not even going to apologize for not checking in last night?"

"Checking in with you?" I'm surprised at the inference. "I didn't think you were watching when I come and go. Mom, I'm honestly surprised you would be worried."

"What is that supposed to mean?"

"It means that I wasn't aware that you would care if I didn't come home at all."

"So now I don't care about you?"

This is the part where the me before yesterday would have started fighting, would have taken this chance to lash out.

If Heath had done that to me last night, I would be on a bus ready to start a new life someplace where I would be miserable. Instead, he'd wanted to know why I was saying the things I'd said, and he'd asked me patiently to explain.

"It often feels like I'm a burden," I admit quietly. "Or like you're ashamed of me."

She seems to think about that for a moment. "I don't understand you. I'm sorry if I made you think that I was ashamed. I suppose if anyone feels shame, it's me. I didn't do a great job with you."

"See, the way you put that makes me feel like I'm damaged or something. I'm not. I know I couldn't hold onto Jensen Medical, but I'm working with Heath on something." I remember what she said the other day and decide to let it go. "It doesn't matter. I'm going to grab my laptop."

"Ivy, I'm sorry about what I said to you."

Her words stop me in my tracks. She'd said a lot since I'd gotten back. I want to make sure we were talking about the same thing. "About Dad?"

A light flush stains her cheeks. "Yes. I shouldn't have said it to you in that fashion."

"But you believe it."

"I think he wouldn't understand," she says after a moment.

I realize in that moment that we're not talking about my dad. Not really. "He wouldn't understand my job?"

"It seems so very ruthless some of the things that woman taught you. He wasn't like that at all. You know at one point he thought about going to seminary."

I've never heard this before. My somewhat hippie-dippie dad had thought about being a pastor? "You're kidding."

She shakes her head and gets that look she always has when she's thinking of my dad. It's a wistful look that makes her seem both young and old at the same time, as though grief places her in both stages of life at once. "We were in high school, and he considered it. His mother was very active in church. He liked parts of it. Feeding the poor. Helping people."

My father had worked for several nonprofits over the years. And he and Mom had done some time in the Peace Corps. Maybe he would be ashamed of his capitalist daughter.

"Anyway, he decided he could do a lot of good outside of the church," she explains. "And I was relieved because I would have been a terrible preacher's wife. I shudder at the thought of having to deal with all those people. Your father was always so much better with people. He could talk his way out of anything. He liked to talk, you know. One time we were walking through Bryant Park after dark. This was years ago. You were a very difficult baby, and the only thing that could soothe you sometimes was to put you in a stroller and walk you around. So there we were at one in the morning and sure enough, a man tries to mug us. I was terrified, but your father talked to him. Turned out the guy was hungry and homeless, and so your dad helped him find a place to stay that night. I would never have done that. I would have called the police and had him sent away."

"I would have done the same, Mom. It doesn't make you a bad

person," I reply. "Wanting to be safe and secure isn't a moral failing."

"No. But what that woman does is," Mom insists, and I know we're right back to talking about CeCe. "This wouldn't have happened to you if your father was alive."

"Your dad sounds awesome." Heath is back, and he slides an arm around my shoulder, seemingly ready to defuse the tension. "My parents did a lot of charity work, too, but it was mostly around the city."

"CeCe does a lot of charity work, too. She has a whole foundation." I feel the need to defend my mentor.

"She throws parties for the wealthy," my mom replies. "That's not the same. She spends all her time with billionaires and celebrities, and she's made sure you're in that world, too."

And I'm done. I gesture around the tiny room. "Yep. I'm in the lap of luxury. I'm going to grab my designer bag and tiara and head out to the next red-carpet event."

"And that wasn't what you did in California?" Mom asks, one brow raised. "Because it certainly seemed like it."

"What I did was work." I'm tired of justifying my life to her. "Pretty much constantly, something you would know if you'd ever once come out to visit me."

"I couldn't come out there. I had to work, too," she replies. "And quite frankly, I wouldn't have fit into that world you're so proud of."

There's a knock on the door, and I have to wonder if it's a neighbor since no one buzzed up.

I hope it is because that will give me the perfect excuse to get the hell out of here before Heath figures out how screwed up my family life is. He's already had to survive my friend drama.

"I don't think you understand that world," Heath tries as my mom goes to open the door. "It's not as glamorous as it seems. It's mostly just hard work. And I'm lucky to have someone like Ivy who's willing to help with the stuff I don't understand. She's really good at what she does."

"Then why is she back here?" My mother knows how to dig the knife in. She opens the door, and my hopes for a low-drama exit are quickly dashed.

"CeCe?" I didn't know she knew there was a nine in the morning. She's more of a late-night person. "What are you doing here?"

She's dressed to kill in an all-white pantsuit that plays off the royal blue of her blouse and shows off the unholy amount of Cartier the woman is wearing. I don't know how she lifts her arms sometimes. She breezes past my mother and into the apartment. "Well, darling, you went missing last night. I was worried."

"You could have called." I look over, and it's easy to see my mom is not happy about the new guest.

She waves that idea off. "I was so worried I had to see your face. Why on earth are you wearing that? It doesn't fit at all. Now tell me why your friends called looking for you last night."

"Well of course they called you," my mother says with an angry huff.

CeCe turns to her. "Yes, of course they did. Harper and the other one know how fond I am of Ivy and that my home is always open to her. I was, quite frankly, surprised she came back to this place."

"Well, it's her home, so naturally she came back here, and that other girl's name is Anika," my mother responds, her eyes narrowing. "I'm surprised you remember Harper's name."

"Oh, she's a very angry girl. I found her amusing, so I remember her name." If CeCe is upset by my mother's vehemence, she doesn't show it. She merely turns my way. "Now, what happened and have you settled things with your friends? Because I need you focused. I've scheduled several meetings for you next month, including a presentation with Gavin Huffman."

"Holy crap," Heath breathes. "Even I know who he is."

He's a mega billionaire, and he got there funding winning projects. He rarely takes on a project that doesn't end up making millions. I'm caught between excitement and utter dread. "I don't know that we'll be ready in a month."

"Of course you will. Hire more people if you need to," CeCe says. "I'm opening the purse strings."

"And what will you get out of it?" My mother is itching for a fight.

"Well, I'm going to end up with a percentage of the company, of course. We haven't settled the details," CeCe explains.

"You're going to take all their hard work for yourself is what you're going to do," my mother accuses.

Her definition of hard work seems to change based on who she's arguing with. I'm still reeling from the news that we're meeting with Huffman. Huffman money could change our lives, could open whole worlds for us. CeCe could fund a small team, but Huffman could put us on the map. If it got out that Huffman is willing to meet with us, honestly, even if he ends up turning us down, we'll have more interest than we can handle.

"Breathe," Heath whispers in my ear. "You can handle it. It's going to be fine."

But he's not thinking about all the things we're going to need for that meeting. Some kind of proof of concept. Proof we're working on the patents that will be so valuable.

"I'm the reason they can work at all," CeCe counters, still arguing with my mom. "I know you think it's noble to live in poverty, but money makes the world move. Especially the business world."

And I realize I'm not sure what we're meeting with Huffman about. "Why is he interested?"

CeCe turns my way again. "Well, the surprising thing is what he's truly interested in is the matchmaking program." She shrugs. "He thinks it's time for something new and that the idea of an actual matchmaker behind it is interesting. So you need to shift your focus."

But everything I've been working on is focused on the AI and possibly opening up the framework Heath's built over the years. I've only got a month.

Heath has the biggest grin on his face, and I wonder what it's taking for him to not fist pump right now.

"What about what she thinks?" my mother asks. "Do you ever ask her? Or do you simply order her around?"

CeCe turns, her jaw going stubborn. "Lady, I don't understand your problem with me but I'm sick of it."

Heath takes my hand as they start to circle each other like two velociraptors ready to rumble. "And it's time to go."

"My laptop." It was the whole reason we came.

"We'll get it later." He tugs me toward the door.

They're still fighting as we make our escape.

Chapter Seventeen

"So that was fun. Are they always like that?" Heath hands me a bottle of water.

I'm on a bench in Balsley Park, still feeling shell shocked. We pretty much ran away, leaving my mom and CeCe to fight things out—I'll pay for that at some point. "Yes. Though they don't tend to do it to each other's faces. They're more behind the back fighters."

He sits down beside me on the bench. At this time of the morning, the park is filled with kids playing on the small playground, and the scent of pizza is in the air as they gear up for lunchtime. "I got the feeling they weren't friends. I didn't realize they hate each other."

"My mom hates CeCe. I doubt CeCe thinks much about my mother. When I said behind the back fighting, I really meant my mom just complains about CeCe all the time." I haven't really thought about what a wedge that had put between us.

"You two seemed to be having a serious conversation when I came back." He says the words cautiously, as though he's not sure he should wade into this particular pool. "Everything okay?"

"Everything is exactly the way it has been since I started working for CeCe."

"That's weird. So things were good between you and your mom before?"

"I don't know that I would say they were good. Look, after my dad died, my mom kind of shut down. I mean she still took care of me, but it was clear even to a kid that she was going through the motions. The only time she's ever really animated is when she's talking about my dad or CeCe and my career. I did invite her, you know." I don't want him to think I cut off ties with my mom when I'd been in California. "When I was settled in San Francisco I asked her to come out at least four times, and she always made an excuse. If I wanted to see her for the holidays, I had to come here."

"And you would have to miss work because I would bet you worked weekends and holidays, too."

"Yeah. So I missed a few Christmases." Too many. "I think it was easier to work than to come home and deal with her. Somewhere along the way she became a problem I have to deal with, and I stopped enjoying being around her. She has her work and her friends, and I think if I move again, it might be years before we talk."

"How do you feel about that?"

I would bet Heath had studied some psych in school. Or maybe he'd learned how to talk to people from his grandmother. Lydia could get me talking, too. "I miss her sometimes. Even though I always felt how sad she was, when I was younger she did things with me. Like she would come to my school plays, and we would get ice cream after. She used to take me out for pizza once a week and we would talk. She would help me with my homework. And then I got to be a teenager and we kind of drifted apart."

"Drifted? Or fought? I remember being a teen," Heath prompts.

Talking about this makes me antsy, but it's a problem I suddenly feel like I need to resolve. "Yeah, there was a lot of fighting. She didn't like all the time I was spending on things like robotics. I think she wishes I was more feminine."

"Have you asked her?"

"I don't know that she would tell me the truth," I reply. "After I started working with CeCe, she blamed everything on her. The last few years we've barely talked. I was surprised when she let me move back in. I now know it's because she sees me as a source of rent. If I'm honest with myself, I feel a little like an orphan, which is ridiculous because I'm a grown woman."

"That's not ridiculous at all. I feel that every day. I was fifteen when my parents died. I was actually in the car," he says. "I was asleep in the back. They think that's why I came out of it with relatively no injuries. Broken arm was all I got from a head-on collision with a truck running with its headlights off. Still hurts from time to time, but the point is I woke up in a hospital bed and my grandmother had to tell me they were gone."

I sense he's going to say more, but I turn and wrap my arms around him because I can't stand the thought of these two people I've come to…appreciate so much being in that position. I hug him tight and do that thing where I wish him all good things.

I feel his lips on my forehead, and he squeezes me back. We sit for a moment.

He kisses me again, and then eases away though not far. "I don't know that you ever get over a loss like that. I don't think your mother has."

"She's never dated." I lean back, letting the sun hit my face. I don't like talking about things like this, but it feels right with him. "I think time stopped for her, and she's just waiting until she gets to see him again. It made her bitter. I wish I could have been the kind of daughter she wanted. Apparently that's Anika."

"I find it interesting she's made such a connection with your friends. Did she have that before you moved out?"

"No. I mean, she was nice to them. She liked Harper and Ani, but I wouldn't say she took a special interest in either of them." It was why it felt so weird for them to have a whole relationship with her.

"Have you considered that the friendship with Ani is so she can keep up with what you're doing?"

I snort at the idea. And then wish I didn't snort at all. It's not a sexy sound. "I highly doubt that."

"I don't know." Heath sounds unsure. "She said she feels uncomfortable in the world you move in."

"She doesn't understand it." And the truth is I don't understand her. I get that there are things about the tech business people who live outside of it don't get, but in the end it's all the same hard work and the same hard workers getting screwed by the top dogs. It's capitalism at its finest, and I would think she would applaud me for learning how to navigate those waters.

"Most people don't, and it changes constantly," Heath points out. "All I'm saying is her problems with CeCe might be more about losing you than you think. Even people who don't express them have emotions. For a while after my parents died I shut down. I barely made friends in high school because I didn't want ties that could be broken."

I can't stand the thought of him as a lonely teenager. Heath is a light in the world, the guy who everybody can be friends with. "But you had your grandmother."

"Only because she wouldn't let me shut her out." He takes a long breath, as though thinking about that time weighs on him. "She made me see a therapist, and when that didn't seem to work, she tried something else. One night she brought a bunch of files into my room and told me she would pay me if I would make a database for her. I was already into computers, so it seemed like a way to make some cash."

"She gave you her client files." I've wondered exactly how he'd gotten so invested in her business. I'd thought it might simply be because of the family ties, but this makes more sense.

He nods. "And I started building this database. The next weekend she asked me to join her for a client meeting. So I could take notes. I was a faster typist, she said."

Of course Lydia had found a way to bridge their worlds. "She brought you into her business and got to learn about something you were interested in."

"She did, and I was weirdly fascinated by the idea that she could take two people and figure out if they had a shot. I've gone with her on over two hundred meetings at this point, and I've followed up with a lot of her older clients. What I figured out during those meetings was that it was worth it."

I'm not following him. "Worth it?"

"I figured out that what my parents had, the love they felt for each other, it was worth it no matter how it ended. Grief is a weird thing. It can warp the way you look at the world. Especially depending on where a person is in life. You were very young, and I know you felt grief…"

He doesn't have to qualify it for me. "I was very young. I felt the loss of my father, and I still feel it, but it's a wistful thing. A wish that didn't come true. Sometimes I barely remember him. I can remember that he loved me, remember I loved him. Or maybe that's a trick of my mind, a way to stay close to someone I never truly knew. It's not the same for my mom. They had been together since they were in high school. They should have been together for fifty or sixty more years. Her world ended that day, but the problem was I was still in it."

His hand covers mine. "I don't think so. And I don't think she would exchange you for your dad. I know I'm glad you're here."

I lean into him. I'm so glad he's here. I know this can't last, but I want to pretend for a while. I want to be a normal girl with the guy she likes sitting in a park on a Saturday with nothing more to do than hold his hand and watch the world go by.

"You don't think they would go full-on Housewives on each

other?" Heath asks the question with the trepidation of a man who's known a couple of table flippers in his time.

"CeCe and my mom?" I shake my head. "Never. They'll shout at each other for a while, and then CeCe will get bored and leave. I'm still trying to figure out how CeCe snuck up."

"Do you honestly believe a simple door can stop the fabulous CeCe Foust?" he teases.

I was sure she'd simply tell the door to open and it would. Or she would sit in her limo until the driver managed to catch someone going in or out. She certainly wouldn't hit a buzzer and ask to be let up. Probably because my mom would tell her where she could go. "Nope. How do you feel about going in front of Huffman?"

"Terrified out of my mind, and also excited. It means we need to buy some data," he says. "CeCe said she was opening the purse strings, right?"

"Yes." I'm going to have to call her to get that money flowing. I hope my mom doesn't do too much damage. "And that's the first thing we need to do. I've got some contacts."

"The AI needs food," Heath says and then frowns. "And a name. I thought about calling her Lydia, but my grandmother will kill me if I name an AI after her. I don't know a bunch of other famous matchmakers. Wasn't there one in *Fiddler on the Roof*?"

I knew the song, but that was about it. "Call her Emma. From Jane Austen. Women like Jane Austen, and a lot of men won't get the reference."

"Uhm, wasn't she kind of terrible at matchmaking? Like all the people she put together were actually wrong for each other?" Heath asks.

He probably remembers it better than I do. "I got nothing else, babe. If it were up to me, we'd name it Love Doctor."

He nods. "Emma it is then."

I'm not good with the sentimental stuff. I like to call a thing what it is. We should talk more about this, but it feels too good to sit in the sun with him. "I know I said I needed to work today."

He kisses the top of my head. "We are taking the day off. Tomorrow's soon enough to deal with the fact that we got an invite to the big show."

I take a deep breath and settle against him. Tomorrow will be here before we know it. I want to enjoy today.

Chapter Eighteen

"What is all this?" Lydia looks down at the mess I've made of her dining room table.

It's Monday morning two weeks later, and I'm in full-on panic mode. Not that I show it. "It's paperwork for the patent we're filing. It's several patents, really."

Lydia pulls up a seat and settles her glasses on her nose as she inspects one of the many forms I'm filling out. "To protect Heath's artificial thingee? The one he thinks can replace me?"

"I don't think he's trying to replace you."

"Oh, he is. It won't work, but I find it fascinating," she admits. "So this patent will make it so no one can steal his program?"

It's a bit more complicated than that. "The US patent system is set up more for machinery than software. It's had a hard time keeping up, so what we're really patenting is a bunch of processes, including how the AI learns. In this case he's got a combination of supervised and unsupervised learning."

This morning Lydia is wearing another of her fabulously colored caftans, purple and yellow and red today. Her hair is up in a turban, and she's wearing the biggest hoop earrings I've ever seen. "What is unsupervised learning?"

"That's when we feed the AI a bunch of data and the AI has to find the patterns on its own."

"What kind of data do you feed it? I know he's using the databases he built for me. Is that part of this patent?"

"Oh, that's not nearly enough data. Honestly, that's being used more as a part of supervised learning. It's very specific and will teach the AI what kinds of patterns to look for, and then we hit that sucker with the big stuff." I was glad I had some more cash because we needed to get the train moving. CeCe had transferred us another fifty K the same morning she and Mom had their knock-down, drag-out, and then she'd sent me to some intellectual property lawyers to get the ball rolling on the patents, hence me with tons of paperwork. She'd told me that she was sending some more by this morning, so I'm waiting for the courier.

And wondering if I can sneak into the office where Heath is so we can make out a little. We've tried to keep this thing we have quiet around the new employees, but I'm sure they've noticed we often leave together. We'd hired Ria Basu and Ye Joon Park after Lydia had told us she whole heartedly approved of them, and so far they've been great.

I have to hope they're not too observant when it comes to me and Heath though.

"We buy data that we think we can use, large amounts, and we let the AI learn from it."

"Buy data?" Lydia asks.

"Yes." This is the part not a lot of people like. Especially people who remember a time when privacy was a thing. "So companies on the web collect tons of data. You know the saying if you're not paying for the product, you are the product? Well, this is where that truth comes into play. I buy a bunch of data from social networking and other sites, and that will serve as an education for the AI. How Heath programs that is what we will actually patent."

"So you'll teach the computer to match people up by letting it read Facebook posts?" Lydia seems a bit horrified at the idea.

"Not exactly, but you know that we can often learn things like what a person values from what they post." I haven't talked to her extensively about how she did her work. "I know you started back before computers were a thing, but in recent years did you use your clients' social media to help you?"

"Somewhat," Lydia replies. "I found it helps me to sort out who's hedging on information to look good. Like the girl from the Bronx who swore she only listened to gospel music and then posted pictures of herself at a Metallica concert. She would have been miserable with the young man her mother wanted her to consider. Now she's married to a guitarist and spends most of her time on the road. She seems happy. But *seems* is the critical word here. Often social media doesn't show the whole picture."

"No, and we'll allow for that." I glance down at the endless paperwork the lawyers have given me. They can do some of the work, but the description of processes is something only Heath or I can do, and he went a shade of green when he saw the stack. "But there's valuable information in there, too. If Heath has set this up right, then the computer will learn to assign value properly, and that should offset some of the problems that come with socials. He's quite brilliant, you know."

That earns me a smile. "I do. He's such a bright young man, and I wish he wasn't using all his skill on something that can't work."

I'm surprised because this woman is almost always positive. "Why do you think it can't work? It's not exactly new technology. I mean the way he's going about it is, but there's been matchmaking apps for ages. Some have quite a good rate of success."

She shakes her head and puts the paper down. "But Heath isn't looking to do what they do. He's looking to do what I do. It's not the same. I don't simply match people up. I feel a connection between two people. Or three. That was a very odd job. I knew something was wrong between the couple, and then I met his best friend and realized what was missing. Live and let live, I say."

I kind of want that story, but I charge forward with the question that comes to mind. "Then why fill out all the paperwork?"

She made me go through her whole process of filling out about fifty pages of preferences and questions about my childhood and if I make my bed when I wake up. The answer is a resounding *no* because I'm just going to get back in it. Making beds is for people who have way more time and energy than me.

Like Heath. He's a bedmaker. At least he's done it all the mornings I've woken up beside him. I've spent a lot of time at his place in the last couple of weeks, and we'd gone over much of this stuff while lying on that bed together.

It's probably the dumbest thing I could do, but I can't help it. I'm drawn to that man, and I'm going to pretend like it's all normal and won't blow up in my face.

"Because sometimes I need clues so I know who to get into a room together, and then I'll know if it can work. The first meeting is always supervised. Usually the clients bring their parents or siblings or a close friend along to that first meeting. I'll feel that spark if they should be together. Even when the two people don't feel it themselves, I know.

The computer can't replace human instinct."

"I'm not sure human instinct is a good way to pick a match," I argue. "Humans can be very foolish. I should know. I thought my last boyfriend was a great match."

She stares at me over the glasses perched on her nose. "Why did you think he was right for you?"

I shrug. "It felt like the right time. I was approaching my late twenties, and that seemed like a good time to settle down. We had shared interests."

"Like what?"

"Like work." I struggle to find another thing Nick and I had in common. The sex had been pretty good in the beginning. Although nothing like what I'm having with Heath. I'm not going to tell his grandmother though. Despite what Heath said, she hasn't pointed my way and accused me of robbing her grandchild of his innocence yet, and I'm happy to keep it that way. "We both liked dogs."

"How many did you have?"

This isn't going well for me. "None. We worked too much."

She nods as though she expected that answer. "So you found someone who validated your existence."

"I don't know that I would put it like that."

"How would you put it?" Lydia asks.

"I don't know. He made me feel like…" I really can't come up with another way to define it. She's done it perfectly. "Okay, he didn't bug me about working too much. I thought we were on the same page and that building the business was always going to take priority and he wouldn't mind. Then he changed and showed his true colors, and I was so invested in work that I didn't want to rock the boat."

"That's not instinct, my love. That's your very logical brain trying to solve a problem that can only be solved with the most elusive gift in the universe." She pats my hand. "Faith."

She uses a word I do not understand at all. "Oh, I wouldn't say I'm very religious."

She shakes her head. "They don't have to go together, Ivy. Religion is something men made as a way to find and honor the divine. I'm Catholic. Catholicism is how I relate to the idea of God. But a person without a particular religion can have faith. Faith is simply allowing that which is divine to lead you. Faith isn't knowing. It's the opposite. It's accepting that you cannot in this life understand what this existence itself means and still believing there is purpose. And that purpose is simply love."

Her words make my chest feel tight. "Yeah, I don't have much of that."

"You have more than you think," she assures me. "There's a well inside all of us. We have to find it and believe. You're here, aren't you? After everything that happened, you're still here and trying to rebuild."

I feel myself flush. "You know about my last job?"

"Of course. When I found out you were going into business with my grandson, I checked you out. I might not know how to train an AI, but I do know how to use the Internet. They were hard on you."

Yeah, there was a reason for that. "I was on top of the world one year, and six months later I ran what should have been a thriving business into the ground."

"I doubt that. It sounds like you weren't given good advice."

"I trusted the wrong people, but that's still on me." I trusted Nick, and he'd been asleep at the wheel. Then he'd used a clause in his contract to extricate himself from all the fallout of his mishandling and landed in an even better position than before.

"Companies get sold off all the time," she muses. "The press was brutal with you. I suspect if you'd been a man, then Jensen Medical being sold would have barely made the news much less had big articles with glossy pictures all over the magazines. You made *People*."

They'd tried to make me sound like I was another Elizabeth Holmes. My paperwork software never pretended to be a diagnostic tool, thank you very much. "As a society, we're obsessed with women making it big, and when they fall, we're every bit as obsessed with that. I was also a tad arrogant."

"No, you were confident," she argues. "You were promoting your business and yourself in the same way a man would have. You know you take a lot on yourself."

I wasn't sure what to do with that. "Where else would I put it?"

Lydia waves a hand. "Oh, any number of places, dear. I've lived a long time, and I've seen people deflect in ways you can't imagine. You don't, but you also don't take credit for the good you do. I read a lot about Jensen Medical and how it ended up being sold. You know you could have declared bankruptcy and still come out of it with the company."

I'd considered that scenario. "It wouldn't have been intact, and it would have hurt my employees in a way I couldn't handle."

"Employees are used to layoffs," Lydia says.

"Selling the company meant I got to keep my H-1Bs on. That's my employees in the US on a work visa. They have to maintain employment or get deported." They had been my main priority when I'd realized how much trouble we were in. The tech world employs a lot of talent from other countries. We run on them, but the US government can be unforgiving when it comes to keeping them here. "The economy wasn't pretty then. It's recovered a little, but I had fifty I sponsored. Selling the company meant they still had employment, at least long enough for them to find other jobs if they needed to. I had it built into the contracts that they couldn't lay anyone off for a year. Anyone except upper management. We were always going to have to go."

"You protected everyone but yourself," she points out. "You see, you have faith, Ivy Jensen."

She was wrong about that. I wasn't known for having faith in much of anything. "No, I have an amazing well of guilt."

"You take these things on because deep down, you believe you can change the world. You believe you can help people. You hide behind the whole ruthless-girl-boss thing. It's armor. You want the world to think you're impenetrable, and I can understand that. But I worry that the world will grind you down and you'll become your armor if you don't have someone to lift you up. That's what you need in a partner." She taps the table as though enunciating the point. "You don't need someone similar to you. You need someone who can see the opposite side, someone who can pull you out of work and remind you to live."

"And this person exists?" This was why it wouldn't work between Heath and me. The only thing we were compatible in was work, and if that went away, we wouldn't need each other. He would find someone sweeter than me, someone who would take care of him and not bring never-ending drama into his life. Someone who would let him take the lead.

She sits back. "Oh, he does. The question is will you recognize him or will you pull in on yourself and let him pass you by? Or worse, push him away because deep down the one person you don't believe deserves good things is yourself."

The words hit me straight in the chest, and I feel them so strongly I have to deflect. "I assure you I'm very good at rewarding myself. My mom will tell you one of the reasons I had to come back home was I spent far too much money on designer things." I still missed those pretty handbags and shoes I'd sold on consignment so I had a little money to float by on.

"Then she doesn't understand that what you actually did was toss yourself on the fire to save your employees." Lydia sits back, one hand on her chest. "But then I doubt you've explained that to many people. You know, dear, I think I need a project. Heath has told me about your friends and how close you are. Bring them by. I think I'd like to do some work, too. I can't promise I'll find them matches. I haven't taken on new clients in the last few years, but I can assess what I think they should look for."

I'm kind of happy she's changed the subject. I don't want her thinking I'm some kind of martyr. It isn't true. I'd only done what most people would. "And you'll write reports for them?"

"Assessments," she corrects. "Just some pointers on what to look for when they decide they're ready to find a partner. And some...what do they call it these days? Some red flags they should avoid. It'll be fun. Amuse an old woman."

"You are not old." She seems so full of life. Lydia is a force of nature. After what she'd survived the year before, no one would be surprised if she lived quietly. Not Lydia Marino. Lydia is still going out with friends and having fun. Just the night before Heath and I had picked her up at the crustiest cowboy bar I've ever seen. I know crusty is a weird way to describe a bar, but there's no other word for it. She'd gone out with her line dancing group, and I swear the woman had been tipsy when we'd gotten her in a cab.

"Oh, I assure you I am. I feel every year some days." Her hand squeezes mine. "Yes, a project is exactly what I need. Please think about sending your friends to me. It would be fun to meet them."

"Of course," I say as she starts to walk into the room she calls the parlor. It feels like a living room to me, but with old-school furnishings. She looks perfect in it. Like it's a place where she can hold court like the queen she is.

She stops at the archway that connects the spaces. "And Ivy?"

"Yes?"

"Make sure your birth control is up to date. You should know Marino men create strong sperm, and condoms can break," she says without turning around. "Be careful. Or not. I wouldn't mind a great-grandchild."

A pure wave of embarrassment washes over me and I want to deny it, to challenge her because there's no way she can know for sure. But I don't. "I will check on that right away."

She disappears, and I'm left alone with my paperwork.

Chapter Nineteen

It's around noon when there's a knock on the door and I push the chair back. "I'll get it. It's probably the courier."

I don't want Lydia to have to get up. She's been relaxing in her parlor, a mug of tea Heath made at her side as she reads a book.

Heath gets there first. He grins my way. "Oh, I know why you're rushing to the door. Do you think I haven't picked up on CeCe's tricks? Behind that door is some superhot guy with a bunch of paperwork. Two of your favorite things."

Nope. I don't love paperwork, and I've learned that if the superhot guy isn't also a charming nerd who gives great hugs, I'm not truly that interested.

Now if he's holding a couple of tacos, a really nice burger, then maybe...

"Superhot guy?" Ria joins us, her eyes on the door. "I would like to see that, too. I'm surrounded by nerds."

"Says the nerd herself." Ye Joon frowns her way. "I saw you at the anime show this weekend. Don't pretend. You cosplayed and everything."

Ria and Ye Joon have a lovely rivalry going. I'm waiting for them to get a room. I glance over and Lydia is smiling their way like she's waiting, too. She'd been the one to tell us those two would be great hires and would get along brilliantly. Now I wonder if she really meant they would start some epic mild annoyances-to-lovers story.

"I just want to get the paperwork so I can add it to my never-ending pile. I'm perfectly happy with the hot guy I'm hanging with now."

Heath's lips curl up. "I thought we were keeping that quiet."

"She knows," I say with a sigh. In the last hour or so I've come to the conclusion I don't like hiding, and I really hate not being able to touch him during the day. I've decided if I can handle Lydia knowing, I can handle the new hires knowing, too.

"Told you," Ye Joon whispers Ria's way.

So everyone knew. I gesture to the door because if Heath wants to deal with the hottie, then more power to him.

He opens it, and then I'd bet everything I own that he wishes he'd been less alpha-male, knuckle-dragging possessive.

"Hello, Ivy's Side Piece." CeCe stands there looking elegant in all black, from the pencil straight slacks to the silk blouse and Chanel jacket. There's a broach on her lapel that could likely feed a small city. She's also wearing a hat and sunglasses, as though she's trying to hide from the paparazzi. And she's not alone. Lady Buttercup peers out of her handbag. It's a massive Louis Vuitton CeCe only uses as a dog carrier.

"Uh, not a side piece, Ms. Foust," Heath says with a strained smile. "Not in any meaning of the phrase. I need to get you on Urban Dictionary."

God, no. That would make everything so much worse.

"No, I think he's the main piece," Ria adds helpfully. "Wow, you're CeCe Foust."

"I am indeed, and you must be one of the coders Ivy hired." She stares my way. Or at least I think she's staring my way because I feel like a laser is focused on me. She's still wearing her sunglasses, but I can tell.

"I heard you speak at Brooklyn Tech when I was a freshman. You're why I went into tech," Ria says.

CeCe's expression softens. "I'm glad to hear that, dear. I might not have the technical skills of someone like Ivy or yourself, but I do know what our business needs and that's more intelligent young women. How is the project going in your estimation?"

Ria seems to realize a spotlight has been turned her way, and she straightens up. "It's great. I'm working on debugging a couple of problems we have with integration, but I think Emma's ready to learn even more."

"Ye Joon is writing most of the new code." I don't want to leave him out. "He and Heath have been working on the learning system. I've been filing all the paperwork your lawyers sent over. Thanks for that."

An elegant brow rises over her sunglasses. "For the ridiculously expensive intellectual property attorney who you couldn't even get an appointment with, much less afford?"

She does have a way of putting things. "Yep. That very one. Thanks."

Her head shakes slightly. "You're welcome. Now, I need to speak with Ivy. Ivy's Ill-Advised Boyfriend, take Lady Buttercup. For some reason she can't stand the waitstaff at Bergdorf, and they're whiny babies who can't even take a little love nip. She didn't even break the skin. Come along, Ivy. We're having lunch with Benjamin and going over a few things."

"She actually doesn't like that word. Boyfriend, that is. She's not into labels," Heath says. "And shouldn't I be at this meeting?"

She looks him up and down. He's wearing sweats and a T-shirt that claims he is a code ninja. "No."

He nods and reaches out to take Lady Buttercup. "All righty, then. I'll stay here and hold down the fort."

Ria is already moving in to pet the Maltese, while Ye Joon looks like he's just trying to stay out of the way.

I grab my bag and start to follow CeCe out. "You know I'm not dressed much better than Heath."

I had on jeans and a sweater, Vans on my feet.

She's moving toward the elevator. Again, no idea how she managed to get up without buzzing in. Lydia's place has an actual doorman, and apparently CeCe had gotten past him. I often think she could have made an excellent spy. Not the stay undercover kind. She would have been a female version of Bond, walking boldly into every European casino and announcing her full name and taking down the bad guys, but only after she'd slept with them a couple of times.

The elevator doors magically open as she nears them. A man steps out and then scurries away as though he knows a predator is near. I have to hustle to catch up. Naturally she leaves it to me to push the button for the ground floor.

"At least your sweater isn't covered in sarcastic sayings," she says, glancing down at her watch. "Also, I want to talk to you away from him."

That doesn't sound good. "Anything you can…"

Her lips form a flat line. "Do not complete that sentence. I knew you would likely end up enjoying that young man, but I need the illusion that you're not making a foolish mistake with him."

I turn and face the elevator doors. "I'm not making a mistake at all. We're nothing more than friendly business associates who enjoy a physical connection."

That is starting to sound dumb to my ears. I've said it over and over the last couple of weeks, trying to make it feel more real to me.

"I think that you might want to keep it that way."

I'm really nervous now. "What can you not say around Heath?"

"I'm not sure," she hedges as the doors open and we enter the lobby. "Benjamin said he's heard something he'd like to talk to us about, and I'm worried it's specifically about you."

That makes my gut tighten. "But he didn't want to do a conference call?"

"You know how he enjoys a good luncheon," she says as the doorman holds the door open for her.

"Ms. Foust," he says with a nod.

I would be shocked if the man knew my name and I've been coming in most days for the last several weeks.

"But today is ziti," I argue because sometimes CeCe's version of luncheon is very froufrou and involves things like microgreens infused with the essence of steak. You know what's better than the essence of steak? Steak.

"You know pasta makes you bloat, and then the reporters will all wonder if you're pregnant and you'll be right back in *People* again." CeCe moves out into the sunlight but only for a moment because somehow her driver is right in front of the building, holding the door open at precisely the right time. She moves in effortlessly, and I'm left scrambling to not get hit by a car as I stumble in via the other side.

"You're in a mood today. You don't usually body shame unless it's something really bad." I've barely gotten my seatbelt on when the driver takes off.

He moves the old-school Rolls-Royce through the streets like the expert he is. Thomas is the only member of CeCe's staff who's roughly her and Benjamin's age. Not that he's not attractive. He's former British SAS, and has served as her bodyguard as well. He deeply enjoys cutting off taxis and Ubers. Sometimes I think CeCe instructs him to *Fast and Furious* a drive just so she can get a jolt of adrenaline.

I prepare myself to die. It might be good since apparently I'm going to be given shitty news over lunch that won't be ziti piled high with sausage and cheese.

"I have other things to talk to you about. Things I don't like to talk about."

Damn. CeCe isn't afraid to talk about anything. She gave me a sex ed talk when I was in college that I to this day still cringe about. So this is bad. "You want to pull out of the project?"

The thought panics me utterly. What will we do? She really is paying for the lawyers I can't afford. Will I still be able to file for the patents? I can try to find funding outside of the normal investors.

What will I do if I let Heath down?

What will I do if Heath no longer has a reason to see me? He's not going to want to put up with my drama if he's not getting something out of it. Will he?

Yeah, I keep those questions to myself because I've promised to keep up the illusion that I'm not an idiot.

"This isn't about the project," she says. "It's about your mother. I've been thinking about this for two weeks. Ever since our fight. I didn't want to talk about it, but I fear I must."

I knew that would come back to haunt me. "I'm sorry if she was awful to you. She doesn't understand our relationship."

"Oh, she understands it all too well. She knows exactly how I feel and what I'm doing. She simply hasn't been able to stop it." She leans forward. "Thomas, maybe you should take 3rd to 59th."

That requires a hard right, and I hear the horns start up in angry unison. I also catch Thomas's lips curling in satisfaction in the rearview mirror.

I clutch the armrest, but CeCe isn't fazed at all. I manage to sit back up. "What do you mean she understands? I assure you she tells me all the time that she doesn't understand anything about my life."

"Well, she certainly doesn't understand the technical aspects of your life, and what you have to accept is your mother is not a risk taker. Not at all. I'm sure that has everything to do with losing your father. Grief makes us act in odd ways. After I lost George, I took some crazy risks. I felt unmoored to reality and that things didn't matter if he wasn't around to enjoy them. It's a common reaction in the first stages of grief. But your mother couldn't do that. She had a child, and so her pendulum swung the opposite way. She tried to block out all risk."

CeCe has a point, but I'm not buying it entirely. "I'm not going to die if a company goes under. I think I've proven that I can take that pain and still end up standing for the next round."

"Risk is more than physical," CeCe counters. "There's a reason your mother's stayed in the same place for over twenty years. She can't risk losing the last place where she was happy. She can't risk that if she tries to find something else, she'll lose what little she has. After all, she lost you."

A weary sigh goes through me. "She didn't lose me. She pushed me away."

"And that is a fear of risk, too."

"How did she lose me?" I need someone to explain this to me. "And what do you mean she understands what you want from me?"

There's more loud honking and some four-letter words thrown around as Thomas weaves the Rolls through traffic. We have to go through Midtown, which should give us plenty of time to talk through whatever we need to because it's always a parking lot. Not for Thomas. He's a master at wedging himself in and getting through lights right before they turn.

CeCe leans forward and opens the small panel in front of her seat. It's a minibar, and someone has kindly left what looks like a gin and tonic sitting there. How that sucker didn't spill I have no idea. I have a mental picture of Thomas playing bartender as he waited for CeCe outside Lydia's building. She takes a long swig and then pulls her sunglasses off and turns my way. "There's one for you, if you like. Or a bottle of water."

I open the panel on my side and sure enough, there's a second G&T and some water. There's also my favorite candy bar sitting there along with single bags of Chex Mix and Flamin' Hot Cheetos I shouldn't eat but love.

She used to have a big tray of snacks at her penthouse when I would come to work after school and during the summers. She claimed they were always there for anyone who wanted them, but since when did CeCe have junk food around? When she served guests, it was whatever Chef had created, not deliciousness shoved into a bag at a factory.

She'd done it for me.

I'd been planning on taking the water, but this is a CeCe moment, so I pick up the Waterford Crystal glass. Sure enough it's perfect and refreshing, with just the right burn to get me through a conversation that is turning decidedly emotional. "She thinks you wanted to make me your daughter."

CeCe sits back, taking another drink. "Did it work?"

It's my turn to sit back and search for the right words. Now I have to wonder if I haven't failed all the mother figures I've had. "I should have called you. I wanted to. You can't imagine how much I wanted to."

She reaches out, and her hand covers mine. "And you can't know how much it took for me to not ride out there and save you."

I shake my head because that wouldn't have been possible. "You couldn't have saved me. It was too much money. Even for you."

"Well, it's a terrible thing having to watch someone you adore suffer. Note I didn't say fail. Failure is a part of life. It's an important part. We learn from our failures. But they were so harsh with you."

"You couldn't have stopped that either." I hadn't considered that CeCe would feel that pain with me. I'd assumed she would be embarrassed, and now I had to wonder why. Is there an essential piece of me that can't forgive myself for what was basic human error? I'd done my best. When the chips were down, I'd played every card I had to help the people around me. What Lydia said to me earlier seems to have taken root inside me. "They built me up, and that means they enjoyed taking me down, too. You can't know how much it means to me to have you on my side now. I'm not going to let you down again."

"That's what you don't understand. You didn't let me down the first time. Do you know how many businesses I've had fail? How many investments that didn't work out? The only reason I didn't end up on the streets is the enormous amount of money I have. I'm smart with it. I never overleverage, and I think that's a lesson you've recently learned."

"Yes. I assure you I'm not letting anyone else near the money again," I vow.

"You won't be able to do that when the company grows. You'll need someone you can trust, and you'll need oversight," CeCe says. "And it shouldn't be someone you're sleeping with. I'm not trying to shame you. I'm not. I'm worried about you, though Heath seems more solid than Nick ever was."

"You could let him know you know his name."

"Where would be the fun in that?" She slows down, taking a sip of the drink. "Your mother said some things to me that have led me to believe she needs help."

"Help?"

"Ivy, your mother is depressed. She's also stubborn, and I can't tell you the words that came out of her mouth when I suggested she see a doctor."

No. I could believe the words. My mom is perfectly capable of saying all the bad words. "Wow. No wonder she hasn't talked to me for weeks. You think she's depressed?"

"Let me be clearer because that word is misused. I believe your mother is clinically depressed and has been for a very long time. She needs help, but I can't be the one to get it for her because I'm the one who stole her child."

I barely manage to not roll my eyes. "You didn't steal me."

"I would have." She reaches over, and a perfectly manicured hand brushes my hair back. It's the tenderest I've ever seen CeCe. "If you'd come back to New York and asked for a place to stay, I would have moved you right in. I had a room ready, didn't I, Thomas?"

"Absolutely, ma'am. You even had Maid take out all the art because you know how messy our Ivy can be." Thomas looks back at me through the rearview mirror. "She had Electrician put in so many new power sources."

"And your own Wi-Fi hub," CeCe says with a sigh. "He was a lovely young man. Thought he could be an exotic dancer. Terrible rhythm, but I did need an electrician so I sent the lad to school. He rooms with Help Desk. They have a lot in common."

Yes, she'd sent a lot of lads to schools. She was practically a pretty-boy charity, but I'm still reeling at the idea that she changed her place for me. "I didn't know that was an option. I'm going to be honest, I probably wouldn't have ever asked."

"And you would have turned me down had I offered." She seems sure that would have been the outcome. "Likely for the same reasons I worry your mother is depressed. I think you wouldn't have accepted my offer because you think you don't deserve it. You think you deserve some kind of punishment for your failure."

I take a longer drink because she might be right. "I should have seen it coming. I should have paid better attention."

"No, you hired a CFO who had a reputable résumé. Your mistake was letting him talk you into putting his friends on the board. I would love to really delve into what happened. I still don't buy that it was all accounting and purchasing mistakes. Thomas believes it has a malicious feeling to it, and he was in the military," CeCe assures me.

I don't see the point in going over it all again. I want to look forward. Or, more importantly, I want to live in the now for a while. The now includes Heath and the feeling that we're actually building something. The now includes waking up to fun discussions about the state of publishing with Darnell. He'd warmed up to me once I started reading his novel. His eight-hundred-page novel that isn't finished yet.

"Does feel like you got set up, love." Thomas swerves, locking out a yellow cab. The driver proves he knows how to use a horn.

"I'm not sure that matters at this point." I check my seatbelt once more. I might try to convince CeCe I want to walk back to Little Italy or somewhere closer. I might need to go home this evening. I've been avoiding it or sneaking in when I know Mom will be in bed or at work. But if CeCe's right, I need to talk to her. "You really think there's something wrong with my mom?"

"I do, darling girl, and I worry it's affected you over the years," CeCe says as we make it to the Upper East Side and the stores go from over-the-top touristy to blatant shows of wealth. "Your mother might not have intended to do it, but I believe she infected you with a bit of her martyr syndrome. And her need to control the world around her."

"I know damn well I don't control anything," I shoot back.

"Then why is everything your fault?" CeCe replies, her lips tugging up as though she knows she's made her point.

"You walked right into that," Thomas says with a sigh.

Yeah. I really had. And now I had something else to think about. I hoped Benjamin didn't bring even worse news.

Chapter Twenty

When we enter BG, I see Benjamin is already seated at a window table, his head turned so he can look out at the sweeping views of Central Park. It's quieter than normal, and I realize no one is seated near him. The rest of the restaurant is hopping with lunchtime shopping energy, but there's a calm surrounding Benjamin and a basic bubble that says *do not enter.*

"Please tell me he didn't buy all the tables in that section." Sometimes it's weird to be around truly rich people. Most of the time, really.

"Of course he didn't. I did." CeCe follows the hostess, and Benjamin turns our way. "If I wanted to listen to people whine about their lives I would... I never want to do that. Benjamin, darling, have you been waiting long? Thomas is off his game. It took us forever."

It hadn't. Thomas had pissed off every ride share driver and taxi in his path from Lower Manhattan to the Upper East Side and gotten us here in no time at all.

Then Benjamin's standing, holding a hand out. He wears an immaculately cut suit and loafers that had probably come from the menswear department across the street. "CeCe, thanks for coming on such short notice."

"And on so little information," she chides, giving him two air kisses. "I had to leave Lady Buttercup with Ivy's slightly unkempt non-boyfriend."

"He's not unkempt." He is very clean. I know because I shower with him most mornings lately. Benjamin leans over and kisses my cheek.

"Does he own slacks with belt loops?" CeCe asks.

"Of course he does." Now I see it. She's the meddling mother I never really asked for.

"Does he wear them?"

She has a point, but she lives in a completely different world. There are two tech worlds—the one CeCe lives in and the movies fantasize about, and the real one. That's the one where we work in basements, buy our Hot Pockets from Costco (seriously, every company gets a membership), and pray the bank that funds us doesn't suddenly go under. "He's a coder. He's always going to be behind a screen. Don't expect him to be the face of the company."

"Which is excellent since he doesn't like to wear pants," Benjamin says with a shake of his head. "He needs to wear pants to business meetings. I want it in his contract."

CeCe sits down next to Benjamin.

Ah. My business mom and dad are presenting a united front. I slump into the seat directly across from Benjamin. "He wears pants," I assure him.

"Ivy should know since she gets into them regularly," CeCe whispers as a martini magically appears via a bartender who had to have been waiting for her entrance. "Thank you, darling."

Benjamin has a glass of what is likely incredibly expensive Scotch in front of him. He nods my way. "You should order something."

So I'm going to need liquid courage. Or comfort. I still have to go back to work, and I don't want Lydia to think I normally drink my lunch, so I settle on a glass of rosé. We order and when the server is gone, I lean in.

"What is going on? CeCe seems to think the world is ending."

CeCe frowns. "I certainly do not."

"Well, you definitely made it seem like an emergency. Somewhere in Little Italy a guy who should be working is currently walking an overly privileged Maltese," I point out. Or Lydia's feeding her my ziti, and that feels wrong on all fronts.

"How close are you to being able to announce your project?" Benjamin ignores our banter, preferring to get straight to the point.

"Uh, I thought I would secure the funding first." It was kind of how this went. There was no real public project until the money was in place. Once the initial money was in place, hopefully more money would follow, and we would eventually get loans from a bank that would pay for our Hot Pockets and fuel all our anxieties that filled up when Dodd-Frank left the building.

"I know it's not usual, but I think you should announce as soon as possible," Benjamin urges, his fingers playing with the glass. "I was taking some meetings in Silicon Valley, and I heard some concerning rumors. Who have you talked to about this project?"

"You two and Teresa Fleishman are the only ones who know the specifics. She's solid. I told Heath we only talked about the AI innovations to everyone else," I reply. I'm getting antsy because Benjamin sounds worried. He's normally calm, cool, and collected. And I'm surprised that there would be rumors concerning the project since the project didn't really exist on anyone's radar until a few weeks ago.

"She's almost certainly talked with her friends," CeCe corrects.

"Well, yes, but Ani and Harper don't have a bunch of contacts in the tech world." I was pretty sure they both fought to stay awake when I try to explain technical stuff to them. "They would be talking more about me and Heath than what we're working on."

"Well, someone's been talking. One of the banks on the West Coast just approved a rather large investment in a start-up that claims to have the most advanced matchmaking AI in the industry," Benjamin says.

"Bullshit." I've heard nothing about a new AI. The dating apps all use similar engines. What Heath is building is brand new. There's nothing like Emma on the market, and it will take a while for other companies to catch us.

"I have contacts out there. Ones I trust very much." His eyes meet mine, and I realize he hasn't gotten to the bad part yet. "They're excited about a new AI matchmaker, and it's not yours."

There's always competition, but that's not what would put that grim look in Benjamin's eyes. He's been in the business for a very long time. He watched the tech industry grow from computers that filled buildings just to do basic computations, to ones we hold in our hands that contain a universe of knowledge in them. In that time, he and CeCe have made more deals than I can imagine, and never once did he look like this. Even when a project was failing spectacularly. This isn't about business. This is personal.

"Nick Stafford is planning on announcing his collaboration with a celebrity matchmaker. Sherry Carrigan. She's got her own reality show. It's very popular," he says, his tone grim.

The room goes cold on me, and I sit there, allowing my brain to process the fact that Nick is screwing me over once again.

And it can't be a coincidence. It's been a month since Heath and I made our bargain. There's zero chance Nick was working on a project to rival ours before that. Nick doesn't put together deals. Nick is a slick talker in an expensive suit, but he doesn't do what I do. "I thought he took a C-level job somewhere."

"He's working at Golden Tech. I believe he's describing this as a side project," Benjamin explains. "I don't know, exactly. I haven't read the article yet. It's coming out next week. I'll see if I can get an early copy."

It gets worse? "There's an article?"

If there's an article about Nick, I have to assume they'll ask him about Jensen Medical. It's not like Nick's going to own up to his mistakes. If I'm lucky, he'll be demure about it. If he's an ass, he'll blame it all on me.

CeCe puts her martini down. "Can we quash it?"

"I don't think so," Benjamin says. "It's being written by one of Nick's fraternity brothers for a magazine published by his family. We have no real leverage."

I try desperately to find the bright side. "So Nick heard I'm working on something and is trying to fuck with me. If you haven't read the article, then this could all be speculation. Even if he does announce that he's backing a similar project to ours, I assure you he hasn't done the kind of work Heath has."

"You know he doesn't have to." CeCe sits back, and her expression has gone tight. "All he has to do is toss some glitter on the right investor and he'll be able to pay someone brilliant through the nose to do the work he needs. I've heard of the woman he's working with. She's known as the matchmaker to the stars. Mostly she pairs up ridiculously wealthy men with trophies."

"I assure you she's not as good as Lydia Marino." Sherry Carrigan is on one of those reality shows that spends as much time on her employees' relationship drama as it does her actual work. Because the show is likely what makes her money, not the matchmaking.

Lydia is the real thing.

"Lydia Marino doesn't have a television show, and no one outside of the city knows who she is." Benjamin seems determined to drag me into the reality of the situation. "Can we announce the project tomorrow?"

"No. We promised Gavin Huffman first crack, and he's out of the country." CeCe takes a long breath. "And you know if we panic, he'll pull back. He can sense desperation."

"He can also sense when he's getting into a horse race," Benjamin counters. "The whole reason he was willing to look at this project was how different it is from what's on the market. He liked the idea of it being associated with a real, old-school matchmaker."

Then I didn't see the problem. "None of that has changed."

"Huffman might know who Lydia is. He might respect her. But he'll also know that Nick has the glossier package," Benjamin argues. "He's already got his first round of investment."

They're forgetting something. "So do we. Hello, sitting here with my investors. The Foust Foundation is one of the biggest capital investment firms in the world."

CeCe shakes her head. "Private firms. Benjamin and I are considered private investors. It's not the same as having Huffman or a national bank invest, and you know it."

"And there's the fact that what CeCe's given you barely covers a few months, and you know they won't say the Foust Foundation is backing you. They'll say CeCe is feeding her favorite pet," Benjamin explains with stark honesty.

CeCe groans but concedes. "That's somewhat fair. To be honest, I wasn't all that interested in the project in the beginning. I wanted Ivy to have something to work on while she came up with her next big idea."

I want to argue with her, to point out this is a big idea, but I didn't think so in the beginning. However, I'm starting to really believe in Emma and what Heath is trying to do. We are so disconnected these days. Why not give every person the best chance they have at finding someone to help them with life, to make it all more meaningful? "I think Emma could change the game, and I assure you whatever shiny thing Nick is pursuing doesn't have a tenth of Heath's brilliance."

CeCe puts up a hand. "We can't be certain of any of this. At this point it's all conjecture, and I want us to remain calm. Panic is always a mistake. And while Benjamin is likely right about the community's assessment of my and Ivy's relationship, they also know how smart she was when it came to Jensen Medical. Not the end of it, but the actual company. No one questions the technology behind the company. I've been trying to make sure the right people know I believe she's doing the same thing here."

Benjamin turns her way. "Yes. You've already put money in this, and Ivy's put in an enormous amount of time. This is supposed to be her comeback. You've been teasing the whole tech community here in the city with Ivy's big new project."

"You have?" I'm slightly horrified by the thought. I've been under the assumption that there isn't a ton of pressure on me. I mean, I knew I could let Heath down and Lydia. But CeCe really has been treating it like it's a little project to get me back on track.

"This business runs on gossip, and I have to keep your name in the conversation. But while I did talk you up, I assure you I didn't discuss the specifics of the project. How many people besides Teresa did you talk to the night of the party?" CeCe asks.

I search my memory. Mostly what I remember about that night is Heath kissing me and then sitting with me on the fire escape. "We talked to probably ten people, but everything was vague. I kept it that way. He certainly didn't go into anything technical. I couldn't have at the time. I didn't fully understand the processes. Though I do know some of the people there knew him and who his grandmother is. Do you think someone there talked to Nick?"

"I think it certainly could have gotten to him that way, but I didn't hear anyone talking that night," Benjamin replies. "I do, however, remember your gentleman walking back into the house with one of Nick's friends. He'd taken Buttercup outside."

There had been a reason for that. "Because CeCe treats him like the dog walker."

CeCe waves a hand. "If he wants to move up in life, he should dress better. Besides, it was a test. I trust Buttercup's instincts. She didn't attack the man so he's likely trustworthy to a point."

Or he was smart enough to sneak the dog meatballs. I don't buy into Buttercup's psychic powers. CeCe always has a cute, tiny puffball of a dog. They are always named after some kind of royalty, and always have the power to predict who is good or bad. Buttercup had totally not bitten off Nick's balls, so I would say her powers are off. "Heath wouldn't talk about the project to one of Nick's friends. If he talked to someone, then he didn't know who he was. But he wouldn't have talked at all because I made it clear to him that I was doing the talking. I knew who to talk to. I knew who to avoid."

"Well, it appears that your friend might not have followed your rules." Benjamin picks up the menu. "You should discuss it with him. We need to figure out if we can get in front of Huffman before that article comes out. Even if it means flying Ivy to wherever he is."

"I doubt it will come to that. This is going to be all right. Nick is being an asshole. I'm filing the patents on Heath's process in the next couple of days. I assure you he doesn't have anything close." I try to let the words bolster my confidence. Nick is trying to make quick money. It won't come to anything, and it certainly shouldn't scare anyone off.

"Ivy's right. We should move forward with the project." CeCe nods my way like I'm a toddler who's done something new and fabulous. "But it might be good to see if we can get Lydia a bit more involved. Maybe we can get our own press. I'll reach out to some of my contacts. This could be interesting. We frame it as an East Coast/West Coast fight. You know we always win those."

We don't, but I'm going to ride CeCe's certainty for as long as I can because anxiety is bubbling in my veins.

I pray that article doesn't ruin everything. I settle down as the server brings the first course, but I've lost my appetite.

Chapter Twenty-One

Two hours later I make my way into Lydia's apartment. Ria had been the one to bring Buttercup down and return her to CeCe's loving arms. CeCe had told me not to worry and then Thomas had taken off like a bat out of hell.

I'm back in my world, and worry is pretty much all I have.

"You should know there's an experiment going on upstairs." Ria pushes the button to take us to the right floor.

"Experiment?"

"Ye Joon thinks he's got the restaurant app working. He wants us all to test it and Lydia said she wasn't feeling up to cooking this afternoon, so he asked her to let Wendy choose for her."

"Wendy?" This is new to me. Because of all the paperwork I've done, I haven't really seen most of the progress being made. It makes me realize how much I miss sitting in front of a computer trying to figure out how to make things work. I've spent all my time on administrative things, and it's got me anxious.

She shrugs. "He's from Ohio. Apparently they have a lot of Wendy's there. Heath let him name her. We had to talk him out of Popeye. He likes his fast food. Anyway, Lydia agreed to let Wendy select lunch for us. Ye Joon wants to test the group feature. It not only picks an overall restaurant, it cuts the selection down to three or four items to match the individual diner's taste profile."

"That sounds fun." I had eaten very little of the truffled gnocchi CeCe had pushed me to order. I'd sat there and listened to her and

Benjamin go over all the scenarios on how this project could crash and fail.

And the whole time I'd been wondering who had talked. There's not a chance in hell Nick came up with this on his own. There's no coincidence here.

"So it took all of our data, and our lunch was delivered a few moments ago by Star India." Ria grins. "I'm pretty sure she blames me. Lydia went a little pale. I think she's worried her mouth is going to explode, but she's going with it. How do you live in New York all your life and never eat Indian?"

"You live in an Italian community known for their food," I point out as the doors open.

I hate the fact that I'm wondering if Ria might be the one who talked about the project. I hate that I'm going to have to ask the question. I hate that I'm going to wonder if someone on our team hasn't been giving Nick information and maybe more.

"Well, Wendy was so easy on her. Chicken tikka and butter chicken were her only options. Our AI understands gateway foods." Ria is beyond cheerful as we make it to Lydia's door. "And when Heath tried to order too little naan, Wendy pointed out Ye Joon is a carb addict."

"What did it order for you?" Despite my worry, I'm happy the app is working.

"Fish curry. It's absolutely what I order from there," she responds. "I know there are going to be people who enjoy spending half the night trying to figure out where to eat, but I'm all in on Wendy. I think she's a game changer."

I'm glad because Emma might be dead on arrival. We might still be able to salvage something.

My head hurts, and an ache is starting to go along with my anxious gut. I follow her inside and Heath is there looking stupidly cute and huggable, and I realize how much I've started to count on his affection as comfort.

I'm making the same mistakes again, and I'm preferring to be the girlfriend instead of the boss. I want to be a part of them. I want to sink into the fantasy TV and movies try to sell us—that work proximity can somehow turn a group of disparate strangers into a family.

I don't talk to my old friends at Jensen Medical. They don't call me up, and I don't check on them except on LinkedIn where I breathe a sigh of relief every time one of them gets a new job.

I'm letting emotion rule my brain.

Those ridiculously hot lips of his curl up as he catches sight of me. "Hey. How'd it go? We've been having fun here. Nonna discovered butter chicken."

Lydia points down at her plate. "This is delicious. Who would have thought it?"

"Wendy works." Ye Joon is all smiles.

"In a limited capacity," Heath qualifies. "We're only integrated with about ten restaurants here in the city. And Wendy can view menus on the Internet. But we're getting there. You hungry?"

"No, but we need to talk as soon as you're done."

His brows rise. "I thought you would be hungry. I got extra samosas."

Normally I don't turn down fried food, but today is special. "I just had lunch."

"With CeCe, who barely eats." He's joking like the day's normal and the sky isn't falling. But then he seems to realize something's gone wrong. He puts down his plate. "What's going on?"

Ye Joon looks up at Ria. "Told you something was going down."

His expression goes tight. I know that expression. It's one every person who's ever worked for a start-up sees in the mirror at some point. The one that says I'm going to have to find a new job because all the people above me are idiots.

I can't even blame him for having the thought.

"Come on, Ivy. Let's get whatever bad news out of the way," Heath says.

Fine. He wants to do this here, I can do it here. It's not like they won't find out soon. "I need to know if anyone's been talking about Emma and who they talked to."

My words effectively snuff out the joy that had filled the room.

Ria sits down next to Ye Joon. "I signed an NDA. I take that seriously."

Ye Joon shakes his head. "I only talk to you guys. My parents know I have a new gig, but all they really want to know is when I'm going to get a real job. The only real job is doctor, by the way. They genuinely expect me to drop everything and go to medical school so they can say their son is a doctor."

"Is something wrong?" Lydia asks, setting down the naan she'd been scooping up sauce with.

I spoke too soon. I hadn't been thinking about the fact that Lydia is here. The last thing I want to do is cause her anxiety. I school my expression. "No. There's some rumors going around. That's all. Just wanted to make sure we keep things tight, if you know what I mean."

Ria looks Lydia's way. "I think Ivy's heard something and now she's worried one of us is… The word *spy* is so overused."

"Spy?" Lydia's eyes widen.

Ye Joon offers her more naan. "We're not and she'll figure that out, but she's been in the big leagues before. Ivy, you can look through my system. I'm not sending anything on Emma out. I know you've been screwed over before, but we're good here."

I kind of want to hug him because I'd been expecting a fight. Not that I wouldn't understand a fight. It sucks to be accused of something you didn't do, and I'm not trying to accuse anyone. "I don't need to check anyone's systems. I just think we should have a talk about security."

Heath puts a hand on my elbow. "You guys eat. We'll be right back."

He steers me to the terrace, opening the heavy glass door and letting me through.

He stares at me for a moment. "What did CeCe say that has you in this mood?"

"Nick is announcing a project very similar to ours, and it looks like he already has full funding." There's no point in sugarcoating it. "In fact, he's got Sherry Carrigan working with him."

His arms cross over his chest. "The Hollywood lady who runs an escort service?"

"It's a matchmaking service," I correct.

"It's always an old dude and a twenty-year-old."

He obviously hasn't watched the show. I'd joked about it, but she is considered a serious expert at putting people together. And it's LA, so some of the "twenty-year-olds" are likely in their forties. They kind of all meld together. "It's not that bad. The show, I mean. The fact that Nick is going to go public first is very concerning for us."

"How would he even know?" Heath asks. "I mean this has to be a coincidence. You've only been broken up for what? Six months? How did he build a working model in less than six months? Did you get a hint he was working on something like this?"

"He wouldn't have done it himself. He's working with someone, and it's very likely they have an AI they were building or one they think they can repurpose." I lay out the most likely scenario. "Nick is the forward face of this project. Or rather the money face. Sherry Carrigan will be the one doing all the advertising. So Nick finds out what we're doing and wants to cut me off at the knees. He finds someone with a program he can use to make it look like he's farther along than he really is, goes to Sherry Carrigan, convinces her this is a great way to make money, and voila, he gets to the big investors before we do, and we're left with very little money."

"That doesn't make any sense. Why would he go to the trouble? I mean they have to put out something that works, right?"

He was such a sweet summer child. "Or they collect as much money as they can, and it never works. There's a reason they call it venture capital and not a no-risk investment sure to pay out."

Heath shakes his head like he can't quite grasp the whys. Or hows. "I don't understand how he would even know."

"Because someone talked about the project," I reply. "It's why I was vague about things the night of the party. It's why I gave you the lecture about letting me do the talking. Many a great idea has been stolen at one of those things. You have to be specific enough to pique an investor's interest so you get a meeting, but subtle enough you don't give away the project."

"Well, I didn't…" He stops, his expression going blank.

And I know it was him. At least I don't have to put my employees through anything unpleasant. "Who? I told you we had to keep this quiet."

His eyes meet mine, a bit of desperation in there. "Ivy, I didn't think about it. He was outside smoking when I was waiting for that dog to poop, and he asked some questions."

I could see the scenario play out in my head. "One of Nick's friends. You had met them. You knew they were with Nick. Why would you talk to them?"

He shrugs, turning away and looking out over the terrace. It's one of those stunningly beautiful New York days that usually energizes my whole being. "I don't know. I'm friendly."

I stare at him. Today the sun just feels hot, and I don't care that there's a lovely breeze and the sky seems like endless blue. I don't see anything but Heath and the way he's obviously trying to find an angle so he can handle me.

He starts to pace. This is the first real fight we've had, and I hate every second of it. I hate the fact that he's tense and I made him that way. I hate that we're squared off like enemy combatants.

"Fine. I didn't like the way they talked about you like you were some kind of failure, and I wanted them to know you're working on something cool."

Oh, I'm not buying that. "I was perfectly clear about who we did and did not talk to. I was also clear that I don't care what they say about me."

He's back to looking my way, his focus lasered in, and I know he thinks he's got me. "But you didn't mind me kissing you and pretending to be your boyfriend."

Humiliation washes over me. I don't expect it from him, and I know he's right. I did that. I appreciated the save at the time, but this is different. "That didn't give you the right to walk around giving out all kinds of information because you were trying to spare my reputation. In fact, you barely knew me that night. I doubt it was about me. Did you hear them talk crap and feel bad to be associated with me?"

He hesitates. It's only a second, but I can easily see the truth. "Ivy, that's not what happened."

But it was. I blame myself. He's human, and for weeks I've played him up to be something far more. I've put him on a pedestal, and that's on me.

I'm making the same mistakes again. I'm choosing a personal relationship over business, and it's going to hurt everyone—including Heath. Heath will likely hate me in the end.

It seems like Nick does, and I'm not entirely sure why. Nick seems to feel the need to bury me, and it's that emotional reaction fueling me forward.

"I'm sorry I gave you the impression I needed you to save me." Even as I say the words, I pull back from him physically. I can't risk getting close to him. I don't trust myself to make good decisions. "I don't."

For a second I think he's going to apologize. He's that guy. We might be able to save this if he admits he was wrong. Not the relationship. I've proven I can't handle that. But we might be comfortable still working together. We don't have to have this big fight. We can be cool with each other. It didn't work. We weren't the right fit.

Then a gleam hits his eyes, and I realize this is going to get bad. "Oh, you do. You absolutely need me to save you, but I thought it was from a little embarrassment about a bad relationship and some business mistakes anyone could have made. It's deeper than that, isn't it? The person I need to save you from is you."

"What the hell is that supposed to mean?" I've spent too much of the day under a microscope, and it's starting to get to me.

"It means you're being ridiculous about this," he replies. "This isn't anything we should be worrying about right now. I know CeCe needs to bring massive drama to what is essentially a minor problem."

"It's not minor. It's huge. It could derail everything we're trying to do."

He points my way. "Everything you're trying to do. You're the one who needs to be the best at everything, Ivy. All I want is to build my project and hopefully help a few people along the way, and that's good enough for me. But it's never going to be good enough for you, is it?"

Oddly, I know he's the one saying the words. I can hear them coming out of his mouth, but it's my mother's voice I hear.

The things I care about are all wrong. What I need is wrong. How I work is wrong.

"Ivy, I didn't mean it that way." He takes a deep breath, and his expression has softened. "Baby, I'm sorry. I didn't mean it like that. I only meant I wish you didn't feel like the world is on your shoulders."

"Well, it has to be because no one else takes it seriously."

"You don't trust anyone enough to handle it," he says, and there's very little accusation in his tone.

But I don't need much to get me going. "Heath, you told me flat out you didn't want to handle it. You wanted me to do all the heavy lifting so you could be the creative genius. And you are. I'm not arguing with you about that, but you can't have it both ways. You can't hand over all the business responsibilities to me and then accuse me of taking them too seriously. You might be content with what you have. Hell, maybe I would be, too. I know we joke about your crappy apartment, but at least you have one. And I know what it costs, and you can't afford it. How big is your trust fund, Heath?"

His mouth goes tight. "I'm not living some high life."

"No, but you're also not worried about money," I point out. "Seriously? How big is it?"

"Not so big I can fund things myself but big enough I don't have to worry about making money," he admits. "And since you're so interested, one day it'll be even bigger because I'm my grandmother's only heir. Do you want to accuse me of being rich?"

"I don't want to accuse you of anything. That's what you don't understand. I am so sick of being vilified for having dreams and goals, and yes, they include money, but when you grow up like I did, you realize how different the world is without it. And you might be perfectly fine with this all imploding, but we have two employees who count on us for a paycheck. They don't have trust funds. I will not play with their livelihoods."

His expression falls. "I'm not doing that. Look, I'm sorry. This is a stupid fight. I will admit that I was feeling insecure the night of the party and I was stupid. I puffed up and tried to save face with a guy who I normally wouldn't give the time of day to. I don't even know why. Maybe it was because I sort of fell for you the minute you walked in my door."

"It'll pass." I can't help but remember that once Nick had said something similar to me. He'd told me he'd known how right we would be for each other within a few minutes of meeting me.

The problem isn't meeting me. It's living with me. It's dealing with the complex and often frustrating person I can be. I'm never going to want to play a costarring role in my own life. I cannot simply be someone's girlfriend. If I have to choose between having a man and being the person I think I should be, I made that choice long ago.

I will always choose me.

I just thought for a little while he wouldn't make me choose at all.

"No, it won't," he insists.

I shake my head and start for the door. "It will. It always does. I'm going to take the rest of the day off and you can decide if you want to continue this working relationship or if you want to find someone else to handle that side of the business. I can give you a few names, but you'll have to pay them."

His arms cross over his chest, a sign he's going to be stubborn. "I don't want anyone else."

"But you seem to," I counter.

"I was talking as your boyfriend, not your business partner, and don't give me that crap that I'm not your boyfriend," he argues. "We fit, you and me."

"We don't, and you proved it. If you loved me, you would love all of me, not only the parts that make you feel comfortable."

"I do." His voice goes low, and he gets in my space. His hands come up to touch my shoulders, and he lowers his head to mine. "I do love every part of you, and I hate watching you tie yourself up in knots. I just want you to relax a little."

That's the problem. If he merely wanted me to take an afternoon off or something I could understand that. I could deal with that. He's already gotten me to concede weekends, and that's something I would never have done before. I don't know why but I have this drive to build something that I can't deny. I've had it since I was a teenager and I dreamed of making robots not only because I thought they were cool, but because I thought I could make my mark that way. "So what are you proposing? How should I relax?"

"I feel like this is a minefield, baby, and you've laid about a hundred traps for me," he whispers.

My damn heart clenches. "Because it can't work. The things we want are too different. Our values are too different."

"Not true. I'm not handling this well. I know I screwed up, and I'm panicking."

"It's better we know now." I step back, shoving down the need to reach out to him. All I want to do is wrap myself around him and pretend like the day hadn't happened, but it had. I can't pretend. I have to live in this world. "Can we be friendly?"

"I think we're past friends now."

"Can we be civil?"

"Don't do this." He moves in again. "Baby, we hit a rough patch, so let's take a breath and figure out how to make our way through it. I know you think we're only together because of convenience and proximity, but you're wrong. You've been happier with me."

I have. I've been happy with him, and it made me forget what I want. Or rather made me think I could have both. I can't let go of what he said, of the resentment I feel. Of how much he sounded like my mom, and I don't think I can have two of those relationships in my life. "I need some time to think."

"If you think, you'll walk away."

He's probably right.

"Don't," he says. "Stay and fight it out with me."

I don't know what to say to him. I feel stuck standing here because I don't want any of the options in front of me.

He straightens up. "Let Emma decide."

I'm surprised at the turn. "What do you mean?"

"I mean we've put everything we have in this company and you're betting your business future on it, so why not your romantic future? She's not ready yet but when she is, we feed her all our data and if she says we're a match, we get married and that's it."

That is the craziest idea I've ever heard. "Married?"

He shrugs. "If I'm in, I'm all in. And no prenup. I'm betting everything I have on you. If you're brave enough though, we can just do it. Tonight."

I feel like all the air has gone out of the room, but we're not in a room, so out of the city, I suppose. He's got to be joking.

"I am not joking," he assures me. "Three weeks. That's how long it's going to take to work out the bugs, and then I'll prove it to you. I'll prove Emma works. I'll prove we work. If you feel like we need to be business partners and nothing more until then, that's how it will be. But, Ivy, you should know I'm going to be very professional. Right up until you tell me I can take you to bed, and then I'm just going to be determined to make sure you understand we do fit."

I have no idea how we went from fighting to him…asking isn't the right word…betting we're going to get married, which is not a thought he's expressed thus far in our extremely short relationship.

He said he loved me. Mere minutes ago he'd said he loved me, and I hate that the first time he said it we were in the middle of a fight and that I can't go back and make him say it again.

And I've only thought about it a couple of times. Being with him for the rest of my life. Getting married to him. I think about it when I'm weak and he's sweet and I think the world is so much nicer because he's here with me.

"That is the most ridiculous thing I've ever heard." I've got nothing else. I finally understand the word *poleaxed.*

He steps back and shrugs. "Stick with me, baby. I assure you I can come up with much more ridiculousness. And I promise you I won't let you down again. I had a moment's weakness when I didn't understand."

"Didn't understand?" I was getting a little lost.

He stares at me for a moment. "That you're worth more than my pride. That my pride is a silly thing compared to how I feel when I'm with you. I need you to understand that whatever that article says it's bullshit. It's because he lost you, and he knows how much that means now. No man attacks someone this hard because they don't feel anything for them. He's still in love with you, and that makes him dangerous."

Heath is the one who doesn't get it. "He never loved me. I don't even think he's capable of it."

"Well, then he's jealous as hell because he didn't pull any of this until that night," Heath points out. "You want to know what really prompted this? It wasn't me being a moron. It was me kissing you. It was you holding my hand."

I shake my head. "He left me."

"Of course he did. He failed you, Ivy, and he wasn't man enough to take responsibility for it. He knows you did what he couldn't, and he can't stand it. Baby, he's jealous of you on so many levels, and I know he's in your head. He's in there telling you this can't work because I'm going to end up failing you like he did. I won't. And I promise you even if I do, I'll stay at your side and make it right. I won't use you as a stepping-stone to greater things because you are the best thing that is ever going to happen to me."

I have no idea how we got here. "It can't work."

"Three weeks." He says those two words like they're a vow. "You'll see. Now come inside. We have work to do, and Ye Joon probably ate all the naan. The good news is Nonna baked cream cheese brownies."

They were my favorite. "Heath, we should talk."

"Talking gets us nowhere," he replies. "Do you want a hug?"

I want that hug more than anything in the world, but I can't ask him.

"Ivy, I could really use a hug," he says quietly.

Damn him. He knows. He knows I need it. Knows I can't ask for it. Knows I'm scared and tired and angry at the world.

I open my arms because I will never deny him this. Not even if we never fall into bed again. When I'm a cranky old lady, if Heath Marino shows up on my doorstep and says he needs a hug, my arms will open wide.

"Thank you," he whispers.

And I hold on tight because I know this storm isn't even close to being over.

Chapter Twenty-Two

"He said what?" Harper's eyes have gone anime-character wide as she stops, the slice of pizza that had been heading to her mouth dangling now.

Anika's mouth is hanging open.

Well, it's good to know I can still shock the hell out of my friends. They didn't react like this when I told them my world fell apart and I had to sell the company. They'd taken that news like champs, but the idea that a man had asked me to marry him was too much for them.

He hadn't actually asked, though. "He said if Emma decides we're a match, we should get married."

"It's like tossing a coin in the air," Ani finally says and reaches for the wine.

We're sitting in her tiny apartment in Greenwich Village. It's what passes for an efficiency in the city meaning we're sitting at a table Ani will move out of the way later on when she hauls the Murphy bed down to sleep. It's fine because the table is from IKEA, which like all things Swedish weighs very little and neatly packs into a space in a highly creative way. Her place has one tiny bathroom and a kitchen with a hot plate and a microwave, and somehow it's also brimming over with judgment.

Now I'm offended because Emma is absolutely not a coin toss. She's a superpowered high-tech AI with all the wisdom of Lydia Marino, albeit pared down in a way a nonhuman can understand. "It's not. It's really not."

"You know what I'm saying." Ani looks to Harper for support.

Harper puts the pizza down. "Nope. I'm with Ivy on this one. Emma is a highly developed system meant to make decisions based on logic. If she gets it up and running, I might try it myself. But she should be used to shrink the dating pool down. Not to decide if two people who haven't known each other long enough should get married."

"I don't think time has anything to do with it. They've known each other for a month, but they've been thrown together on an everyday basis. It's not like they're dating and seeing each other a few hours a week. They've been together pretty much twenty-four seven since the day they met," Ani points out. "I think they know each other, but it's weird to bring a computer into it."

"A month isn't long enough." Harper is insistent. "I don't care how much time they spend together."

I agree with her fully. "He's being obnoxious. He doesn't mean it. He realized he screwed something up, and he's trying to make sure his money person doesn't walk away. I told him I'd find someone else to run the business end, but this is how he decided to go."

And it had worked since I hadn't quit then and there. He'd distracted me with hugs and his manly body and his grandmother's brownies.

Ani frowns. "That does not sound like the Heath I've come to know."

"Not in any way," Harper agrees. "It sounds like he was feeling desperate."

"What makes more sense? That he's worried about his company, or he's fallen madly in love with me and can't stand the thought of losing me?" He told me he loved every part of me, but I don't tell them. I don't know how much I trust those words. I've thought of nothing but this since I walked back into Lydia's apartment and joined the group for the rest of lunch. I'd then sat back down to work and Lydia had fed me cream cheese brownies and asked if she could help with the paperwork.

I'd forced myself to leave at five, and Heath had walked with me to the subway station talking all along like nothing had happened, but he hadn't kissed me good-bye. He hadn't tried to convince me to come home with him. When my train had come he'd looked sad and told me he hoped I had a good night.

I wondered what he was doing.

It had taken a lot not to text him about some random business thing that would lead to figuring out where he was and if he was lonely.

I thought about grabbing my things from his apartment. My brain had buzzed with all the reasons I should show up on his doorstep.

And Darnell owes me a new chapter. He'd left me hanging in the last one. The captain of the starship had found out the man he was sleeping with was actually a changeling who was an operative for the opposing fleet. I'm not sure if he's going to kill his lover or they'll work it out, but I'm damn sure I want to know what happens.

I should go by. Just to talk to Darnell, of course.

Nope. This was why I'd called an emergency meeting. I need my girls to get me through the night without making a complete idiot of myself.

"Love," Ani says, a dippy look on her face. "It's the love thing."

Harper winces as I look her way. "I know it sounds stupid, but I gotta go with the love thing, too. Heath isn't terrifically invested in building a business. He's kind of a happy-go-lucky guy. Don't get me wrong—he's a hard worker—but he doesn't have your ambition."

"That's why it works," Ani says.

"That's why it can't work," I say at the very same time.

Harper sits back and takes a sip of the Cab she brought to share with us. Luckily I brought a bottle, too, though mine is far cheaper than hers. Which is why we opened hers first. "It's only not going to work if you don't let it. Now you said he did something wrong."

I've not explained the full situation to them yet. I thought the more interesting hook was the marriage thing. I've already forgiven Heath for being a dumbass. We're all dumbasses from time to time. "Turns out he talked to one of the Bro Coders the night of CeCe's party and that asshole went straight to Nick, who decided what I'm doing is a fab idea and he walked into Sherry Carrigan's overly pretentious office in LA and said 'hey, lady, wanna help me screw over my ex.' Can you guess what she said?"

"No, because I think you're making part of this up, but I do get the gist," Harper allowed.

Ani leans in, an unholy gleam in her eyes. "I bet she said yes. I hate that woman. I know her producer. I can fix this."

I suddenly do not want to know how Ani would fix this. It's always the quiet ones. Besides, she's not on the best ground with her bosses. If she puts out a hit on the headliner of a rival show, she'll likely be out of a job.

Or she'll get her own show… I can't be sure. Her world is a mysterious place.

Harper brings us all back to reality. "So he went to LA's plastic version of Lydia and is doing his own dating app with a matchmaker deal." She seems to think about it for a moment. "I hate to say it, but it could work."

"Not if I put out the before pictures," Ani vows.

Remind me not to really piss off that particular bestie. "It's not Sherry who's the real problem. She's just listening to what seems like a good idea and running with it. Despite what I said, she probably doesn't even know I exist."

Ani's eyes flare in that oddly optimistic way of hers.

"And no, I'm not going to talk to her in hopes that she'll back down out of the kindness of her heart." I have to shut the naïve shit down fast.

"Oh, I wasn't going to suggest that," Ani replies. "There is no kindness in that woman's heart. I was going to say we should blackmail her into supporting Emma instead. Seriously, I've got the before pictures. Her makeup artists all hate her. I think her plastic surgeon does, too. Let me say not his finest work."

"I think Ivy's saying Nick is the real problem here." Harper's fingers drum along the edge of the table. It's something she always does when she's thinking through a situation. "I don't understand the inner workings of your business the way you do, but I assume this is a bad thing since you're still looking for capital."

She understands perfectly. "Investors tend to like to back a winner, and Nick looks like the winner here. After all, he came out of the Jensen Medical debacle with a shiny new job, and I got dragged in every major tech journal. Even the people who understand what happened will likely give him a pass because he didn't get the bad press."

"Which was completely unfair." Ani takes a long drink. "But I suspect Sherry's celebrity status will help him out, too. Despite the fact that she's got a crappy rate of return. I mean no one actually watches her show for the love stories. You watch for the train wrecks, and boy does she provide them. The rich can be weird as hell."

"That's a good point." Harper takes up the thread. "Sherry Carrigan is more of a celebrity than an actual matchmaker. Lydia's got a much better reputation. And Emma's got other uses besides matchmaking."

"I don't know that it will matter. Sherry's name is glitter, and investors love some glitter. It's surefire publicity, which helps any new project get off the ground. At this point I'm filing the patents as fast as I can so Heath has a leg to stand on if the AI processes turn out to be even close to the same. Look, all is not lost here." I'm trying to take a more optimistic approach. "His framework is stunning. He's been working on it for years, and it's got an ease of use like nothing I've ever seen. It's incredibly adaptable."

"So you can make money off that?" Ani asks.

"Yes and no, but mostly no. Framework is the kind of thing you open source, meaning you put it out and let developers use it for free. The money you can make is through offering support services. I intend to do that. It should be out there," I explain. "But it's not what Heath wants. Emma is his baby. It's the way he's stayed close to his grandmother. He's emotionally invested in this."

"But you said he's not ambitious about it." Harper's eyes narrow like she's making a point. "That's why you claim this thing can't work."

"It's been working fine," Ani counters.

"He's dedicated to the project. There's no doubt about that, but I don't know that he's going to like what can happen if things go well. It's a hard grind being at the top." I don't know how else to explain it. Running a business like that takes up your whole life. Heath seems to have the expectation of some kind of balance. Likely because he's never been as hungry as I am.

"What if you compromised?" Ani asks.

"Compromise?" I do in fact know the definition of the word, but I'm not sure how it fits into the current situation.

"You always shoot for the stars. You have since we were kids," Ani begins, and then her mouth makes that tight line that lets me know she's not sure she should say what she wants to say.

"Just be honest. I can handle it. Trust me. If I can handle my mom's constant criticism, I can handle whatever you're about to say," I let her know.

Ani nods and seems to make the decision to move forward. "Well, you know I worked on the Dr. Janice show for a couple of years, and while she's a TV psychologist, she actually knew what she was doing. I learned a lot from her. I think you're still that kid everyone made fun of for having crappy clothes."

"We all had cheap clothes." I'm not the only one who'd survived being a poor kid in one of the richest cities in the world. Despite how stunning the Upper East Side is there's another side of Manhattan.

"But it bothered you more," Ani points out. "There's something inside you that was always going to need to achieve at a high level. When we were kids, your definition of greatness was set by watching the wealthy people around us and deciding the only way to achieve what you need is to be the absolute top of your class in whatever you do. Hence the relentless drive to be valedictorian and get every scholarship you could. To win every competition. You can't full throttle your whole life, Ivy. You'll get to the end of it and you won't be happy you worked more. You'll wish you'd gotten some living in. When I say compromise what I'm really asking you to do is to redefine what you need to be happy because you had that. You made it to the top."

She's not telling me anything I don't already know. "And I lost it."

"Did it make you happy?" Harper seems to catch on to what Ani is saying. "When you were in the thick of Jensen Medical and everything was amazing, were you happy? Were you content that you were doing the thing you were born to do?"

Born to do? I'm not sure I believe in destiny in that way. I'm surrounded by people who started off with one life and ended in another. For better or worse. The universe throws things at us and we deal, and that's the measure of a life. But they're right. I've viewed success as something only achieved at the very top of the field. Because if I got there everyone would know I was good. Everyone would know I was worthy. My mother…

"Oh, god. I'm still trying to find a way to make my mother love me." So much of my life comes into focus, and tears blur my eyes. Even the rebellions were a way to try to make her see me, to see that even though he was gone, I was still there.

"I know you don't believe this, but she does," Ani says quietly, not arguing with my revelation. "She talks about you all the time."

"In a happy way?" I can't help but remember what CeCe told me.

Ani's lips curl down. "She's not a positive person. She's mostly worried about you, but that's kind of her love language."

"She's still grieving. I don't think she ever got over losing your dad, but we knew that," Harper says. "I'm reminded of that every day because my mom is grieving, too. It's hard."

"CeCe thinks she's clinically depressed," I say. Ani and Harper share a look, and I know they've talked about this. "Why didn't you say anything?"

"Because you're not a therapy kind of girl," Harper replies. "And your mom is definitely not. But I am worried about her and about you. I don't want you to let Heath go because your mother's disease convinced you you're not lovable."

"I don't…" I begin even as I can feel my chest tighten because we're getting to the heart of the matter.

"You settled for Nick." Ani's expression goes stubborn. "You didn't love him, but you thought you could give him something that would satisfy him, mainly a job and status. You basically bought a boyfriend to go with the job that you thought would give you everything you need."

"That's a rough way of putting it. But looking back, it's probably fair. When it ended, I didn't exactly throw a fit and try to save the relationship. I waved good-bye and went back to work. Honestly, it was a relief because he annoyed the hell out of me those last couple of months. He was always trying to get me to…" It's a night for hard truths to roll over me. Those last few months with Nick came back in full technicolor. "To pay attention to him. I mean he did it like a toddler, but looking back I think he was trying to get my attention. Heath thinks he's doing this to get back at me for not loving him enough."

"And you couldn't consider it because…" Harper leans forward. "Come on, sweetie. You're so close. You can't fix the problem until you admit it exists."

Stupid tears. They roll down my cheeks. I can't deny it. "Because I don't think I'm lovable."

If you ask me how I would describe me, it would be words like tough, hardworking, tenacious. If you ask me what I want, it's to be the best. I filled out all those forms for Lydia and now I realize not once did I say one of the things I wanted in a partner was that he love me. I asked that he respect me, acknowledge my contributions, give me space.

I didn't ask for him to love me for who I am.

My friends push back their chairs, and I'm surrounded by them.

"You are so lovable," Ani whispers. "I've loved you since we were kids."

"I'll love you my whole life, sister," Harper adds. "There is nothing unlovable about you."

Ani kisses my cheek, and they both sit back down. Ani passes me some tissues. "So what I mean by compromise is that you stop viewing success the way that little girl did. The one who thought the only way she could be happy is buying a freaking mansion on Park Avenue so her mom would be proud of her. You have to let that go. You have to define what success means to you as a functional, practical adult. What will make you happy? I'm not saying you give up being the badass you are. The world needs you, but maybe you shoot for the stars but you land on the moon and there's a really great guy there who loves you and makes you want to slow down because being with him helps you enjoy this life we have. Maybe that could be success, too."

"I haven't worked a Sunday in weeks." Because Heath always teases me until I give in and watch a movie with him. I would vow I would work after, but I never do. After the movie or the park or hanging out with our friends, we inevitably ended up lying on the couch together letting the day move around us because we were content to simply be together.

"I know. A few Saturdays, too," Harper says with a smile. "And you usually quit working when you leave Lydia's. I can't tell you how much I've enjoyed having my friend back."

Ani reaches out and holds my hand. "Me, too. I like planning things with you and being about half sure we're really going to do them."

I'm that bad. Or maybe I had been in the past. I squeeze her hand. "I'll be more reliable. I promise. I think you're right. I wasn't happy in San Francisco. I was scared all the time, and I felt removed from everyone because I always had to be the boss."

"Let Heath take some of that," Harper urges. "Code some more. You love it. You know you miss it."

I do. I miss creating. It was what I loved about the field in the first place. I created worlds where I didn't have to feel like the outsider.

What if I'd somehow managed to do that here in my real life and I'm letting my past screw it all up? What if I'd felt like the outsider for so long, I don't realize I'm inside and warm and surrounded by people who genuinely cared about me? "Maybe I will. Ria is working on Emma's voice. That could be fun to play with."

It would be, I realize. I've been so bogged down in the business that I forgot how exciting it could be at this point. Everything is new, and every day brings some intriguing challenge.

"That sounds perfect." Harper picks up her pizza again. "And what are you going to do about Heath?"

On that I had no idea. "I've got three weeks to figure it out, right?"

Ani's palms go flat on either side of her plate, and a slightly panicked look hits her eyes. "What if Emma says you're not a match?"

Harper's head shakes. "It won't matter. This is about emotion not logic, and she's never cared about any guy the way she does Heath. See. I'm smart. I could be a matchmaker." She grimaces. "Do I really have to do the thing with Heath's grandma? She seems nice and all but..."

On that I will insist. I've been helping Harper with the company's finances, and it has proved challenging. She owes me. "Absolutely. I'm helping you work through years of financial statements saved by a man who did not believe in organization."

She nods. "I found tax forms under the bathroom sink. They had Old Spice soaked in. Like old Old Spice, if you know what I mean. Yep. I will do it."

Ani grins, back to her infectious self. "I'll let Lydia find me a guy who doesn't stare at my boobs and then yell at me when his coffee is too hot. Seriously, men in the entertainment field are the worst."

We start to talk about the future, and for once I let myself think about something other than business.

Chapter Twenty-Three

I wake up the next morning and reach for Heath, turning from my left toward him. I'm used to waking up next to his radiator of a body. He's big and warm and I feel cold today, so I start to wrap myself around him and get nothing but pillow.

Because I'm alone. Because I didn't manage to talk myself into going to him the night before and apologizing and begging him to still love me.

That sounds pathetic, but last night with Ani and Harper left me with some gaping wounds. I'd had to tear them open and let some of the poison out so they could heal. Properly this time.

There's still an ache inside me, but I also feel freer than I did before, like when I finally know what's wrong with a program I'm writing. I haven't debugged it yet and I know there's hard work ahead, but I'm satisfied because I can do this. I can make this program work.

I might be able to make me work the way I should. To make my life what it should be.

I glance over at the clock. It's still dark outside. Long before I need to be at Lydia's. I've got three hours before I can start work. It sounds like a backslide, but it's not merely about business. It's about being in a place where I feel comfortable. I want to be at Lydia's because I belong there, because it's where I get to be around her and Heath and Ria and Ye Joon. It's where I intend to play around with Emma and see if I can make something new.

I hear my mother out in the kitchen. She'd been asleep when I came in the night before. We haven't talked in days, so she likely doesn't even know I'm here unless she saw that I hung my jacket on the hook by the front door.

I think seriously about lying here until she's gone. It would be so much easier, but I've vowed to not be this person anymore. When I was a child she should have been the one to bend to my needs, but I worry she wasn't capable of it.

My eyes close as I ask myself some hard questions. Do I want a relationship with her?

What do I owe her? Do I owe her anything at all at this point? So much of my damage was inflicted by her.

But what if she couldn't help it because there was something chemically wrong with her brain?

I don't owe her. Children do not owe their parents a relationship, especially if it was toxic at some point, but I find myself sitting up and then wrapping a robe around my body. After a trip to the bathroom, I'm walking down the hall. I can smell coffee. The same brand she's made since I was a child. She'll be drinking it out of the same mug she's had since I was fifteen and someone had given it to her as a Secret Santa gift at the office.

Is this what her life turned out to be? An endless round of routines? Wake up at six. Coffee and toast. Make it to the subway platform by 8:15. Work. Lunch. Subway ride home. Come home and microwave dinner. Watch TV until she falls asleep. Start over.

She hadn't been able to throw herself into something new when my dad had died. She couldn't take off and find herself. She'd had me, and she'd sunk into a routine that I then blasted when I was old enough to. I remember all the times I told her how boring her life must be and that I wouldn't get caught in it the way she had.

She wasn't the only problem.

I stop at the corner of the kitchen. She's sitting at the small table, the mug of coffee in her hand as she stares out the window at the slowly encroaching light. Her hair is in a neat bun at the back of her head. She always wears it up when she's working. I want to see it down, to brush it and see if we can find a new look. The way she did when I was a kid.

We don't talk anymore. We fight. I push. She pulls.

What if we can find a way out?

"I like this time of morning," I say quietly so I don't startle her.

She glances my way. "I didn't know you ever saw this time of morning. There's coffee if you like."

It's as much of an invitation as I'm going to get. I grab a mug and pour some in. "The whole sleeping routine is a recent development. You know I used to wake up at five every morning so I could be sure I had everything ready for school."

"Yes, that's a habit you picked up after CeCe made you work for her in the afternoons and evenings," she says, her mouth turning down. "You would do your homework in the early mornings. It was too much for a young girl."

I hadn't been so young, and it hadn't been too much since I'd managed to do it all. I don't mention that a lot of my homework had been done with Benjamin while CeCe drank a martini and discussed all the reasons I would never need algebra.

She'd been wrong. I'm one of the people in the world who actively uses higher mathematics on a daily basis.

I could point out I still managed to be the valedictorian of my class, but I'm done fighting with her.

It might be time to see if I can fight *for* her instead.

"I like how quiet the city seems," I say as I sit down opposite her.

She nods and her head turns again, going back to staring outside. From this window she can see the streets below and the other buildings around us. The sun starts to peek through. "In half an hour it'll be loud again."

It's never really quiet, but there are a few hours when one can pretend. "How is work going?"

She's been a legal secretary for one of Manhattan's oldest law firms for years. She hadn't started there. She'd gone to secretarial school after my father died because she had to find a way to support us. She'd had no family or friends to rely on and had been left with nothing but a traumatized kid and a rent-controlled apartment.

I never asked her what she'd wanted to be. I simply assumed she was one of those people who fell into a career and had no real dreams of their own. I've been looking at her through a child's eyes, the kind that don't quite understand a parent is a person first and foremost. It's a selfish thing, to believe a parent only ever wanted to be a mother or a father, that their lives are defined entirely by the child's. And yet that's what I've done for years and then judged her for it.

"It's fine." She seems a bit startled by the question.

"Working on anything cool?" I kind of like that I've thrown her.

"One of the lawyers is working on a big case, and we've all been pulled in. I've spent days combing through emails. It's actually more interesting than one would think. I mean it's mostly stuff about work, but every now and then you get the idiot who sends his mistress emails from his work computer." She shudders. "And did you know some men send pictures of their…"

"I know what a dick pic is, Mom. Sorry you have to know, too." There should be some privileges that come with age. I can't help but smile though.

Her lips curl up slightly, too. "Well, it was quite a shock that first one. Now Mattie and I compare them. I think there's something wrong with one of those men. It's very small and he's not good at grooming, but he keeps sending it out. There's a certain level of optimism and tenacity I would appreciate if I wasn't also disgusted. The things people keep. Well, I don't think they mean to keep them. I don't think most people understand how systems work these days. Not that I'm telling you anything you don't know. We still use the system you designed. My bosses always talk about how smart it is."

It's the nicest thing she's said to me in a long time. I'm proud of that system. There were backups of backups. I keep everything. I learned that from Benjamin. He'd taught me to keep every email, every text, every voice mail. A few years back I'd designed some protocols that connected my backup systems to my computer, phone, and tablets. It's an easy way to ensure nothing gets lost. I'd let my mom take it to her bosses, and they'd implemented it, too.

I love doing things like that—making things easier, streamlining processes. I love the daily work of taking a system and making it better. Somewhere along the way I'd lost that. "I'm glad."

"Well, I wish the defendant in this case had our software." She grimaces. "Not that they would give us what we need in a neat package. It's one of the tactics all firms use. Overwhelm the opponent in discovery. Although we would have to actively screw everything up if it happened to us. That system makes it easy to search for things. When that biddy Pauline Maxwell tried to pin her screwup on me, I easily found all the emails I needed to prove her wrong."

I find myself relaxing as we talk for the first time in a long time. "Glad I could help, Mom."

"So what are you doing here? I thought you spent all your time with that young man now. Heath, isn't it? He seems nice. Not like the last one."

"I'm not sure I'll be seeing him on a personal basis anymore," I say carefully, trying to make myself believe it. "I think we should concentrate on work."

I can plainly see she's disappointed in me. "Well, that shouldn't be surprising. Can I ask what he did to offend you? Or did you have enough of him and wanted to get back to work?"

It rankles. Her words are like nails on my own personal chalkboard, but I take a deep breath and choose not to scratch back. It might be time to treat her like a mom and see how she responds. "I'm scared. I'm scared that I'm making a huge mistake and I'm going to come to really love him and he'll figure out what a bad bet I am."

Her expression softens in a way I haven't seen in years. "Sweetheart, what is that about? You shouldn't be scared. He seems very nice."

"He is. That's the problem. He's too perfect." He's not. He snores sometimes and he makes the bed too fast in the morning, and often when he's playing a game with Darnell, he loses track of time, and that annoys me. And even his imperfections somehow make him perfect.

"No one is perfect. Not even your father. He could annoy the hell out of me at times, but it was worth it. Are you sure this isn't a work thing? Did he do something at work that made you push him away? You have to understand that it's his business, too. He should have a stake and a say in it."

She thinks I'm the bossiest boss on earth. "He doesn't want a say in it. He wants me to do all the business stuff so he can let his creativity flow or something. I don't know. I mean yes, what prompted it was about business, but not in the way you think. Nick founded a competing company that looks like it might get to market before we do. I'm pretty sure he did it to get back at me. How can Heath not resent me for that? He swears he doesn't, swears he doesn't expect anything except we do our best, but won't he hate me someday?"

She seems to think about it for a moment. "You might be right. You might be wrong. We can't know how things will go. We can only move forward with the knowledge we have at the time."

I let those words sit between us before I ask the question I really want to know the answer to. "Would you change the past?"

"What do you mean?" Her whole body goes tight.

I decide to press on. "If you could go back, would you do it all over again?"

She holds the mug between her hands as though soaking in its warmth. "Of course."

"Mom, it's okay. I'm not a kid. You can say it out loud. Do you ever think about what your life would have been like if you hadn't married him? Hadn't had me?"

Her hands tighten around her mug. "No. There's no use in regrets."

"But you have them." I keep poking and prodding. "We all have them. I regret not seeing how much pain you're in."

Her eyes flare. "I'm not…" They close and when they open again, she seems older to me. "That's nothing for you to worry about, Ivy. And I know you think I wish it had been you, but I don't. Not for a second. I wish he was still alive. I don't wish anything else. That's not true. I wish…I wish I could still cry about it. Isn't that the oddest thing? I miss crying. I did it so often in the first years and then it's like they all dried up."

It's the opening I need. "Mom, have you considered talking to someone?"

"I'm talking to you," she points out.

"I'm not a professional."

She frowns as though she doesn't quite understand. "Why would I need to talk to a professional? I'm not thinking of hurting anyone."

I don't tell her how much she's hurt me. That's not what she needs to hear. "But you're not enjoying your life."

Her head tilts, and I can tell she's looking for a way to turn this around. "From what I can tell, neither are you."

I nod. I'd made a bunch of decisions the night before. "And that's why I'm going to figure some things out. I'm going to find a way to be okay with who I am. I'm going to figure out how to be content and how to stop pushing for something that won't ever make me happy. I'm going to try to love me a little. I think I've cried more in the last six months than ever in my life, and you're right. It's felt good. It felt freeing, like a weight's lifted. What if someone could help you find that again? What if it's all a chemical reaction in your brain and you need some help to rebalance?"

I see the minute I lose her. She stands, smoothing her blouse down. "I do not need medication, and I don't like the implication that I am mentally ill. If you don't like me, feel free to leave."

My heart aches because she's not listening to me. She's taking everything wrong, so I say the only thing I can. "I love you, Mom. I want you to be able to love you, too."

She stops, the words seeming to freeze her in place.

I seize the moment. "I never said thank you. I never thanked you for moving forward. I know you wanted time to stop, but you moved on the best way you knew how. You tried to make a life for us. You made sure I knew who my dad was and that he loved me."

I wonder now if all the times she reminded me how much my dad would have wanted to be there wasn't some odd code for how much she wished she could be there, too, wholly and fully, without the heavy weight of grief dragging her down. When she told me my dad loved me, had that been her way of saying she loved me, too?

"I know I'm not the most demonstrative parent," she says quietly. "That was him. He was the one who couldn't go an hour without hugs and holding my hand. He drew me out of myself and back into the world. He made it all right for me to accept affection. Then he was gone and you didn't seem to need it."

"Because I was so like you. So much more like you than him," I muse. "Heath hugs me all the time. For no reason other than he thinks I need one."

She shakes her head. "He knows you need it, and he finds a way to give it to you. And after a while you'll find yourself reaching for him because you're so used to having him as comfort. I should have done that with you. I should have made it a routine so we learned the behavior because it's something we needed."

"It's okay." I'm getting misty again. This is the first real, honest talk we've had in years and years.

"I miss it, too, you know."

It's all I need. I get to my feet and I hug her. It's a moment before her arms come around me, one hand coming up to smooth my hair. It's awkward, like she's trying something out for the first time in a long time. I stay there, letting the moment live, letting it connect us in a way we might have never been before.

"Ivy, I still can't cry," she whispers. "I feel it. I want to. But it won't come. Why won't it come?"

"Because you need help. Mom, let me find it for you. We can be more than this."

That's the moment she holds on to me, her arms tightening like she's afraid to let me go. I hug her back.

"I'll go see whoever you think I should, but you have to talk to Heath."

I was going to do that anyway. "Deal."

There's a knock on the door, the sound separating us. My mom takes a deep breath and turns to it.

"I wonder who's here at this hour," she mutters as she walks toward it.

When she opens it, I worry all the work I've done will be for nothing because the one person in the world who can irritate my mother like no other is standing there.

CeCe. She looks past my mom at me and holds up a magazine. "Ivy, I got an early copy. It's worse than we could have imagined."

And my day goes to hell before the sun is fully up.

Chapter Twenty-Four

"What does it mean?" Ye Joon frowns down at the magazine.

It's all there in glossy color. Nick is staring out, his gaze so hawklike I wonder if he practiced it. He's got on a three-piece suit, a cigar he would never actually smoke in one hand. He looks like the douchebag Bro Coder fantasy of what a captain of industry should look like.

"It means we might be dead in the water." Ria slumps back as she says absolutely nothing I haven't thought. "That sucks. I like this job. It's the most fun I've had in forever. I don't want to go back to an office."

It's been two hours since CeCe brought the magazine over. I've read it three times. My mother read it and vowed to find a way to sue Nick for libel. CeCe had promised she would pay for all the lawyers in New York. I'd argued that a lawsuit wouldn't fix my reputation and would only take up more of my time, but they'd actually left together after saying if I couldn't help, they didn't need me.

I shudder at the thought of them plotting. I'd thought them being at each other's throats was bad, but now I realize a unified Mom and mentor is much worse.

"That Sherry person is all for show." Lydia is every bit as upset as my mom or CeCe, but I can't tell if she's upset about the project or about what Nick said about me personally.

Because that was a lot.

Heath was reading through the copy I'd made off his printer. After Mom and CeCe had left to plot legal revenge, I'd gotten dressed and made my way over to Lydia's because I couldn't hide this from the team. I'd had to hit them with the brutal truth the minute they'd walked in the door. Heath had been the last, and he'd walked in carrying a big box of donuts and he'd just started to tease me when he'd realized something was wrong.

He'd sat down to read, and his expression was so serious now.

He's discovering exactly how fucked his project is.

"So he's working with Taisir Jatt," Ye Joon says.

I've heard the name before. He's a big name in artificial intelligence. He's a Standford grad with serious skills. "That's what he claims in the article. Now I need to know who his investor is because Jatt won't come for cheap, and he's not putting in sweat equity. He'll want money upfront along with a stake in the business."

The thing was the article had alluded to Nick's project looking for big funding after Nick had put his own money in. It was practically an advertisement to attract investors.

"Ivy, did you do those things he says you did?" Lydia asks. She's wearing a vibrant red housedress and a matching hair wrap, long earrings dangling. She could be a fortune teller at an upscale carnival.

I could guess what she would say about my future. "I did, though not for the reasons he's attributing to me."

"He's trying to make himself look good," Ria says with a shake of her head. "He was the CFO. The company had to be sold because of mismanagement of funds."

"Then it sounds like it was his fault," Lydia replies.

"It was." Heath doesn't look up, merely keeps reading.

"And it wasn't." I had a part in my own downfall. "He's right that I wasn't paying attention the last couple of months before we sold. I was working on adjusting the software, and I took my eyes off the ball."

"You mean you didn't do the CFO's job as well as your own," Ria points out.

"I also didn't check into rumors that I heard. I should have done my due diligence," I reply.

The article was part showcase of a young man on the rise and part misogynist fantasy. When the "reporter," who also happens to be Nick's buddy, asked if he learned anything from working with me, Nick had gone on a tirade about how emotional I was, how I didn't appreciate his advice, how if he'd been at the helm, Jensen Medical would still be around. Oh, and the only reason he put up with my megalomaniacal bossiness was the somewhat abusive relationship we were in. He hadn't used those exact words, but it was there.

That man hates me.

Heath's eyes are suddenly on me. "Don't."

I'm not sure what he's talking about. "Don't?"

"Do not pull the martyr card on me now, Jensen." He stands, his shoulders squaring. "This is bullshit and you know it. You standing there trying to take the blame is bullshit, too. They didn't even call to get your rebuttal, did they?"

"I don't think they want it. Look, that was a hit piece on me, but the reasoning behind it is to effectively stop the backing of this project so the money can flow to his. He knows he can't beat us any other way. If he halts our capital flow, he halts the project." I'd decided on a path on the subway ride. There would be no three weeks for the two of us. "I'm stepping out of this project. We can find someone else to run it and once the distraction is out of the way, I think you might be able to still meet with Huffman, and if you can get in the room with him, you can sell Emma."

His head falls back, and he groans.

Actually, they all kind of do that.

Except Lydia. Her small body stiffens and seems almost supercharged with anger. All of it directed my way.

This is going to hurt like hell.

She points a finger my way. "Ivy Jensen, you will do no such thing. You will not walk away from your friends and family and let that terrible man win. I did not fight for women's rights so you can wilt at the very first hint of some man insulting you."

I'm pretty sure my jaw is on the floor. Does she have any idea the kind of crap I have to put up with on a daily basis in this industry? "I'm not wilting."

"Yes, you are, and I won't have it," Lydia announces. "You will give me this CeCe woman's phone number. I will speak with her myself, and you, young lady, will get back to work. Think about how you're going to take this man down because we are going to do it. I don't know where your relatives are from but mine are Sicilian. I assure you, we do not let a slight against our family pass easily."

Lydia turns and her housedress flows behind her as she stalks down the hall.

"Damn, I'm scared of Nonna now," Ye Joon says.

Ria simply smiles and nods like she knew she had it in her the whole time. "Nonna's a badass."

I'm intimidated, but I have to say something. "I'm only trying to spare you and Heath. If I leave…"

Lydia stops, turning toward me.

Heath actually puts a hand over my mouth. His whole hand. "She's going to go to work now, Nonna. I'll send you CeCe's number." He leans over, whispering in my ear. "You should do whatever she says when she gets like this. It goes poorly if you don't."

I'm still thinking about the fact that she called me family. She didn't mean it like that. She was surely talking about the family project. Yeah. She was talking about Emma.

Heath doesn't give me a chance to seek clarity from his grandmother. He simply turns my body and starts marching me into the office. We're set up in the big office that Lydia used to use. Once it was a delicate feminine space complete with a sitting area where I was sure she would invite clients in and share tea with them as they talked about what they were looking for in a partner. Now it's covered in computer equipment and more monitors than any room should have. I'd tripped more than once before Ye Joon had told us we were all barbarians and used some magic to organize the cables.

He closes the door when I'm fully inside and turns to me. "What the hell, Ivy? You cannot be this calm. He eviscerated you. He made you look like you have no thought or care for anyone but yourself."

It wasn't the first time. "There's always someone who is willing to believe that of a woman in a position of power. Anyone in a position of power, really, but it gets particularly nasty when it's a woman. And I can't get mad or I play right into a bunch of stereotypes. If I try to shut the story down, I'm covering something up. If I rant about how it's all his fault, I'm the woman scorned. Honestly, the best thing I can do for the project is to walk away. The best thing I can do for my career is to lay low for a while."

I feel a little numb, and I have ever since I'd read that article.

"Okay. Then I'm going to go let him know what I think." Heath starts to turn.

Now I feel a spark of panic. I don't see what the three moms can do, but Heath can get himself in real trouble. "Don't you dare. Do you have any idea how a fight between you and Nick would play in the press?"

He looks down at me, and I'm shocked at the stark expression on his face. "I don't care how it plays in the press. He doesn't get to do this to you. He doesn't get to put you in this place where you throw up every wall you have and sacrifice yourself so… I don't even know why you're sacrificing yourself. You are this project. I started it for one reason, but now I do it because it feels like we're building something. Something I would never be able to build by myself. You and me. I know that might be naïve, but it's true. I got through to you yesterday, but I can't fight him every day. I can't win if he's still here always lurking around, waiting to show you how you screwed up once. You did. You screwed up and fell for an asshole. We all do. I once dated a woman who went viral for trashing a Duane Reade when they stopped stocking her favorite flavor of gummy vitamin."

"You dated Raspberry Karen?" I remember that video. It made me swear off both drugstores and vitamins.

"That is not the point. The point is I made a mistake, and then some more after her, but if I'm making a mistake with you, I'll take it. If Nick is in the way, well, I need to handle that. I've still got three weeks. Maybe you'll forget about him in three weeks if he's dead."

He's not serious. Not about the dead part. He was totally serious about my fear coming between us. My fear has me locked in a place I hate, a place I've spent far too much time in.

I blink because suddenly there are tears in my eyes. Angry tears.

Nick lied about me. He's pushing his failures off as mine, and he thinks he can get away with it because I've always played by the rules. Always. He knows I won't cause a scene, that I'll take the hit and find a way to move on, and he can take whatever he wants.

I feel my fists clench.

"That's it, baby. Let yourself feel it. You can't work through it if you don't feel it." Heath gets into my space. "It's okay to feel it here. If you need to, take it out on me." He brings my fist up to his chest. "I can handle it. What I can't handle is you standing there with an expression like a blank doll because you can't imagine anyone is going to protect you. I need to say this so you understand me. You are more important to me than any project. That is true now, and it will be true if this thing makes a billion dollars. If I have to pick between you and Emma, I will always pick you, and I know that might not be the same for you right now, but I don't intend to get between you and your work. I understand you. I know who you are deep down and I love you. Even if it takes years, one day you're going to love me, too."

I don't want this. I don't need this. My chest feels too tight, the world seeming to shrink in until I don't have any other sensation except this feeling. I slap at his chest, not really hurting him, but he's the one who woke up this awful emotion inside me. "I told you what I want."

I want to walk away. I want to bury my damn head in the sand after I help Ye Joon and Ria get new jobs. I can walk away and not come back this time.

I do not want to stay here with him. The idea of letting this man love me is too scary. It's too much. If I fail him…

He doesn't say a thing, merely stares down at me with those soulful freaking eyes of his.

He'll never be in this position. No one is ever going to accuse him of being too hormonal to be a reasonable boss. He'll never have his board talk over him to the point that he has to shout to gain control and then know every single one of them is calling him a bitch behind his back. He doesn't have to work twice as hard to be considered half as good. He doesn't have to be made of steel. He can get mad. He can show everyone how he's feeling and they'll shrug it off as all part of his creative genius.

I hate him.

Not Heath. Never Heath, but I do hate that part of Heath who gets all the things I'll never have, the respect I've worked for that can all be snatched away because a man decided he didn't want to take the blame for his own failure.

I scream. It's a sound that's been building since I was a child. A sound that started the first time Mr. Collins told me he wouldn't waste tutoring time on me because I was a girl and math was just a passing fancy for me. A sound that built when none of the guys on the robotics team would work with me. A sound I kept inside when I realized the guy I liked in college spiked my drink and only Ani's quick thinking saved me from something that could have destroyed me. A sound I shoved down the first time I had to let a man take credit for my work because I needed to be a "team" player. A sound that Nick has amplified until I can't hold it in a second longer.

I scream and I hear the door open, but Heath is moving to close it again. He swears he can handle it and I need time, but I don't care because I scream again.

How fucking dare he?

He thinks he can break me.

"He can't break you, baby," a calm voice says.

I hadn't realized I said the words out loud. Heath is standing there, his back to the door, barring anyone from entering. He's there, a grim protector who watches me with tears in his eyes as though he feels my pain.

And suddenly it doesn't matter that I've sworn to keep our relationship professional. There's nothing professional between me and this man. I walk straight up to him. I need more from him. The scream was satisfying, but I need more.

His eyes flare and then his hands come down from around his chest, and he gets in my space. I feel savage as I go on my toes and wrap my arms around him. I kiss him, but it's not a soft, sweet thing. It's carnal. I'm running on pure emotion, and I realize it's because I can. It's because I can let out all this poison with him in a way I can't with anyone else in the world. Not even my friends who I love.

I love Heath in a different way. I can acknowledge that in all its scary glory. I don't know how brave I'll be in ten minutes, but in this one I feel a fierce love for him. He gets a side of me no one else will ever see.

A side of me I didn't understand existed until this moment.

I don't stop kissing him as I drag his shirt overhead and my greedy hands find his skin. I can't think of anything but him in the moment, how much I need him. How fucking much I will miss this man if I leave him.

"You don't have to miss me," he says, and now there's something savage about him, too. My always laid-back boy genius sinks a hand in my hair and twists. I gasp because I feel that everywhere. "I won't let you miss me, Ivy."

He holds me still, and I feel his tongue surge inside as he takes over the kiss. The world tilts and I'm whirling along with it, running on emotion and the feel of his body against mine.

Somehow we end up on the big couch, Heath sitting and pushing up the skirt I'm wearing. He tears at the fly of his jeans, freeing himself. I don't bother taking off my undies. He pushes them aside as I straddle him and then, oh then he's inside me and it's like the world falls away. The pain I'd felt seems manageable again as he holds my hips and thrusts up. We kiss over and over, his hands soothing me even as he pushes me toward something spectacular.

I hold on to him as I go over that wild edge. His arms wrap around me, tightening as he joins me.

I'm exhausted as I let my head rest against his, let his warmth surround me.

"It's going to be okay, baby." He whispers the words against my ear. "I promise. No matter what happens, it's going to be okay."

I'm starting to believe him.

"No, Harvey, there's nothing wrong." I hear Lydia talking outside in the hallway. "I was watching a horror movie. You know I love a horror movie."

"Oh, no." I hug him tighter like I can disappear inside his body and not face the fact that I just primal screamed inside a New York apartment building and probably freaked everyone out.

"Oh, that." Lydia's voice is getting further away, but unfortunately my hearing's pretty solid. "Well, that was when I changed channels. Yes, I was on the pornography channel."

Heath's body shakes with the force of his laughter.

"I can't believe we did that," I whisper.

He flips me over so I'm lying on the couch, his big body covering mine. "I won't let you take it back. And Nonna can handle it. Now kiss me again and then we should get to work. My boss gets crabby if I slack off."

"I am so not your boss." But he's got me smiling.

And when he kisses me again, the world doesn't seem so cold.

Chapter Twenty-Five

I feel so much better three hours later. After I managed to force myself to face my friends, I realized I wasn't actually all that embarrassed. It was weird. Something happened in those moments when I finally let it all out, and I'm able to take the problem and examine it in a way I haven't before. I'm not embarrassed that I had an extremely emotional reaction to something hurtful that happened to me. I'm not embarrassed that I cried and screamed, and I'm really not embarrassed that I screwed my superhot boyfriend on his grandmother's couch.

Heath is definitely not embarrassed. He'd simply opened the door after we'd made sure everything was cleaned up and started working again. He was cool, calm, and collected and showed no signs he was freaked out about his grandmother having overheard us having sex.

I'd spent the whole afternoon working with Ria on Emma's voice. She sounds a bit like Lydia now. It's a no-nonsense voice that's also somehow warm and inviting.

And I realize I thought the word *boyfriend* and it feels right to me. I've been avoiding it, trying to float along living in the now because the future feels like a scary thing to contemplate, but I hate the idea of a future without him, so I'm going with it.

"She sounds great." Ria grins as she runs Emma through a set of basic protocols. "Emma, what should I look for in a man?"

The monitor blinks and then Emma's voice comes over the speakers. "Compatibility with your basic morals and values is important, but personality traits are important, too. And check to see if he has an arrest record. You can't be too careful, sweetie."

I can't help but snort because that sounds so like Lydia.

"Should she do the pet name thing?" Ye Joon frowns at us from the doorway. "Shouldn't she be more professional?"

"Every user experience will be different," I explain. "This one is matched to what Ria values in a mentor. She prefers a more personal experience. Like Emma's her grandma giving her advice. Here. I set one up for you, too. Emma, what should Ye Joon look for in a partner?"

Emma's voice goes a little flatter, far more professional and artificial sounding. "Someone who can survive his mother."

Ye Joon barks out a laugh. "You programmed her to say that."

I shrug because I had. "You complain about your mom a lot."

He nods. "I do, but I love her. Although I do worry about whoever I eventually bring home."

Emma decides she's not finished. "You should find a nice doctor and then you will have brought a doctor into the family."

"Wow." Ye Joon looks down at the monitor. "She's really been listening in on us. That's crazy. Also, Emma, I don't know that would work. My mom would just point to my partner and ask why I couldn't be more like her. Mom's coming around a little. My sister can't fix her computer or her Internet, so I'm absolutely good for something."

"I will add that to my data files," Emma replies.

Emma has a user function that allows her to listen in to gain more information about the user. She's also got a handy *stop listening* function for those who think it's creepy for a computer to listen in on your everyday conversations. I expect our users are going to trend younger. We've been testing the function by letting Emma listen in on us.

"Emma, do you think Ivy and Heath would make a good couple?" Ye Joon asks.

"Hey." I'm not sure I want the answer to that question yet.

"They better after what they did in the office this afternoon," Emma replies.

I wince. Yep. Her listening function is working well.

Ye Joon pats my shoulder. "Heath is a genius. She took in all the data and knows about your quickie. I want you to think about that. She was able to figure out what was happening."

Ria sends him a glare. "Come on. You know that wasn't a quickie. That was an emotional and physical connection that Ivy needed very much in the moment. I thought it was beautiful."

"I thought it was loud," Ye Joon counters, and then his hands come up as though staving off an inevitable attack. "And beautiful. I'm glad we're all cool now, and we can get back to work."

I look at these two who've become important in my life. Despite the fact that I feel better, my problems haven't gone away. "I'm going to do everything I can to keep us moving forward. I believe in this project, too. It might not happen overnight, but I'll find us the funding."

"I don't care what that asshat says he has. It's not better than Emma." Ye Joon sounds confident. "And I don't want you to worry about me. If the worst happens, I can find a job to pay the bills and help out during my free time."

"Me, too," Ria adds. "Though I'm with Ye Joon. I don't think any other system can beat Emma. We just need to be able to get her in front of investors. I don't think we're more than six months from being able to take her to shows, and a year from market."

I like that timeline and I think she's probably right, but it's the getting her in front of investors that might be hard. We need those patents, and the fact that CeCe is paying our legal fees might be the one leg up we have.

I hear the bell chiming from the front of the apartment and the sound of someone rushing to open it. I wonder if someone ordered food. I could definitely eat. I wonder what street vendors they have around here. I got so involved in work I forgot about lunch until Heath put a sandwich in front of me, but now I realize dinnertime is close.

"Ria, Ye Joon, could I have a moment alone with Ivy?"

Lydia's voice has me turning. It's odd because I've been listening to Emma all day and when Emma's directed toward me, she really sounds like Heath's grandmother. I chose that. I now wonder if she's going to give me an earful about what happened earlier. I haven't seen her since the incident. I've been locked back in here working with Ria, and I realize I might have been avoiding this confrontation.

Ria looks at me sympathetically, but I nod to her. She and Ye Joon leave, and I worry as Lydia shuts the door behind them.

I'm still not embarrassed by what happened between me and Heath, but I realize Lydia might be. "I'm sorry about the noise from earlier. I promise it won't happen again. I can apologize to your neighbor if you like."

She waves off that worry as she sits down in the chair Ria had been using. "Oh, that was Harvey. Busybody. He's going to spend days trying to find the pornography channel. I'm not worried about that. I am worried though. Ivy, I have to ask you what your intentions toward my grandson are."

Wow. I had not expected that. "Uhm, well, I probably am going to have dinner with him tonight."

She frowns my way. "You were going to leave him yesterday."

"Not because I don't..." It feels weird to think about the word I kind of want to use, but I settle on an easier one. "Not because I don't care about him. I was doing it because I do care about him. It was the same reason I was going to leave this morning. That article could hurt the company."

"Heath doesn't want the company more than he wants you," Lydia points out. "And I know what you're thinking. You're worried he could change his mind down the line."

I'm not going to lie to the woman. "It's a possibility. I hate the idea that he might come to resent me, but I have to balance that with who he is as a man. He promises me that won't happen. So I have to figure out if I believe him. It's not that I think he's lying to me. I know he's not."

"You're worried he's lying to himself," Lydia deduces.

"I worry that we don't always know how things will work out, and he can be very optimistic about business." Heath is optimistic about most things, despite some painful turns in his past. He keeps going, and maybe I need that in a partner. I've spent a lot of time thinking about how a partner and I would fit together like we're all puzzle pieces, and if we don't snap into place then it can't work. But maybe it's more about finding someone who can round out our edges. The fit won't be perfect at first, and it could even be uncomfortable for a while, but over time if we learn and grow together, we ease into place.

"And you can be pessimistic, but that doesn't mean you're not compatible," Lydia says.

It was exactly what I've been thinking. "I know, and I'm afraid I'm so worried I might fail him that I could actually will failing him into existence."

"The only way you'll fail Heath is to walk away from him. Do not underestimate the importance of the hard times. Don't take away his right to stand beside you. If the shoe was on the other foot and it was Heath's past that was going to drag the project down, would you tell him to walk away?"

"Of course not, but it's his project," I point out.

"I think he would say it's yours now. He's been working on this weird version of me for over a decade. He tinkers with it for a while, then gets distracted by some other project and then comes back and works for a couple of weeks before he sees another shiny object," Lydia explains. "You're the one who's brought him focus."

I could see Heath squirreling from time to time, but he was always so eager to get to work. Was that about me? Did I bring him something no one else has?

Lydia leans toward me. "I'm going to tell you a story that not even Heath knows. I don't talk about it because it happened so long ago, and it doesn't seem to matter now, but it might to you. There's a dark secret in my past."

"Dark secret?" I can't imagine Lydia doing anything dark.

"Heath's grandfather was not my first husband," she says slowly, as though forcing the words out. "I got married at fifteen to a boy I thought I loved. He was a friend of my cousin's, the one my parents thought was a terrible influence."

"You got caught in a bad boy trap."

"I suppose I did. Oh, I was rebellious when I was young. I didn't want the life my mother had, and I thought I was smarter than everyone else. I know having money is a lovely problem to have, but at that moment in my life I felt so trapped. I was trapped in a society where I didn't feel like I had a voice. Looking back now, I know my parents weren't the problem. My mother encouraged me to go to college, to see some of the world, but I thought I knew what I was doing."

My heart aches for her because I know there's no happy ending to this story. "What happened?"

"Angelo was two years older than me. We went to my parents and told them we were going to get married, and they did not take the news well. They explained I was too young and they would not support the marriage. So we eloped. I think he thought my parents would come around and support us financially when they realized where we were living. I was fascinated by all of it. I got a job at a bakery to help support us, and he would work on a construction crew until he was late too many times and they inevitably fired him. I wanted to build something new, but he wanted a meal ticket. When that didn't happen, he became very angry. We were only married for a few months when he started hitting me. I'm ashamed to say it took me a while before I could leave him, before my fear overcame my pride."

I reach out and put a hand on hers. "It doesn't matter when you left. All that matters is that you're here and you have a good life with people who love you and would never hurt you."

Her hand flips over and squeezes mine. "Yes. That is the point of this story. It doesn't matter what happened to you in the past. Your future is the important thing. I was terrified that I would make another mistake. My parents let me move back in and my father handled the divorce, which was scandalous at the time. I helped my mother with her business, and I think I might have never gone on another date had I not met my Gabe. He worked at my father's firm, and I met him at an office party. He asked my father's permission to take me out, which he gave. I turned him down, but he would come over for dinner once a week and we talked. He was the most patient man. He was kind and gentle with me, and I took over two years to let him in."

I see what she's saying. "I obviously did not need that much time. I know Heath isn't Nick."

"He isn't, and he knows what he wants. I hope you give him a chance because I think the two of you could be very special together," Lydia tells me.

I hesitate because I don't know how I'll feel if she can't give me the answer I want. And then I realize it doesn't matter. I don't need some mystical force in the universe to tell me how I feel about Heath. I don't need to wait three weeks and let a computer program tell me how I should feel about the man I've come to love. But it could be a fun story to tell later. "You said you could feel it. When a couple is really right for each other, you told me you can feel it. Do you feel that spark with me and Heath?"

Her gaze is steady on mine. "The minute you walked into my apartment. I felt it. I know it deep in my heart, even if the two of you aren't perfect on paper because one of you hasn't figured yourself out yet."

That would be me. I'd filled out those worksheets without really considering what I truly want. "I think I might have overemphasized work on my questionnaires. I might go back and look at them with a different perspective now. I think I was trying to be the person I thought I should be. The warrior boss bitch."

"Oh, my darling, you are a warrior and you are a boss, but there is nothing bitchy about you," she says. "I know Heath made that ridiculous bet with you about Emma pairing you up, but you don't need her. You know."

"My intentions toward your grandson are entirely honorable," I vow. "I'm hoping to have a long, happy relationship with him. And I promise to stay off your couch from now on."

Lydia stands and smiles down at me. "Don't you dare. Heath's father was conceived on that couch. Once I let my Gabe in, he was all in, if you know what I mean. Every room of this house."

"I'm never telling Heath that." I will protect him from that knowledge until the day I die.

She laughs, a light sound that makes me happy. "Well, I'm glad we had this talk. Now come along because your army is assembling right now. I hope I have enough food. When they told me they were coming by this evening, I made a big batch of sauce. I've got to get the pasta going. If I understand correctly, CeCe won't actually eat anything, but Darnell will make up for her. The boy can eat."

She walks out the door and I hurry to follow her. "What's going on? What do you mean by army?"

When I reach the living room I have my answer. It's full of people. My mom and CeCe, who has already foisted Lady Buttercup off on Ye Joon, who does not look like a dog person. Harper and Anika are talking to Darnell, who's sitting by Heath.

CeCe has brought her own bartender. Thomas has taken up a place at Lydia's bar, and it looks like she brought her own gin. And glasses. I recognize the Tiffany martini glassware from her home bar.

And Mom is drinking one, too.

What fresh hellscape is this?

Heath stands and makes his way to me, slinging an arm around my shoulders. He leans down and whispers in my ear. "If you leave, you better take me with you. I will never forgive you if you leave me alone with your mom and CeCe. They seem very cozy now. It scares me."

Hell has frozen over. The apocalypse is upon us. It's the only explanation.

CeCe looks up and sees me. "Darling, your mother, Lydia, and I have come up with a plan."

"A plan?" I am equal parts fascinated and terrified. "A plan for what?"

"To save you, of course," Lydia says, as though I should have known the answer to that question all along.

"And to totally fuck over that dirtbag, Nick," my mom adds, raising her glass.

Anika nods. "That's the content I'm here for."

Darnell sits back. "I'm here for the food and the drama."

It looks like my army has my back. I lean into Heath. "I think we're going to stay, babe. It's time to take a stand."

Chapter Twenty-Six

"So the plan is to catch him doing something illegal." I'm glad I have a big plate of pasta in front of me. It's soothing, and Lydia's meatballs are to die for. I need some comfort because so far the moms' plan isn't working out in my head.

"You know he's dirty," my mom announces. She seems far more animated than I've seen her in forever, as though spending time with the enemy invigorated her. She digs into her food and seems to actually enjoy it.

"We all know he's dirty. I think he's likely already done something illegal." CeCe nods Mom's way. She's got a plate in front of her but it's salad and a single meatball. I don't know how her body runs on alcohol and the occasional grapefruit, but it does. "I want to take a look at his finances. I called some people I know in Silicon Valley, and he doesn't have bank financing on his project yet. He's meeting with potential investors along with that reality person next week. He does have one name attached to the project. Lance Norfolk, and I find that very interesting."

I'm confused. "He didn't know Lance Norfolk. I thought Benjamin set up that meeting. How did he convince the man to invest so quickly?"

CeCe finishes off her martini and Thomas swoops in with another. "Benjamin is looking into that. Neither of us believe they had any ties before the night of the party. Now we're wondering if we were wrong, and wouldn't that be interesting? From what I can tell Lance is backing them, but for now in a hands-off way. I've heard a rumor the majority of the money to hire the actual programming staff came from Nick himself."

This is what I don't understand. I lived with the man. I know his finances. "Nick makes a great salary, but it's not like he's ever had a ton of cash. He mostly spent everything he made. The man drives a Bugatti. I know how far out on a limb he went for that car."

His car note is more than most mortgages. Far more.

"You didn't have a joint account?" Heath asks.

At least I hadn't been that dumb. "I wasn't going to join our finances unless we got married. We kept everything separate, and we each paid half of the monthly bills."

Harper snorts at that statement.

I know what she's saying, but I wish I didn't have to react. "Fine. I paid most of the bills because he always had an excuse. One of which was the Bugatti, which he claimed was really for both of us since we needed to look like a power couple. I rode in that car maybe three times." I look to Heath. "We can be the power couple that takes the subway."

He grins my way, and my heart threatens to stop. "Baby, I'll spring for a Citi Bike, too. It'll have a nice basket on the front. Nothing but the best."

Lydia frowns at Heath and looks Mom and CeCe's way. "He's joking. He's got a very weird sense of humor. He certainly has enough money for a car. He's excellent at saving. I taught him not to go into debt."

"A sensible lesson." My mom seems perfectly happy with Lydia. She'd gone into the kitchen and helped her bring out our dinner.

Ria and Ye Joon had left for the day, and I'd promised to fill them in on the plan tomorrow.

If there was an actual plan. Because so far it seemed like Lydia, Mom, and CeCe had spent the afternoon simply bashing Nick.

"So the question is where did Nick get the money to bring in Taisir Jatt," CeCe muses. "Taisir apparently left what he was working on to start this project. Benjamin called around, and he estimates it would have cost Nick roughly two hundred and fifty to bring him on."

Darnell's eyes narrow on something other than his plate. He's on seconds. "We are not talking two hundred fifty dollars, are we?"

"Of course we are. Isn't that what I said?" CeCe asks.

I don't think CeCe knows there's amounts of money that small. "Thousands. She means two hundred fifty K."

Harper whistles. "That's a hell of a golden parachute."

I shake my head. "I joked about that. Nick left the company with less than fifty K severance. We didn't have anything at the end. His golden parachute was really more bronze."

"Because he mismanaged your funds," Mom points out. "He invested money in risky ventures that didn't pay off and brought the entire company down. You came out of it with far less than he did."

Lydia nods her way. "And that should be illegal."

"I think we call that capitalism," Darnell points out. "He sounds like a cartoon villain. Any way he made a little money on the side as he slithered off into the sunset?"

Anika leans in, her eyes lighting up. "Yeah, I bet he did. I certainly wouldn't put it past him."

I'm not following. "What are you saying? Do you think Nick embezzled funds? Shouldn't the accountants have found that? Our accounting department went through every test they could before we sold. Surely they would have found something."

"And how would we even prove it at this point?" Heath asks. "Could we hack his bank records?"

"You will not be hacking anything, young man," his grandmother announces. It's good to know we have a voice of reason. "I'm sure CeCe knows plenty of people we can hire to do that job for us."

Or not.

CeCe nods. "I do, of course. I have a special young man who does all sorts of jobs for me. Thomas, what is his name again?"

Thomas is still here, though he refused to sit down and eat with us. He said it wouldn't be proper. He pokes his head out of the kitchen where he's been hanging out. "No idea, ma'am. You simply call him Hacker."

CeCe nods as though this is normal. "Yes, Hacker can help us."

"We're not hacking Nick's accounts." I was pretty sure Nick wouldn't have the balls to physically steal from the company. There were a lot of things the man might do, but it wouldn't be anything so blatant.

"We set a trap for him." Anika's hands come up animatedly as she speaks. "For him and Sherry Carrigan. They think they're going to a business meeting but then they meet with a shit ton of cocaine and oops, the cops show up and everyone believes it because in some circles she's known as *Snowy* Carrigan for both her superwhite skin and her love of cocaine."

Harper turns her way. "Sweetie, I'm worried about you."

"I'm just saying, it wouldn't be so bad if everyone involved went to jail," Anika says with a shrug. "For a very long time."

"I like her," Darnell says with a nod to Heath. "She seems ready to cause some trouble. The one you have seems to have calmed down a lot."

The arrogant grin on my boyfriend's face has me groaning. "Yeah, I made that happen."

"Heath," I hiss under my breath.

"What?" Harper has sensed gossip, and she narrows in on me and Heath. "How did you calm Ivy down, Heath?"

"Is everything okay?" my mother asks.

CeCe leans in. "I believe the inference here is that Heath gave Ivy a physical release for her perfectly normal in her given situation anxiety."

"He fucked her calm," Darnell says with a grimace. "Would you please stop? His head is big enough. You would think he invented sex."

My mom blushes but still looks my way. "You're okay now?"

I nod. "I'm good. I'm afraid I came over to quit the company, and Heath talked me out of it."

"Good for Heath," CeCe says approvingly.

"I thought you were against the whole dating while they're working together thing," Anika points out.

"I was until I saw Emma." CeCe had asked Heath to walk her through what we've achieved so far. She'd been impressed, to say the least. "Now I'm sure we're going to make millions, if not billions, and I'm all for keeping the boy genius happy. Ivy, use your body as you wish. You might be able to negotiate another ten percent."

"My daughter is not a prostitute," my mom announces.

"Sex worker," Harper corrects.

CeCe shrugs as though she doesn't understand the problem. "I don't see anything wrong with it. The young man is getting something out of it. I've found young men often need an extra push to achieve their goals."

Darnell got the biggest smile on his face. "I love that woman. She's one hundred percent going in a book."

This feels right. Not the sitting around talking about me exchanging sexual favors for artificial intelligence part. The part where we're joking and laughing and eating delicious food and feeling like a weird family.

Or maybe all families are weird in their ways. But this one feels right.

"I don't think it was Ivy doing the pushing," Lydia says. "Heath knew she was on the edge after that terrible article, and she needed some physical affection. That's all."

I could do with less talk about my sex life, though. A lot less talk.

Heath sits back, that dumbass sexy smirk on his face. "She needed some affection. As her boyfriend, I gave it to her. Now stop making Ivy blush. We need real solutions. Unless we can access Nick's systems, I doubt we're going to figure out where he got the money."

"We're not…" I'm about to say the word *hacking* when I realize we don't have to hack anything. Not anything at all. "My backup system. I didn't even think about it."

My mom sits up, palms flat on the table. "He used your system when you were living together? For his laptop?"

We might not have shared a bank account, but we'd shared a freaking cloud. "For his everything, and he didn't understand how to use it. I dumbed it down for him because he refused to learn. I set the whole thing up so all he had to do was plug his system in and everything got pulled to our personal cloud."

"But that's for business," Harper replies. "I get that he would need a backup for his laptop. He would do all his business stuff there."

Darnell snorts. "Not that dude. I assure you, that dude does the majority of his business on his phone or a tablet. I work with these guys. They're all flash and no actual substance. He says he works in tech, but I would bet he's never programmed anything on his own. He's probably got a group of guys and one or two of them are the actual smart ones, but he's convinced them he'll show them the way to nerdvana if they carry him on their shoulders."

He's pretty precisely summed up Nick's friends. "The Bro Coders. They love coding and misogyny. Nick met them in college. I think they're the reason he went into tech. His actual degree is in management, but somewhere along the way he figured out he could manipulate talented people so he looked like he was one of them. He takes a lot of credit for smart people's work."

The table goes super quiet.

I wince. "Including me. The point is Nick let me do anything technical, and the backup system was used for everything. When he plugged his phone in to charge it, the system pulled down all the new data. Same for his laptop and tablet and smart watch. I've got over a year's worth of data. When he left I offered to send it to him, but he said he didn't need anything from Jensen Med since he was starting a new life."

"Did he not understand?" CeCe asks. "That you were downloading the private files, too? He might have a right to privacy argument."

I feel a smile slide over my face. "If he didn't understand it's only because his ass didn't read the user agreement."

Heath snorts. "You made him sign a user agreement?"

"Oh, she makes everyone sign one," my mother says. "I had to sign one when she set it up at our office. My boss actually wrote it, so I assure you it's legally binding."

I shrug. "I was storing his data. It seemed right at the time. I guess I was covering my ass."

Heath leans over. "You installed that system for me weeks ago. I do not recall a user agreement."

Because I don't need it with him. Because he's never going to use it against me. I wrinkle my nose and brush my lips over his. "Like I said, it seemed right at the time."

Darnell makes a vomiting sound. "Could we get back to the part where we potentially use this asshole's own data against him? I think at my next writer group we can revisit the meaning and use of irony in fiction. In real life it's just sweet karma."

Harper finishes her last meatball and sets down her fork. "So we're going to legally violate Nick's privacy because he's lazy. I'm ready."

I don't know that they understand how massive this job could be. "It's a lot. It's every email, text message, voice message, document, picture he's taken for years. We can start with the time surrounding the Jensen Med sale, but it's still a ton of stuff to sort through."

"Not for Emma." Heath isn't done but he stands. "All we have to do is feed her the data, set the parameters of what we're looking for, and see what happens. Maybe he's perfectly clean and then maybe he's not."

"Maybe he does a ton of crime and takes pictures of it, and we can get him hauled off to jail." Anika is thinking positive.

"Do you still have the data?" Lydia asks. "You didn't dump it when you dumped him?"

CeCe's smile is positively predatory. "She has it. She would never dump it because I taught her that information is the most important thing in the world."

I have to hope I find something useful. Something that might prove it wasn't all my fault that Jensen Med failed. "I can access it from my laptop. Let's see what Emma can find."

It's not as easy as simply loading the data. By almost two in the morning, Heath and I had written and rewritten a dozen protocols. We have to push and pull and get things just right so the AI understands what it's looking for and is able to make connections.

There's so much on the drive—a near complete documentation of Nick's life. The one I hadn't realized he had. I thought we'd shared the same values, but it was clear we hadn't.

I was surprised to find that he went out with the boys on several nights when he told me he was working. There was picture after picture of him and the bros partying it up around town. And they appeared to have enjoyed numerous men's clubs.

I look through the pics and wonder if I knew this man at all. There are a couple of us, but I'm barely smiling. Had I thought I was happy? Had I decided I didn't deserve to be happy, and I would settle for whatever I had with him?

"Now I know he didn't think it worked on his phone." Heath shakes his head as he looks at the screen. "He couldn't have wanted you to see those."

The whole time we've been working there is a sense of peace between us. This is the kind of job that should make me anxious. I should want to hide whatever I find from Heath to salvage my pride, but I hadn't thought twice about letting him open those pictures. It's not that he doesn't irritate me at times. He does, but then he brings me coffee or kisses my forehead. The man knows how to soothe my inner beast. It's something I've never felt before, and I don't know if I trust it. This thing between us feels way too good to be true.

"I told him it worked on all his data." I feel the need to defend myself. I hadn't been trying to trick Nick. I hadn't once looked through the data despite the fact I'd known it was there. The only times I'd ever accessed his files was when he'd lost his laptop and I'd needed to pull the data down into a new one.

Maybe if I'd looked I would have known he was cheating on me in so many ways.

"Did you know her?" Heath's tone is grim as Emma pulls up pictures of Nick with another woman. She's blonde and far prettier than me. She looks like the kind of girl who's super impressed with a Bugatti and some jewelry. I do know her.

"She worked in sales." I don't still love Nick. There's zero affection for the man in my heart, but I ache for the me I'd been at the time. I hadn't even had a hint that Nick was screwing one of the sales support staff. She answered phones. There's nothing wrong with that, but Nick was the guy who constantly talked about how he needed a woman on the same level, a woman who could keep up with him in business. This was a bit of fluff looking for a husband to take care of her. Again, nothing wrong with that, but I wish he'd been honest about what he really wanted.

Heath puts an arm around me. "I'm sorry you had to see that. Especially since it doesn't help us."

Nick cheating on me would bring shrugs and nods and conversations that began with *well, of course he did*. It's not illegal to be a douchebag.

"Look for anything concerning Lance Norfolk," a familiar voice says.

I turn and CeCe's still here. Everyone else, with the exception of my mom, has gone home with promises to help more tomorrow, but CeCe is still here. Somehow she looks perfect at two in the morning. Not a hair out of place, and her makeup looks like she'd just put it on. Mom is half asleep on Lydia's couch, and Lydia is fully asleep in her lounge chair. Thomas had taken Lady Buttercup home and was probably circling the block, waiting for CeCe's command.

"He didn't know Lance Norfolk back then," I say. As far as I knew he'd met the well-known corporate raider the night of CeCe's party. "Nick didn't have a lot of ties to New York before he met me. He's always been a West Coast guy. He wouldn't have any reason to know him." The idea slices through me. Lance Norfolk is exactly what I'd said he was. A raider. An investor who likes to take apart companies as much as he likes to build them up. How far did this go? What had he done to me? "You think he knew Norfolk all along. Norfolk is the one who got him the job, not old fraternity contacts."

"I've been looking into it. I think it's very possible. I think it's how Lance works," CeCe explains. "I'm curious. The fact that Lance is quietly funding him means something. Lance doesn't invest in any company he's not sure he can steal at some point. He's very careful. I've not known him to go into business with someone so quickly."

Heath is already typing away, resetting the parameters for Emma's search.

I'm shaken at the idea that there might have been more to my "failure." I join CeCe out in the hall as Heath works behind us.

"Are you okay?" CeCe asks.

I don't know that I've been okay for a long time. "I'm finding out that my whole life was a lie, but I think I already knew that."

"And now you're questioning if he's a lie, too." CeCe says the quiet part out loud. There's no question which *he* she's talking about.

I look back, my voice low so Heath can't hear me. "I don't think he's a lie. I think Heath is exactly who he says he is. The problem isn't Heath. It's me. I worry I can be a lot for any guy. Lydia thinks I should jump in with both feet."

"Yes, you do that often," CeCe replies.

"I do not." I'm careful. I think through every relationship I've ever had. I'd made a thorough list of pros and cons before moving in with Nick.

"You went into business with Heath the day you met him. You had the idea for Jensen Med on a Tuesday and an LLC filing by Thursday morning. That game you programmed. Same thing. You had the idea and it was available for sale within a year. You leap all the time," she points out. "You follow your gut, and your gut is usually correct. Deal with the Nick problem. Confront him and get some closure no matter what we find. He's noise in your head. Once you shut that noise out maybe you can listen to your gut again. I think it's important that you and Heath continue the way you're going."

I roll my eyes. "I'm not sleeping with him to motivate him."

"Of course not, darling. You're sleeping with him because you love him." CeCe's eyes shine suspiciously. "He's your George, and I wish you all the time in the world with him."

I have to blink because I've got tears in my eyes, too.

"Ivy." Heath is standing behind me, and I worry he's heard too much. "I found something. Something big."

I join him and hope I can find the closure CeCe talked about.

Chapter Twenty-Seven

I sit outside Nick's beautiful corner office and I'm surprisingly calm.

I'd expected an adrenaline rush, but all I feel is sad that it's come to this.

The admin looks over from her desk, hanging up the phone. "I'm sure he'll be with you soon."

She says it in a way that lets me know he could be a while. I was surprised he was willing to take the meeting with me on such short notice. I'd texted him this morning as I'd sat in bed with Heath. We'd stayed at Lydia's because it was so late when we finally had all the evidence we needed. We'd fallen into the bed in her guest room and hadn't even taken off our clothes. At some point in time he'd wrapped himself around me, and despite the fact that I was sure I'd looked like hell, he'd kissed me in the morning and gotten me coffee and bagels.

Nick had told me that he would love to see me. Why didn't I come by his office around eleven and we could catch up? I was sure he was expecting me to shout at him or cry.

I'll be lucky if he doesn't have security escort me out once he realizes what I've done.

I've been sitting here for twenty minutes despite the fact I was right on time, but I should have known he would leave me hanging. It's what he does.

When he's not busy feeding me to the wolves.

"You don't look like I thought you would," the admin says. She's a beautiful brunette who appears to be in her mid-to-late twenties.

Everyone on Nick's team seems young and stylish. I'd caught sight of one of the Bro Coders as I'd walked in, and I wonder if he'd gotten them all jobs here. He seems to have taken care of his friends.

I glance down at my jeans and T-shirt. I'd forgone the armor. I hadn't even thought about putting my Chanel on. I'm saving it for a special occasion. Heath hasn't seen me in it.

It's not armor anymore. It's just a dress I look pretty in.

"The great thing about having nothing left to lose is you get to be comfortable," I reply, though I know I'm lying.

I do have a lot to lose. I could lose the fledgling relationship with my mom. I could lose this family I seem to have found. I could lose Heath.

But I won't lose them because I wear the wrong clothes or make a stupid business move. I will never lose them because I tried my hardest and still failed.

"Must be nice," she says with a turn of her head.

I do not care what she thinks. It's not even a worry in the back of my head. She doesn't matter. What does matter is getting what CeCe advised. Closure.

I can get closure in jeans and a T-shirt and hopefully be back to Lydia's in time for lunch. I won't have to stop by my mom's and change. I'm working with Ria on Emma again this afternoon, and Heath's filling out the last of the patent forms.

I'm looking forward to it. I love work in a way I haven't in a long time. Unlike the last years at Jensen Med, this work fills my soul, but it doesn't consume it. I enjoy it, but I don't feel like I am nothing without it. This might be what Anika means by balance.

The door opens and Nick walks out in his thousand plus dollar designer suit and Louis Vuitton loafers. He looks every inch the successful young businessman. Dark hair slicked back to perfection, broad shoulders, and the man knows how to stay young.

I'd liked the whole package and had never gotten to know the man underneath.

"Ivy." He frowns as I stand, and he looks me up and down. "You look...good."

I actually do. These jeans make my butt look nice, and the T fits just right. The truth is I feel more comfortable in casual clothes, and that makes a difference in how I present myself. I feel more confident, more like myself, and not the me who so desperately wants to fit in.

He stares for a moment. "Different, but good. I don't think I've seen you without a power suit on in a long time."

I shrug. "My new office has a more relaxed culture. Thanks for seeing me."

He steps back and allows me in his office. It's every bit as luxurious and masculine as I'd thought it would be. Wood paneling and a mega desk along with a bar in the back that has only the most expensive of single malt Scotch. The floor-to-ceiling windows show off the buildings around us. It's everything he dreamed of.

"Nice office."

He smiles, a genuine expression this time. "Yeah. It feels good. You can't beat the view. It's kind of what we dreamed of, right? When we talked about someday moving Jensen Medical to the East Coast."

I turn and face him. "Yes. A lot like it."

We'd talked about one day moving Jensen Medical into a posh office. I'd wanted a place on Park Avenue, somewhere close to that mansion Harper, Anika, and I dreamed about. It's funny how dreams can change, how we figure out what we really want in life.

"I imagine you're upset about the article," he says with a nod, as though I've caught him doing something juvenile and not committing a couple of different felonies. "I should have known you would hear about it. You might not believe me, but I was going to warn you."

I was sure he'd been planning on calling me a couple of hours before the sucker came out. "I don't care about the article."

"They decided to post it online early," he says as though he didn't hear me. "There's not a lot I can do about stopping it at this point. Are you here to threaten me with defamation?"

"No." I shake my head because spending a shit ton of money on a lawsuit that would drag on for years isn't my plan. Though I'm pretty sure I could win given what I found in the data he'd left behind. "I came to apologize. I've been thinking a lot about our relationship and how I treated you back then. I've been seeing this new guy and being around him has made me change the way I think about what a good relationship means."

He sniffles like he's caught scent of something he doesn't like. "Marino. Yes. I did some research into him. Seems to be very creative but a little slow. I'm afraid Taisir is going to end up being the better bet. He's moving fast. You know it's all about who moves the quickest in our business."

I ignore the obvious bait. I didn't come here to fight with him. I came for closure. "Good luck with that. Our patents should be filed soon."

"Well, then it'll come down to whoever has the best lawyer, won't it?" He's staring at me like we're about to throw down because the sexual tension is far too much for either of us to deny.

I feel nothing for this man. How could I have not seen it? I hope I'd felt something in the beginning. I can't remember because he didn't matter. How awful is that? He could have been any guy. With the exception of how he screwed me over in the end, I would barely notice he was gone.

"I'm sorry. I wasn't fair to you," I say quietly.

I notice when Heath's gone even for a couple of minutes. I wonder where he is and what he's doing. I know he's probably thinking about me, too.

I love Heath, a love that lives inside my bones and makes my eyes work differently than they did before. A love that I can trust.

A brow rises over Nick's dark eyes. "Wasn't fair?"

"I didn't love you the way you loved me, and I should have known that. You tried in the beginning." He wasn't very good at loving a person, but he tried at the start of our relationship, and then what he'd felt for me had turned nasty.

He starts to open his mouth, his expression turning ugly, and then he stops. A moment passes. "You used me. I was a fucking prop to the great Ivy Jensen."

I shake my head, though I know there's a kernel of truth to his words. "You were something I thought I needed. A smart, gorgeous guy at my side. I thought we could conquer the world."

"We could have. That's the sad part. We could have had it all, but you wouldn't listen to me. You cut me out." He points a finger my way, shooting accusation across the room. "You didn't want me to sit in on interviews with you or big meetings because it might make you look weak. Your feminist bullshit held me back."

"And my emotional distance hurt you," I acknowledge. I don't mention that no male CEO would be expected to bring his partner to interviews or meetings with investors no matter their work relationship. It doesn't matter. He'll never understand. "I'm sorry for that. But you have to acknowledge that coming after my new company isn't going to make that better. That's one of the reasons I'm here. I've recently realized that letting go of past hurts is the only way we can really move forward. So I apologize for hurting you, Nick."

He takes a step back like I've done something threatening. "You can't hurt me. I came out on top. You're the one who got her ass kicked. And I'll make sure your little company means nothing. And when you start the next one, I'll be there, too."

Heath is so right about this. I might be making it worse because I realize the opposite of love isn't hate. Not at all. It's this indifference I feel for him. I've done what I can as a human being to make amends for the wrongs I did to him.

And now I can settle all the accounts between us without regret or guilt.

"I don't suppose you want to apologize for cheating on me." I'll give it a shot.

Ooo, I do feel something. I feel a building wave of anticipation. He might have been hurt by some of my actions, but his response has been nothing but malevolent.

"I never cheated on you," he lies, stepping right into my trap.

"You never dated Kelly Belton from sales? Because you sure took a lot of pictures of the two of you."

He stops, and I can see his brain turning. "Where would you have gotten pictures of us? Did she come to you? That little bitch."

"Not at all. As far as I know she's still in California looking for the next you. I got the pictures from the backup system." Yes, this is the part I've been waiting for. I've gotten the martyr part out of the way, and I'm ready to let my justice warrior off the leash. "You know the one I set up for the house. The one that saved the data from all your personal electronics. Including your phone."

He physically pales. "No. It just charged my phone."

I reach into my bag and pull out the user agreement he'd signed. It's a copy. I'd originally done it because I didn't want him to sue me if the data got lost. I should have known then and there the relationship was a mistake. "Nope. I made it clear at the time that it was all electronics. You knew. You even used it once when you lost a bunch of music off your phone."

"I didn't think…" His jaw tightens as the ramifications hit him. "That's not right. That's my data. You don't get to use my data against me."

It's seriously the most naïve thing I've ever heard him say.

There's a knock on his door and the admin pokes her head through. "Lance Norfolk is on the line and he…you should probably take the call."

Ah, CeCe has excellent timing. "CeCe and Lawyer are paying your friend a visit this morning. I know. I should know the lawyer's name, but she seriously only refers to him as Lawyer. Sometimes I think CeCe went to the Karen Walker school of public relations. I'm sure, though, that Lawyer is extremely good at his job and is informing Norfolk that he will be handing over evidence to the feds later this afternoon that you two colluded to bring the value of Jensen Medical down so he could have one of his shell corporations scoop us up. I'm sure we'll call that person Agent."

Nick ignores my sarcasm. "You can't be serious."

I am so serious. I was the naïve one back then. I never dreamed he would do something like this. I'd blamed myself for everything, and I'm pretty sure he'd known that would happen. I hadn't gotten to know the real him, but he'd known me. At least that version of me. "It was clever, but it didn't take long for Hacker to put things together. He wasn't happy to have to leave the rave he'd been at, but CeCe made it worth his while. And you should know there was a lot of discussion about hacking your systems now, but I said no."

"You can't prove anything."

"Oh, I can. Did you record the conversations so you could cover your ass?" I ask. "It seems like you were smart enough to not trust Norfolk entirely."

The room goes silent, even the admin going still as though she knows what's happening in front of her will change things.

"You can't download those conversations. They were private," Nick finally says.

"I bet they were so private Norfolk didn't know he was being recorded." Norfolk would sue him into oblivion whether or not the feds came calling.

"California is an all-consent state." Nick leaps on the possibility. "You're right. Norfolk didn't know he was being recorded. You can't use them."

I'd already fixed this for him. He doesn't have a great memory. "But this wasn't a phone conversation. You used the personal recording function on your phone to record a private meeting you had with Norfolk. I'll have to pull your phone records, but I listened to the conversation. You were here in Manhattan, and New York is a one-party consent state, and even if you somehow find a way to get it thrown out, I can prove you sold all your stock in Jensen right before you announced we were broke. You were the only C-level employee who did it. Norfolk did as well. He owned quite a bit of Jensen Medical stock through a couple of different companies."

He's going to prison. Oh, it would probably be Club Fed, but he would have a couple of convictions and the fraud charges, and when the feds got involved, who knew what else they would find.

"You bitch." His eyes nearly bulge out of his head.

It's time to leave. I know when I've pushed delicate male sensibilities too far. I move for the door. "Good luck, Nick. I'll put a call in to your team to let them know what's going on. Somehow, I don't think they'll stick around. You're going to be very busy with legal stuff."

He moves in and I hear the admin gasp, but I hold my ground. If he's going to get physical, that's one more strike against him. His whole body is trembling with rage as he towers over me. "This isn't over, Ivy."

But it is. "I think I'll let Lawyer handle you from now on. I've got a company to build."

I turn and walk out even as I hear the admin pleading with him to take Norfolk's call.

I take a deep breath as I get on the elevator and the doors close. I'm the only one in the car, and I close my eyes and let go of everything Nick Stafford did to me. It doesn't matter because CeCe is going to handle it so I can do what I love. All I have to do now is listen to my gut.

The noise is gone, and there's only instinct left. Two roads diverged. I can protect myself, pretend I'm protecting Heath because that article is still going to paint me as a man-eating incompetent who only got big because…feminism or some crap.

The doors open, and I walk out.

Heath is standing in the lobby. He hadn't walked me over here. He'd let me do that on my own. He'd known I needed time, but he's here now.

Or I can take the second road. I can believe. I can believe that this man loves me and we can build so much more than a company together. We can build a life. A real one with ups and downs and movie nights and work and friends and waking up next to him.

He smiles as I reach him and he holds up a bag. "Tacos. I thought taking down an asshole who ruined your life deserves tacos."

He really is the most gorgeous man I've ever seen. I go on my toes and brush my lips against his. "Ruin? Not even close. But I'll take those tacos. And Heath, ask me in six months. No Emma required."

His lips curl up. "Ask you? Oh, you're talking proposal. Six months is a long time. Four weeks."

Thank god. The man has a flaw. He's impatient. We'll have to work on that.

I chuckle and take the bag because those tacos smell delicious. "Four months and not a second sooner. You need time to make it good because we're only doing this once, babe."

He opens the door for me. "Oh, about that. I mean, I've asked a couple of women to marry me. Like four or five. No more than eight."

He's evil. "Sure you have. I know your grandmother. I've seen all of your baby pictures and I heard all about every girlfriend you've ever had."

"I'm having such a talk with her," Heath vows.

He takes my hand and we walk out into the sunshine, leaving the past behind.

Chapter Twenty-Eight

I'm shocked to see CeCe's Rolls parked outside Lydia's building when Heath and I walk up an hour later. We'd sat in a park and eaten the tacos he'd bought and then found an ice cream vendor. We'd talked for a long time and I'd told him everything about Nick and the confrontation and how nervous I am about the stupid article. The actual magazine is coming out next Tuesday, but it's posting online…probably now. I don't know. I haven't looked at my phone. Which is weird for me.

He makes me not want to look at my phone.

"I don't think you're supposed to park here." Heath frowns at Thomas.

There is no *think* about it. It's clearly a loading and unloading only zone, but Thomas doesn't seem to mind.

"I've been given the okay," Thomas promises him. "See."

He gestures to the doorman, who gives us a thumbs-up.

"What did CeCe tip him?" Heath mutters.

"The boss is a generous person," Thomas explains and then nods my way. "Ivy, CeCe left Lawyer with that terrible man. She said it was far too many curse words for her tender ears and that the testosterone level in the room made her head ache. Also, Lady Buttercup needed fresh air."

"So she came here?" Heath asks. "We're a working office."

That's the moment the door opens and Ye Joon walks out, or rather is lead out by the Maltese who prances out like she owns the place. His eyes narrow on me. "I am not Dog Walker. You tell her she better start calling me Coder or Programmer. Not Dog Walker. I asked her why she never hands the dog off to Ria and she called me a sexist. It's not sexist if we share the same crappy duties. It's the opposite of sexist. This whole 'only the man should handle the dog poop' thing *is* sexist."

But he walks off with a pink-colored baggie that will be used to handle all of Lady Buttercup's business.

Thomas utterly ignores him. It's certainly not the first time he's heard someone complain about the way my mentor works. "I think you'll find Ms. Foust has struck up a friendship with your mother and Mr. Marino's grandmother. She wanted to give them all the details in person. They're all very invested in taking down… How did your mother put it? Those preening assholes. I don't think assholes are capable of preening, but I found it amusing all the same. Yes, those three are thick as thieves all of the sudden. There's talk of a girls trip."

My jaw drops. "My mother doesn't leave the city, and by city I mean the island of Manhattan. Honestly, she only leaves Hell's Kitchen because she has to go to work."

"I think you'll find many things are about to change for your mother," Thomas promises, sobering in a way that lets me know he understands the situation she's in. "She's taking some excellent steps. Please tell her I stand ready to take her home whenever she's through. Or to her office if she wants to go there. I would prefer she not use the subway."

My jaw stays dropped. Does Thomas have a thing for my mom?

Heath tugs on my hand. "I need to figure out if CeCe is kidnapping Nonna."

Somehow I doubted that. Lydia is kind of a "seize the day" person. She's living it up in her golden years, and if a ridiculously wealthy lady she has ties to asks her on an adventure, she will likely pack pretty damn quick.

We make it up to Lydia's in record time only to find a whole party going on. And it isn't just my mom and CeCe. Harper and Anika are there. Darnell has the biggest grin on his face, and like many of the people in that room, he has a martini in hand. He looks open and happier than I've ever seen him.

"Hey, guys. I got in," he says. "I got the call and by call I mean an email saying my short story has been accepted into an anthology of emerging science fiction writers. I can't quit my job or anything, but it's a start. I'm a writer. A real writer."

He was always a writer, but I know sometimes we need a little validation to believe in ourselves. I feel a huge smile slide over my face, and he and Heath do that manly back pounding thing that passes for masculine affection.

"I'm so happy for you," I say and then remember something. "But you owe me a chapter. You left me hanging."

He's practically gleaming with joy. "I promise. Tomorrow. How did it go?"

"I don't know how it went with Nick, but Norfolk now understands the feds are going to have his balls on a silver platter," CeCe announces. "There was all sorts of talk about murdering me and cutting my cold, dead heart out and eating it. He was very emotional. I was surprised. That whole 'take it like a man' talk only works until said man is actually confronted with something traumatic. Then it's all tears and pleas and murder."

"He threatened to kill you?" Ria asks, her eyes wide.

"Darling, that's my random Tuesday," CeCe assures her. "Think nothing more of it. He's got bigger problems now. Did Nick vow bloody vengeance as well?"

"Nick handled it as well as could be expected," I reply. "He didn't explode. At least he hadn't when I left. I don't know. I don't care. All I care about is getting back to work on Emma. Which I should be doing now, but we seem to be having a party. You know getting them convicted isn't a sure thing."

"I looked over the evidence." My mom has on her normal workwear, but I notice she's exchanged the gold stud earrings she normally wears for a pair of small hoops. It's a tiny change, but a massive step for her. "I've worked in the legal profession for years. They'll do some time. A lot of time if they're foolish and don't try to cut a deal. But that's not what the party is about."

"Ivy, come back here," Harper calls out from the office. "You have to see this."

Before I can go, my mom puts a hand on my elbow. Heath and CeCe start walking toward the office, but I stay behind.

"Ivy, I want you to know I'm going to see someone CeCe recommended. She got me in starting tomorrow morning," she says quietly. "I was wondering if you could go with me. Not inside the room, of course, but I think I need someone with me."

"Mom, yes." I look her straight in the eyes because she needs to understand how I feel. How grateful I am. How hopeful I am.

"Anything you need. I'm here."

She puts a hand on my cheek. "Thank you. I'm going to try very hard." She straightens up. "Of course I might end up like CeCe. I think this therapy might end up being gin therapy. I half expect Thomas to drive us to a bar."

What is even happening right now? "Thomas is taking us?"

My mom shrugs like this is an everyday occurrence. Sure. She normally has a driver take her to her therapy appointments. "CeCe said it might be easier to get there if Thomas took me, and he kindly said yes. I think it might take longer because of traffic, but he assures me traffic is no problem for him."

"We might need that bar after the trip," I say as we start walking down the hall. I'll make sure she's buckled up.

When I enter the office, everyone is huddled around the monitors. There are a bank of them we use when we're collaborating. Ria sits at one of the keyboards, scrolling through a bunch of text I don't recognize.

Lydia looks up at me. She's got a martini glass in her hand, and she looks like she's enjoying it. "There you are, darling girl. Come here and see what's happening. Oh, do you want one of these? They're delicious. Thomas made a whole pitcher of them."

CeCe smiles. "He opened the bottle. He's excellent at opening bottles. You know a good martini needs very little work but must be poured by a master hand."

So they're drinking straight gin. It's going to be a fun afternoon.

"Yeah, Nonna's discovered hard booze," Heath says, his mouth in the primmest line. "And now CeCe is taking her to Monte Carlo."

"I find her deeply amusing," CeCe admits. "It'll be good to have a friend. And perhaps when the therapist dislodges the stick in Diane's ass, she can come, too."

My mom flips her the bird. "I'm coming to make sure no one gets in too much trouble. I have a lot of vacation time I haven't taken."

CeCe winks her way, like that had been her plan all along. "Excellent. You could use a vacation."

"What is happening?" Heath whispers.

"I think the older generation is about to get their groove back on." I, for one, am happy for them.

"Seriously, Ivy, you need to see this." Anika points to the monitors.

"It is pretty cool," Darnell agrees. "A fitting redemption."

"What is this?" I ask as I focus on what Ria's brought up.

"It's the comments section of Nick's article," Harper announces. "It's only been online for an hour, but there are already forty comments. Read them."

This article is bullshit. Ivy Jensen is one of the smartest women in the business and the best boss I ever had. I worked at Jensen Medical and when it went under, she was there for us. Nick Stafford fled like the piece of crap he is along with the rest of the management team. Ivy stayed even when it cost her because she had her employees' backs.

I recognize the username. "He was on our development team."

He'd been an excellent worker with an amazing sense of humor and a great work ethic. I'd pulled some strings and got him on with a rival firm.

"There's so much more." Ria scrolls down to the next comment.

Mr. Stafford has misrepresented what happened at Jensen and Ms. Jensen's part in the failure of the company—not the excellent product she developed. That is still going strong despite the fact the woman who developed it no longer profits from her hard work. What brought Ms. Jensen down was inexperience. Not hubris or a lack of talent. She also might have hired the wrong people, but that is a function of her youth. All geniuses have their ups and downs. I am waiting eagerly to see what she will do next.

I wouldn't be in this country if Ivy Jensen hadn't busted her butt to find a job for me and my whole team when Jensen went under. Who does that these days? She'll get her house in order and come back stronger than ever, and when she needs a developer, I hope she gives me a call.

Tears fill my eyes.

"It keeps going," Anika says, putting an arm around me.

Harper is on the other side, my best friends bolstering me, joining me in this marvelous moment and making it bigger and more meaningful because they're here to share it with me. "There are a bunch talking about you working to find them jobs so they didn't lose their visas. Or how you mentored them. I know it felt like failure, but you proved yourself to so many people."

"And she's going to continue to do so because Huffman called me right before you came in." CeCe looks perfectly satisfied. "He said the article doesn't scare him off at all. He likes a challenge. I think he's already heard rumors, and those comments mean something to him. So get the terribly named Emma ready and force your boyfriend into a suit."

I wink at Heath—who is totally my boyfriend. "Nope. He's perfect the way he is."

As I read more of the comments, I realize I'm on my way to some form of perfect, too. Maybe perfection simply means being comfortable in our own skin, accepting ourselves for who we are. Accepting the love we are offered and giving it back.

I stand here surrounded by friends and loved ones and him.

That feels perfect to me.

* * * *

The Park Avenue Promise series will continue…

My Royal Showmance

A Park Avenue Promise Novel
By Lexi Blake
Coming June 4, 2024

Anika Fox knows exactly where she wants to be, and it's not on the set of a reality TV dating show. She's working her way up at the production company she works for and she's close to achieving some of her dreams. The big boss just wants one thing from her. He's got a potential problem with the director of *The King Takes a Bride* and he wants Anika to pose as a production assistant and report back.

As the prince of a tiny European country, Luca St. Marten knows the world views him as one of the pampered royalty of the world. It couldn't be further from the truth. His country is hurting and he's right there on the front lines with his citizens. When he's asked to do a dating show, his counselors point out that it could bring tourism back to Ralavia. It goes against his every desire, but he agrees.

When one of the contestants drops out at the last minute, Anika finds herself replacing the potential princess. She's sure she'll be asked to leave the first night, but Luca keeps picking her again and again. Suddenly she finds herself in the middle of a made-for-TV fantasy, and she's unsure what's real and what's simply reality TV.

Book Club Questions

1. Start Us Up deals with what it means to be a woman in a business dominated by men. Ivy has many coping mechanisms to deal with this. Do you think they help or hurt her? How do those coping mechanisms affect her core relationships?

2. Grief and how we deal with losing someone plays a major part in the novel. All three of Ivy's maternal figures are widows, and each deal with it in their own way. How do you think Diane, CeCe, and Lydia handle grief, and how has it affected their ties to family?

3. Mental health is a subject touched on in Start Us Up. Ivy doesn't realize her mother has an issue with depression until CeCe talks to her about it. Their relationship has been strained for years. How did Diane's depression play a part in Ivy's arc? Do you think Ivy should have recognized her mother's problems earlier? At one point in the story, the dynamic shifts between them and Ivy takes on the maternal role for her mom in some ways. Can you think of a time when that shift happened for you and your parents?

4. Artificial intelligence is a highly controversial topic these days. The AI Heath and Ivy are developing is a matchmaking app. How would you feel about using an app to find a partner? How do you think AI will change our world in the coming years?

5. Diane and CeCe have several confrontations over the course of the novel. How do you think they handle their respective relationships with Ivy? What forces make it nearly impossible for them to work together until the end of the book?

6. Ivy and Heath are immediately attracted to one another, but physical chemistry is only one part of their relationship. Why do you think they work? How is Heath uniquely capable of understanding Ivy? How does Ivy support Heath in the ways he needs? Do you think this partnership can work in both their personal lives and with their business?

7. At the heart of the Park Avenue Promise series is a longtime friendship between three women who met when they were children. Ivy, Harper, and Anika are a found family. Over the course of the book Ivy examines the relationship and whether friendship can survive the changes that come with growing up. How do you think moving and building a business affected Ivy's relationship with her "sisters"? Have you had a long-term friendship that changed over the years? How did you try to make it work?

Discover More Lexi Blake

Tempted: A Masters and Mercenaries Novella

When West Rycroft left his family's ranch to work in the big city, he never dreamed he would find himself surrounded by celebrities and politicians. Working at McKay-Taggart as a bodyguard and security expert quickly taught him how to navigate the sometimes shark-infested waters of the elite. While some would come to love that world, West has seen enough to know it's not for him, preferring to keep his distance from his clients—until the day he meets Ally Pearson.

Growing up in the entertainment world, Ally was always in the shadow of others, but now she has broken out from behind the scenes for her own day in the spotlight. The paparazzi isn't fun, but she knows all too well that it's part of the gig. She has a good life and lots of fans, but someone has been getting too close for comfort and making threats. To be safe, she hires her own personal knight in shining armor, a cowboy hottie by the name of West. They clash in the beginning, but the minute they fall into bed together something magical happens.

Just as everything seems too good to be true, they are both reminded that there was a reason Ally needed a bodyguard. Her problems have found her again, and this time West will have to put his life on the line or lose everything they've found.

* * * *

Delighted: A Masters and Mercenaries Novella

Brian "Boomer" Ward believes in sheltering strays. After all, the men and women of McKay-Taggart made him family when he had none. So when the kid next door needs help one night, he thinks nothing of protecting her until her mom gets home. But when he meets Daphne Carlton, the thoughts hit him hard. She's stunning and hardworking and obviously in need of someone to put her first. It doesn't hurt that she's as sweet as the cupcakes she bakes.

Daphne Carlton's life revolves around two things—her kid and her business. Daphne's Delights is her dream—to take the recipes of her childhood and share them with the world. Her daughter, Lula, is the best kid she could have hoped for. Lula's got a genius-level intelligence and a heart of gold. But she also has two grandparents who control her access to private school and the fortune her father left behind. They're impossible to please, and Daphne worries that one wrong move on her part could cost her daughter the life she deserves.

As Daphne and Boomer find themselves getting closer, outside forces put pressure on the new couple. But if they make it through the storm, love will just be the icing on the cake because family is the real prize.

* * * *

Treasured: A Masters and Mercenaries Novella

David Hawthorne has a great life. His job as a professor at a prestigious Dallas college is everything he hoped for. Now that his brother is back from the Navy, life seems to be settling down. All he needs to do is finish the book he's working on and his tenure will be assured. When he gets invited to interview a reclusive expert, he knows he's gotten lucky. But being the stepson of Sean Taggart comes with its drawbacks, including an overprotective mom who sends a security detail to keep him safe. He doesn't need a bodyguard, but when Tessa Santiago shows up on his doorstep, the idea of her giving him close cover doesn't seem so bad.

Tessa has always excelled at most anything she tried, except romance. The whole relationship thing just didn't work out for her. She's not looking for love, and she's certainly not looking for it with an academic who happens to be connected to her boss's family. The last thing she wants is to escort an overly pampered pretentious man-child around South America to ensure he doesn't get into trouble. Still, there's something about David that calls to her. In addition to watching his back, she will have to avoid falling into the trap of soulful eyes and a deep voice that gets her heart racing.

But when the seemingly simple mission turns into a treacherous race for a hidden artifact, David and Tess know this assignment could cost them far more than their jobs. If they can overcome the odds, the lost treasure might not be their most valuable reward.

* * * *

Charmed: A Masters and Mercenaries Novella

JT Malone is lucky, and he knows it. He is the heir to a billion-dollar petroleum empire, and he has a loving family. Between his good looks and his charm, he can have almost any woman he wants. The world is his oyster, and he really likes oysters. So why does it all feel so empty?

Nina Blunt is pretty sure she's cursed. She worked her way up through the ranks at Interpol, fighting for every step with hard work and discipline. Then she lost it all because she loved the wrong person. Rebuilding her career with McKay-Taggart, she can't help but feel lonely. It seems everyone around her is finding love and starting families. But she knows that isn't for her. She has vowed never to make the mistake of falling in love again.

JT comes to McKay-Taggart for assistance rooting out a corporate spy, and Nina signs on to the job. Their working relationship becomes tricky, however, as their personal chemistry flares like a wildfire. Completing the assignment without giving in to the attraction that threatens to overwhelm them seems like it might be the most difficult part of the job. When danger strikes, will they be able to count on each other when the bullets are flying? If not, JT's charmed life might just come to an end.

* * * *

Enchanted: A Masters and Mercenaries Novella

A snarky submissive princess

Sarah Steven's life is pretty sweet. By day, she's a dedicated trauma nurse and by night, a fun-loving club sub. She adores her job, has a group of friends who have her back, and is a member of the hottest club in Dallas. So why does it all feel hollow? Could it be because she fell for her dream man and can't forgive him for walking away from her? Nope. She's not going there again. No matter how much she wants to.

A prince of the silver screen

Jared Johns might be one of the most popular actors in Hollywood, but he lost more than a fan when he walked away from Sarah. He lost the only woman he's ever loved. He's been trying to get her back, but she won't return his calls. A trip to Dallas to visit his brother might be exactly what he needs to jump-start his quest to claim the woman who holds his heart.

A masquerade to remember

For Charlotte Taggart's birthday, Sanctum becomes a fantasyland of kinky fun and games. Every unattached sub gets a new Dom for the festivities. The twist? The Doms must conceal their identities until the stroke of midnight at the end of the party. It's exactly what Sarah needs to forget the fact that Jared is pursuing her. She can't give in to him, and the mysterious Master D is making her rethink her position when it comes to signing a contract. Jared knows he was born to play this role, dashing suitor by day and dirty Dom at night.

When the masks come off, will she be able to forgive the man who loves her, or will she leave him forever?

* * * *

Protected: A Masters and Mercenaries Novella

A second chance at first love

Years before, Wade Rycroft fell in love with Geneva Harris, the smartest girl in his class. The rodeo star and the shy academic made for an odd pair but their chemistry was undeniable. They made plans to get married after high school but when Genny left him standing in the rain, he joined the Army and vowed to leave that life behind. Genny married the town's golden boy, and Wade knew that he couldn't go home again.

Could become the promise of a lifetime

Fifteen years later, Wade returns to his Texas hometown for his brother's wedding and walks into a storm of scandal. Genny's marriage has dissolved and the town has turned against her. But when someone tries to kill his old love, Wade can't refuse to help her. In his years after the Army, he's found his place in the world. His job at McKay-Taggart keeps him happy and busy but something is missing. When he takes the job watching over Genny, he realizes what it is.

As danger presses in, Wade must decide if he can forgive past sins or let the woman of his dreams walk into a nightmare…

* * * *

Close Cover: A Masters and Mercenaries Novel

Remy Guidry doesn't do relationships. He tried the marriage thing once, back in Louisiana, and learned the hard way that all he really needs in life is a cold beer, some good friends, and the occasional hookup. His job as a bodyguard with McKay-Taggart gives him purpose and lovely perks, like access to Sanctum. The last thing he needs in his life is a woman with stars in her eyes and babies in her future.

Lisa Daley's life is going in the right direction. She has graduated from college after years of putting herself through school. She's got a new job at an accounting firm and she's finished her Sanctum training. Finally on her own and having fun, her life seems pretty perfect. Except she's lonely and the one man she wants won't give her a second look.

There is one other little glitch. Apparently, her new firm is really a front for the mob and now they want her dead. Assassins can really ruin a fun girls' night out. Suddenly strapped to the very same six-foot-five-inch hunk of a bodyguard who makes her heart pound, Lisa can't decide if this situation is a blessing or a curse.

As the mob closes in, Remy takes his tempting new charge back to the safest place he knows—his home in the bayou. Surrounded by his past, he can't help wondering if Lisa is his future. To answer that question, he just has to keep her alive.

* * * *

Arranged: A Masters and Mercenaries Novella

Kash Kamdar is the king of a peaceful but powerful island nation. As Loa Mali's sovereign, he is always in control, the final authority. Until his mother uses an ancient law to force her son into marriage. His prospective queen is a buttoned-up intellectual, nothing like Kash's usual party girl. Still, from the moment of their forced engagement, he can't stop thinking about her.

Dayita Samar comes from one of Loa Mali's most respected families. The Oxford-educated scientist has dedicated her life to her country's future. But under her staid and calm exterior, Day hides a few sexy secrets of her own. She is willing to marry her king, but also agrees that they can circumvent the law. Just because they're married doesn't mean they have to change their lives. It certainly doesn't mean they have to fall in love.

After one wild weekend in Dallas, Kash discovers his bride-to-be is more than she seems. Engulfed in a changing world, Kash finds exciting new possibilities for himself. Could Day help him find respite from the crushing responsibility he's carried all his life? This fairy tale could have a happy ending, if only they can escape Kash's past…

* * * *

Devoted: A Masters and Mercenaries Novella

A woman's work

Amy Slaten has devoted her life to Slaten Industries. After ousting her corrupt father and taking over the CEO role, she thought she could relax and enjoy taking her company to the next level. But an old business rivalry rears its ugly head. The only thing that can possibly take her mind off business is the training class at Sanctum…and her training partner, the gorgeous and funny Flynn Adler. If she can just manage to best her mysterious business rival, life might be perfect.

A man's commitment

Flynn Adler never thought he would fall for the enemy. Business is war, or so his father always claimed. He was raised to be ruthless when it came to the family company, and now he's raising his brother to one day work with him. The first order of business? The hostile takeover of Slaten Industries. It's a stressful job so when his brother offers him a spot in Sanctum's training program, Flynn jumps at the chance.

A lifetime of devotion….

When Flynn realizes the woman he's falling for is none other than the CEO of the firm he needs to take down, he has to make a choice. Does he take care of the woman he's falling in love with or the business he's worked a lifetime to build? And when Amy finally understands the man she's come to trust is none other than the enemy, will she walk away from him or fight for the love she's come to depend on?

* * * *

Adored: A Masters and Mercenaries Novella

A man who gave up on love

Mitch Bradford is an intimidating man. In his professional life, he has a reputation for demolishing his opponents in the courtroom. At the exclusive BDSM club Sanctum, he prefers disciplining pretty submissives with no strings attached. In his line of work, there's no time for a healthy relationship. After a few failed attempts, he knows he's not good for any woman—especially not his best friend's sister.

A woman who always gets what she wants

Laurel Daley knows what she wants, and her sights are set on Mitch. He's smart and sexy, and it doesn't matter that he's a few years older and has a couple of bitter ex-wives. Watching him in action at work and at play, she knows he just needs a little polish to make some woman the perfect lover. She intends to be that woman, but first she has to show him how good it could be.

A killer lurking in the shadows

When an unexpected turn of events throws the two together, Mitch and Laurel are confronted with the perfect opportunity to explore their mutual desire. Night after night of being close breaks down Mitch's defenses. The more he sees of Laurel, the more he knows he wants her. Unfortunately, someone else has their eyes on Laurel and they have murder in mind.

* * * *

Dungeon Games: A Masters and Mercenaries Novella

Obsessed

Derek Brighton has become one of Dallas's finest detectives through a combination of discipline and obsession. Once he has a target in his sights, nothing can stop him. When he isn't solving homicides, he applies the same intensity to his playtime at Sanctum, a secretive BDSM club. Unfortunately, no amount of beautiful submissives can fill the hole that one woman left in his heart.

Unhinged

Karina Mills has a reputation for being reckless, and her clients appreciate her results. As a private investigator, she pursues her cases with nothing holding her back. In her personal life, Karina yearns for something different. Playing at Sanctum has been a safe way to find peace, but the one Dom who could truly master her heart is out of reach.

Enflamed

On the hunt for a killer, Derek enters a shadowy underworld only to find the woman he aches for is working the same case. Karina is searching for a missing girl and won't stop until she finds her. To get close to their prime suspect, they need to pose as a couple. But as their operation goes under the covers, unlikely partners become passionate lovers while the killer prepares to strike.

About Lexi Blake

New York Times bestselling author Lexi Blake lives in North Texas with her husband and three kids. Since starting her publishing journey in 2010, she's sold over three million copies of her books. She began writing at a young age, concentrating on plays and journalism. It wasn't until she started writing romance that she found success. She likes to find humor in the strangest places and believes in happy endings.

Connect with Lexi online:

Facebook: authorlexiblake
Twitter: authorlexiblake
Website: www.LexiBlake.net
Instagram: authorlexiblake

Discover 1001 Dark Nights Collection Ten

DRAGON LOVER by Donna Grant
A Dragon Kings Novella

KEEPING YOU by Aurora Rose Reynolds
An Until Him/Her Novella

HAPPILY EVER NEVER by Carrie Ann Ryan
A Montgomery Ink Legacy Novella

DESTINED FOR ME by Corinne Michaels
A Come Back for Me/Say You'll Stay Crossover

MADAM ALANA by Audrey Carlan
A Marriage Auction Novella

DIRTY FILTHY BILLIONAIRE by Laurelin Paige
A Dirty Universe Novella

HIDE AND SEEK by Laura Kaye
A Blasphemy Novella

TANGLED WITH YOU by J. Kenner
A Stark Security Novella

TEMPTED by Lexi Blake
A Masters and Mercenaries Novella

THE DANDELION DIARY by Devney Perry
A Maysen Jar Novella

CHERRY LANE by Kristen Proby
A Huckleberry Bay Novella

THE GRAVE ROBBER by Darynda Jones
A Charley Davidson Novella

CRY OF THE BANSHEE by Heather Graham
A Krewe of Hunters Novella

DARKEST NEED by Rachel Van Dyken
A Dark Ones Novella

CHRISTMAS IN CAPE MAY by Jennifer Probst
A Sunshine Sisters Novella

A VAMPIRE'S MATE by Rebecca Zanetti
A Dark Protectors/Rebels Novella

WHERE IT BEGINS by Helena Hunting
A Pucked Novella

Also from Blue Box Press

THE MARRIAGE AUCTION by Audrey Carlan
Season One, Volume One
Season One, Volume Two
Season One, Volume Three
Season One, Volume Four

THE JEWELER OF STOLEN DREAMS by M.J. Rose

SAPPHIRE STORM by Christopher Rice writing as C. Travis Rice
A Sapphire Cove Novel

ATLAS: THE STORY OF PA SALT by Lucinda Riley and Harry
Whittaker

LOVE ON THE BYLINE by Xio Axelrod
A Plays and Players Novel

A SOUL OF ASH AND BLOOD by Jennifer L. Armentrout
A Blood and Ash Novel

START US UP by Lexi Blake
A Park Avenue Promise Novel

FIGHTING THE PULL by Kristen Ashley
A River Rain Novel

A FIRE IN THE FLESH by Jennifer L. Armentrout
A Flesh and Fire Novel

VISIONS OF FLESH AND BLOOD by Jennifer L. Armentrout and
Rayvn Salvador
A Blood and Ash/Flesh and Fire Compendium

On Behalf of Blue Box Press,

Liz Berry, M.J. Rose, and Jillian Stein would like to thank ~

Steve Berry
Doug Scofield
Benjamin Stein
Kim Guidroz
Tanaka Kangara
Stacey Tardif
Asha Hossain
Chris Graham
Jessica Saunders
Kate Boggs
Richard Blake
and Simon Lipskar